SHADOW OF ZELOS

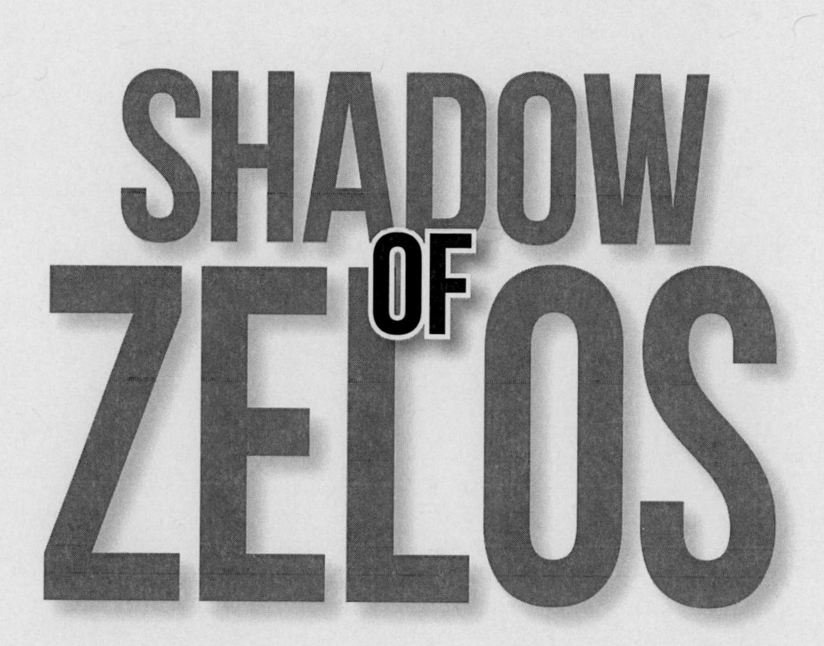

UWE JAECKEL

SHADOW OF ZELOS

iUniverse books may be ordered through booksellers or by contacting:

iUniverse
1663 Liberty Drive
Bloomington, IN 47403
www.iuniverse.com
1-800-Authors (1-800-288-4677)

ISBN: 978-1-5320-5783-0 (sc)
ISBN: 978-1-5320-5784-7 (e)

Print information available on the last page.

iUniverse rev. date: 07/16/2019

CHAPTER ONE

MARS BASE

August 14, 2040
Omega Centauri Log
Colonel Darren Hildure, Mission Commander, reporting.

We have landed on Mars and established a base of operations around the site in question. We found the remains of the first Mars landing from ten years ago; what the wind storms then and since have left of it, anyway. We shouldn't have that problem this time around; the ship is many times stronger, our equipment and suits a lot tougher, that we should be able to stand up against even the four hundred mile an hour winds that have been recorded on Mars. Even so, the first thing we did was to erect a sturdy shelter around the entrance to the lava tubes before constructing the command center.

The command center is built just a little south of the North Pole– the Planum Boreum– about at the far bottom edge of the Chasma Boreale. We've got sheets of ice to our backs and a bunch of red rocks and dead plains before us. Not at all a pleasant place to be without a spacesuit.

The command center is built into the rock to protect against radiation, with four-fifths of its height actually being underground, and a couple of nuclear generators powering everything, including oxygen generation. One end of it even directly connects into the lava tube we're exploring. We should be okay, weather-wise.

Hard to believe it's been ten years, and taken us that long to get back here. I was just eighteen at the time and was on that ill-fated trip as a crewman. I remember those winds picking up rocks and people and hurtling them around. I was only one of two of the crew that made it back to the shuttle and out of here and even then if it wasn't for Feng– that's Colonel Feng Yusheng– pulling me through the airlock I never would have made it. My helmet was cracked and leaking air; another few seconds and I would have been as dead as everyone else. Our suits and helmets have been greatly enhanced since then, of course; those new synthetic spider-silk fibers are as flexible as cotton but a thousand times stronger than steel. Also makes for far less bulk, which makes things much easier with moving around and setting up equipment. Of course, unlike space, Mars actually has an atmosphere– if you like nearly straight carbon dioxide– so we don't have to worry about a vacuum. We should be okay this time around.

My crew is as follows. First myself, Colonel Darren Hildure, mission commander and PhD in computer science and mechanical engineering. Colonel Feng of China is my second in command with PhDs in propulsion engineering and aerodynamics. Professor Andrii Alexander of Russia, world-renowned archeologist hoping to find some actual alien ruins. Dr. Jeremie Claude of France is our medical doctor and physician; he's hoping to dissect some actual alien remains. Next is Doctor Akio Tomoko of Japan, our geologist. Finally, there is Professor Glenda Hayden of Germany, our physicist; a strictly fact-oriented lady, she'll keep us grounded and from engaging in too many flights of fancy.

Our mission now is the same as it was ten years ago: Find the source of the signal.

It was back when the Moon Base was finally completed and its dedication and existence given all the public fanfare you might expect. A fully working moon base built with international cooperation, funded from both governmental and private sources, one that would provide both scientific and industrial opportunities previously only dreamt of. All of this is public knowledge, of course. The part that still hasn't been made public, however, was the signal received nearly immediately after the dedication.

They knew it was an alien signal, if for no other reason than that it came from outside the Earth. We'd finally been contacted by something from another world; aliens. But where scientists might have reasonably expected initial contact to be in the form of some mathematical sequence transmitted at the hydrogen emission wavelength of twenty-one centimeters, or in some other form of universal code independent of specific languages, it came as a UHF signal. In actual words. Repeated in twenty-one different languages. Beamed straight to the Moon Base alone. The message was simple: "Come."

Yeah, ***that*** *got everyone's attention. When the signal was traced it was discovered to have come from Mars so here we are. Admittedly, everyone was a bit eager to find the signaler, so that first mission was rather rushed, but we've planned this one out a lot better this time.*

As best as tracking equipment of the day could make out, the signal came from the North Pole of Mars, from somewhere underground. Suspiciously, the signal persisted just long enough for the Earth-side equipment to get a fix on before abruptly ending. The first Mars mission didn't find out much more, other than that the weather around here is much like being stuck in the middle of a hurricane for months on end. Or if you're feeling ***really*** *adventurous then you can head a little north past where all the ice begins and watch your blood freeze solid. It didn't end well and we never had a chance to find anything.*

For this second mission, the ship is a lot bigger to accommodate the supplies and building equipment required to construct a proper hurricane-proof shelter, not to mention keep out temperatures that make the middle of Alaska look balmy. We also have enough supplies to keep it going indefinitely– if you like the sort of organic pudding-bricks the food synths spit out– not to mention such key equipment as the oxygen converters; picture a really large air conditioner whose sole function is to break down carbon dioxide into oxygen and carbon, the latter remaining stuck in the filters which then have to be changed and cleaned every so often. The main bulk of the Centauri itself is still in orbit directly above us, while the shuttle-segment is kept parked right next to the command center; always ready for launch on short notice, just in case. We're not taking any chances this time.

The trip itself was uneventful, given the months of confinement– another reason for the larger ship size, for the sense of space to keep everyone from getting on one another's nerves. Once we got here, we did a fly-by of the north polar regions with the ground-penetrating radar to see what there might be down here. That's how we found the lava tubes and… something.

Some of the lava tubes are over sixty miles long but what got our attention was the area that didn't show up on radar. Not because the rock was too dense or too light– even that would have made itself clear– but just… nothing. I figure that's our goal, so we've been going through the lava tubes trying to make our way there…

The Mars Command Center looked like a simple hundred and fifty foot-long cylindrical lump lying on its side, its back to the rocky cliffside that protects it from the fierce Martian winds and rivers of arctic chill wafting down from the glacier behind it. From it a covered walkway extends like an umbilical from its mother, to the landing zone where the shuttle-segment of the *Omega Centauri* awaited, secured against the winds by both its bottom-heavy squat design and struts that reached out from the cliff wall to hold the upper portions of the craft in place until ready for launch. The vessel resembled an elongated space shuttle, sleeker in design than the ones that had made the first launch and landing all those decades ago, and far larger. In orbit high above awaited the other, far larger, half of the vessel, that to which it could attach itself for the return trip to Earth.

One space-suited figure was entering into the airlock facing into the lava tube into which the command center was partially built. The suit was far less bulky than the ones worn by those who first trod the surface of the Moon, the pressure gloves fitting more skin-tight with flexible fingers, less padding required about the limbs though still strong enough to take an impact like a bullet-proof vest, the helmet a clear orb that would automatically polarize itself depending on the ambient light, across one corner of its inside displayed a continuous reading of the status of the suit's functions as well as the oxygen levels and atmospheric readings outside. Finally, the oxygen tanks were not the big bulky square tanks they used to be. Instead, there was a far smaller unit on the back that served to convert the available carbon dioxide in the Martian atmosphere into breathable oxygen, with a couple of miniature oxygen tanks fixed onto the outer sides of the legs for emergencies. Theoretically, as long as one remembered to change the suit's carbon filters every so often, one could venture about the Martian landscape indefinitely if the only problem were that of breathable air.

The figure waited for the hatch to slide fully closed before reaching for the first of three levers in the wall to one side. He moved the first lever down and the entire airlock was sprayed with a thick decontaminating mist, then once the ventilation system cleared it away and a green light lit up above the lever, the figure pulled down the second one and in came the air. After a second green light, he then reached for the third lever.

The interior hatch slid open and the figure stepped forward as he began to undo his helmet.

The helmet revealed a slightly tanned face a couple years short of thirty, short trimmed dark brown hair, and an inquisitive look shining out from behind his dark eyes. As he further began to undo the rest of his spacesuit, it was to reveal a well-built six-foot frame.

As he stepped through the airlock into the assembly and locker room, another shorter came over to help him, this a Chinese man of about his same age. Slender, dark ear-length hair kept neatly groomed, and an equally intelligent look.

"Darren," the Chinese man asked, "we have something in from the new weather satellite; I estimate in about two hours we'll be hit with three-hundred and sixty mile an hour winds. Everything will be tossed over half of Mars if it's not secured."

"Don't worry, Feng, supplies are all secured. Most of them are in the lava tube and we got tarps riveted into the ground around the rest of it. Andrii, Akio, and Glenda are finishing it up right now. Don't worry, it's not going to turn out like the first time we were here."

"I hope not," Feng grinned. "I'd hate to make a habit of saving your butt from Martian sandstorms all the time. People might begin to talk."

"Funny man," Darren dead-panned. "Now what about that connecting wall?"

Fully out of the spacesuit, Darren walked over to hang it up on its hook, then over to one of the lockers to change into a fresh set of fatigues as they talked.

"About one and a half meters," Feng replied. "Shouldn't take more than an hour and a half to break through. If the radar scans are right, this little shortcut should save us quite a bit of time."

"Then we can *finally* see where that signal came from," Darren beamed. "Just think about what we might find. Some alien buried himself deep in these lava tubes for whatever reason then sent out a signal that anyone on Earth could understand. *Designed* to be that way. Obviously they must have been monitoring us, but why? And why not just come out and greet us?"

"For all we know," Feng shrugged, "it could just be some alien child playing around with his erector set. Or maybe they're on a picnic and Junior snuck into Dad's radio set."

"Really?" Darren paused briefly to give his friend a look then returned to pulling on his boots. "I don't think I'll be able to sleep until we see for ourselves what's going on in that tube."

"Well, you'll have to," Feng reminded him. "You haven't slept in over twenty hours."

"I'll just take a two-hour nap," Darren said, standing up. "Make sure the others are in before that storm hits, then I want to go over the–"

"You'll sleep a full six hours; a mission commander needs to be alert when History is about to be made," Feng more sternly reminded him. "You're ready to drop. Or do you want me to bring in Jeremie to make it official? He's got the medical authority to sit you down in bed for a week if you need it, you know."

Darren stood up, about to object when a yawn escaped his lips. Then another one. Feng said not a word but just fixed him with a look.

"Okay," Darren shrugged, "so you're in charge while I get a full night's sleep. Happy?"

Darren started walking over to the door leading out, palming the large button that slid it open, then paused for a last remark to Feng.

"But if some alien kid with his erector set and radio kit crawls out of those tubes and you don't wake me up, I'm revoking our friendship."

Feng chuckled in reply and left the room with him. A few minutes later Darren was in his quarters, asleep before his face hit his bed.

August 18, 2040
Omega Centauri Log
Colonel Darren Hildure, Mission Commander, reporting.

Estimates are that the shortcut we made saved us about thirty klicks worth of prowling around these tunnels, but even so, we've been using the electric rover to get around the tubes; have to with the distance involved. The tunnels appear to be a mix of lava tubes with some naturally occurring caves, so it can get a bit confusing down there. The tunnel we broke into looks like it goes pretty deep, but as close as we can figure, it heads in the general direction of the suspected area of the mysterious signal; it's just a matter of finding which of these smaller tubes leads there. We're following the radar map we'd made from the initial fly-by, but can't be completely sure which tube will lead to the blank spot in our map. Or even what we'll find, for that matter.

The rock of these old lava tubes is pretty nonporous, perfect for keeping in any oxygen that we might care to supply. If we could get enough building materials down there, then we could theoretically seal off sections of these tunnels, run the oxygen converters for a while, and have some great staging and storage areas. Heck, there's enough space down there to construct an entire underground city. Something to think about for the possibility of future colonies.

August 19, 2040
Omega Centauri Log
Colonel Darren Hildure, Mission Commander, reporting.

That latest tube we'd been tracking ends in a small cavern that has now presented us with a choice of directions. The decision of which branch to take, though, sort of resolved itself. The radar map had indicated three smaller tubes branch off from here; the problem is, we found a fourth...

The lava tube stabbed down into a stone horizon, a circular tunnel a dozen feet across, walled in red striated rock. Down the length of the ceiling hung the source of illumination: a brightly glowing cable emitting the light of early twilight, alongside it running an electrical cable, both sourced from the command center far behind and ending somewhere up ahead. Along this tunnel, four space-suited figures rode in the electric rover– a vehicle much like a cross between an electric golf cart and the original moon rover the first-generation astronauts used to drive.

Their destination was covered over by a flexible wall of thick durable plastic material sealed into the rock all around. Attached in the center of this heavy tarp stood a large glass door in a fixed frame embedded into the ground. The plastic was just translucent enough to see that it blocked the last ten feet of the tunnel's length before it opened up into the cavern beyond.

The rover stopped just before the wall, whereupon the passengers got out and one by one entered through the glass door. One would open the door, feel a blast of wind from some mechanism above, then watch the door snap closed behind him. A short walk down to the other end and a second plastic wall just like the first, also with its own glass door. In both appearance and function, this was much like an old biohazard tent, acting as a seal to the cavern beyond. With no vacuum to be concerned about, nor masses of water to keep back as for something like a submarine, all the barrier seal had to do was keep the Martian atmosphere on one side and the newly converted oxygen on the other; no real difference in pressure to worry about.

Once all four had gone through the second barrier, they found themselves standing before the cavern the tunnel emptied out into. The oxygen converters had been in there going for two days straight just converting the carbon dioxide in the small cavern into something breathable; they looked like a dozen air-conditioning units ringed around the top of the chamber, fixed into the walls with long rivets, cables going from each unit to the final mass of cabling by the sealed entrance into the cave. A quick check of the reading displayed across the insides of their visors confirmed that enough oxygen had so far accumulated to risk those that had just entered to take off their helmets, though never far out of reach.

Darren and Feng stood there with two others. Dr. Akio Tomoko was slightly older than the other two by a few years, slim, and wearing the usual blue-green jumpsuit beneath his spacesuit. To their other side stood Dr. Jeremie Claude, a Frenchman about twenty years older than Dr. Tomoko, with some grey flecking through his brown hair and not quite as physically fit as the others.

A series of large thousand-watt halide work-lights had been fixed to the ceiling and parts of the wall, cables leading from them through a section of wall by the airlock, and from there on through the tunnels back to the generator at the command base. Hanging from hooks embedded into the walls were more spacesuits, just in case an emergency arose, along with spare tanks of oxygen. Another small portion of the cavern had been reserved for their equipment: welding torches and oxyacetylene tanks, a range of mining explosives and primers, electrical hand-held digging equipment and drills, a compact excavator parked in a corner, and an assortment of hand tools. Next to that was the area reserved for the food locker and a portable toilet booth. Everything one might need for prolonged periods of work away from base.

Before them the cavern stretched nearly a hundred feet across and over thirty feet high; red rock, worn smooth by time and ancient heat, like a bubble frozen in place. At its far end, the four tunnels in question branched off. Three of the lava tubes were small, no more than five to ten feet in diameter, and currently sealed over with more of the heavy plastic tarp but lacking the glass doors. The fourth tunnel was more than twice the diameter of any of the others, and set a few yards into its mouth was another barrier seal but this one with a glass door like the one they had entered the cavern through, beyond which was a short walk to another plastic tarp stretching across the tunnel. Just enough barriers to seal the cavern and keep any carbon dioxide on the outside from mixing with the precious oxygen that the cavern's converters had been working for over forty-eight hours straight to make.

"Air's still kinda thin, I see," Darren remarked after a breath.

"No thinner than climbing to the top of Mount Fuji," Dr. Tomoko grinned.

"Or the Himalayan foothills," Feng added.

"Okay, so I'm the only one here who hasn't climbed a mountain," Darren said with a slight eye-roll, "moving on. I take it the large one with the barrier-seal across it is our mystery tunnel?"

"Yes," Dr. Tomoko replied. "It is very uncharacteristic of the other lava tubes. All the stone around here shows evidence of ancient lava flows, resulting in a smooth non-porous surface, but that one tube is too smooth and regular even to be accounted for by lava, nor does it have the same surface characteristics of such."

"Are you saying it's machine-made?" Feng ventured.

"No sign of chiseling or machining of any kind. If I had to guess, I might say someone used lasers, but even that would leave traces of melting. The rock looks like it was simply sheered away, but I can't tell you what by."

"Then that's the one we take," Darren decided. "Feng, you and I will take point. Jeremie, you're coming along because I figure it might be handy to have a physiologist on hand if we *do* bump into any alien life forms."

"I *was* wondering why I'm not still back in my lab," the man replied, only a slight trace of an accent to his words.

"That," Darren quipped, "and I could use someone besides myself for Feng and Akio to pick on along the way."

"Just our way of showing you how much we like you," Feng smiled.

"Okay, enough of the jokes," Darren decided. "Akio, have that pick of yours ready for samples. Jeremie, you know how to work that hand-scanner?"

The Frenchman gave a nod as he held up a hand-sized device bearing a control-pad and three-inch screen.

"Good, then keep an eye out for radiation and any sort of energy readings, no matter how small. Let's get going. Helmets on, radios set to channel one for local communication, but keep the command channel ready in case someone back at base needs our attention."

They put their helmets back on, each turning on their head-lamps to send a piercing beam into the gloom they would soon be approaching, then started across the cavern. Up to the larger tunnel, then one by one crossing through the barrier's double seal system and into the tunnel beyond where they paused while Darren briefly ran a gloved hand across the slick surface. When he spoke, as it would for all of them, his voice was heard by the other three from the speakers in their helmets.

"Akio, you're right; this wasn't made by lava at all. The surface was fractured, all right, but far too smooth. If I had to hazard a guess… If you could focus sonics like a laser then maybe, but…"

He let the question linger as he led the way, Feng by his side while behind them Dr. Tomoko had his chisel and sample tubes hanging along his belt, and Dr. Claude had one eye on the scanner in his hand. They walked with a wary step, every few yards Akio reaching out to give the wall a slight thump with his small geologist's hammer, while about once every thousand feet Feng would pull out a small round disk and slap it to the wall of the tunnel; the disk would stick there, now emitting a bright light in their wake.

Thus did they make their trek into the empty well of blackness before them, nothing beyond the range of their lights but more darkness, constricting ever closer around them. Soon all they could see behind them was the one line of lights along the wall, but even they looked to come out from an infinity of nothing, a trail to nowhere. Each step they took brought them further down the stone esophagus, nothing outside their suits but a world of night, pressing in ever closer. Four lone explorers, lost to naught but the grip of night.

They were deep into the tunnel, perhaps a kilometer or two, when the eerie peace of the tunnel was broken by a sudden squawk from their suit radios as a Russian-accented voice suddenly blurted out.

"Is Andrii speaking. Am coming in, yes?"

Darren nearly jumped at the unexpected reminder of an outside world, but clicked a button on his suit radio and replied in clear tones heard by all through their own helmets. A video image of the white-blond Russian with the whickered chin appeared in a small corner of his visor's heads-up display.

"The relays we set up are working perfectly, Andrii. What's up?"

"Am wanting to know about mission report. Is already overdue. What to tell Earth Command?"

"Tell them that we finally got all the supplies stored away safely into the lava tubes and are now following up on our first solid lead. We have discovered a tunnel, obviously artificial, that avoided our radar scans. We're walking its length now to see where it leads."

"Commander, perhaps I should come down there. If alien civilization after all, then you will need qualified person to study–"

"Andrii, we haven't found any actual ruins yet," Darren said with a slight grin, "so calm down. I'll let you know when there's something of interest to you, but first we have to make sure it's safe down here. So, just relax and have yourself a bottle of vodka or something."

"Voad-ka, yuk," came the reply. *"Tastes like hairspray. Will tell Glenda to be making report. Andrii out."*

Both Darren and Feng exchanged a grin at that last exchange as the radio went silent once again and the video image disappeared, Feng with a slight shake of his head as he clicked back to channel one to reply.

"He must be the only Russian I know of that hates Vodka."

"And it's still fun to poke his nose in it every once in a while," Darren replied. "Jeremie, anything on that scanner yet?"

"Not a peep," Dr. Claude reported.

"What about the background count?" Akio asked. "What's our baseline?"

"Like I said," Jeremie re-stated, "absolutely nothing. Not even background."

"Re-check that, it can't be right," Darren told him. "There's always some manner of background radiation and that meter should be sensitive enough to pick up even the faintest signal."

Dr. Claude slid a gloved finger across the control-pad of the scanner then replied with a shake of his head, to which Feng stepped over to read it for himself.

"He's right," Feng confirmed. "It's set to the most sensitive scale and there's nothing."

"But how is that possible?"

"I have a better puzzle," Dr. Tomoko stated.

The geologist said nothing, just brought out a pen-light from his belt and aimed it towards the ground before them. The tunnel they had been walking through was perfectly round, but someplace along the way the ground had become flat; no curve to it at all.

"A road?" Darren ventured. "Down here?"

"To where?" Feng asked. "Or what?"

"Not Oz, that much I'm sure of," Darren quipped. "But at this point, anything else is up for grabs. Come on, let's see where this road leads."

Their pace quickened, a mix of curiosity and fear driving their steps. What would they find? Did they *want* to find it? After all, an alien presence does not necessarily mean a friendly one.

"Here's a thought," Feng said as they walked. "What if we find something that it's someone buried? For a reason. That invitation it broadcast could have been a prisoner asking to be let out."

"Then I will still die happy if I have the chance to examine a truly alien life form," Jeremie blandly replied.

"Earth Command figured that as a possibility long ago," Darren told them, "which is why every orbiting nuke back at Earth is now aimed *outwards* just in case."

"A comforting thought," Dr. Tomoko remarked. "If something goes wrong down here, we'll be ground zero for a glowing crater. That gives me two reasons to hope whatever we find is indeed quite friendly."

With that thought in their minds, they continued onward; one kilometer then two, until the light of their head-lamps finally hit upon the end of their journey. A rather abrupt one, in the form of a flat wall; the end of their journey into the stony abyss seemed to be simply more stone. After a quick visual survey for any obvious dangers, Darren gave a nod to Dr. Tomoko who then took the hand-scanner from Dr. Claude and approached the wall with his chisel in his other hand. A single tap with his hammer, puzzled frown, then another somewhat harder tap, then running a hand carefully across the surface as he studied its detail.

"I do not know this material," he reported, "but I can confirm that it is artificial. It's completely smooth, absolutely flat, and while it appears to be stone, it almost resembles a sort of metal."

"What about the scanner?" Darren asked.

Akio took a glance down at the meter, put his pick back into his belt, then played with the scanner's control-pad a bit more while pacing slowly across the front of the wall before giving his report.

"Well, offhand I'd say this is the center of the lack of radiation we've been having, for lack of a better way of describing it. This meter is able to scan up to ten meters through solid rock for the rest of the tunnel, giving any indication of pockets or differences in density there may be. But when it comes to this wall? I can't get so much as a millimeter in."

"Maybe the signal is being reflected by the surface," Feng offered.

"I'm taking that into account," Akio said, adjusting another small dial. "No bounce, which means whatever this material is, it's absorbing the signal. That might be why the radar was having trouble mapping certain sections. No, if I had to say so, beyond this wall is whatever put out that signal all those years ago."

"So," Darren summed up, "we have a road leading up to a dead-end beyond which we can't scan, and no apparent way in. Any suggestions?"

"Knock?" Feng shrugged.

Akio reached out once more with his geologist's hammer and gave a light double tap, waited a moment, then a harder tap. He replied with a shrug to his commander.

"What about the drill," Dr. Claude suggested.

Dr. Tomoko replaced the hammer with a small hand-drill from his belt, started the drill-bit to whirring, then pressed it lightly to the surface while everyone else stepped back. Sparks flew away from where drill contacted wall, but when it became apparent no progress was being made, he clicked off the drill, wiped off some dust from where he had drilled, then looked at his drill-bit with a frown.

"Something?" Darren asked.

"Yes. My drill-bit appears to have been worn down."

"Use a diamond tip," Feng suggested.

"I *did,"* Dr. Tomoko frowned, a slight scowl on his face. "That dust I just wiped away was from the diamond bit."

"Hmm," Darren pondered. "Any *other* suggestions?"

When none were in the offering, Darren made a decision.

"Well, we can start by reporting this in, but I'm not leaving here until we have at least a clue of where to go from here. Someone sent out a signal, rolled out the welcome mat, then locked the door? I don't buy it."

Clicking his suit radio back to the command channel, he called out.

"Colonel Hildure to Command Base. Who's awake over there?"

This time a video of a woman with straight ear-length blond hair and angular features appeared in the corner of Darren's visor HUD.

"Professor Hayden here. What is it, Commander?"

The voice had a slight German accent, spoken with an efficient clip as if the speaker did not want to waste even a single stray syllable.

"Glenda, have you made that report to Earth yet?"

"Just finished. Should be about twenty minutes before they get it. You want to add an addendum?"

"Yes. Report the following. Have followed the one large tunnel that did not come up on our radar scans. About midway down the floor seems to nearly resemble a road, and ends at a flat wall. The wall is of no known material and can neither be chipped nor scanned through. We even tried a diamond drill-bit and still could not even mar the surface. We will continue to try looking for a way in or around, but could use some advice."

"What about energy readings?"

"Absolutely nothing. No ambient radiation that we can pick up, and as for the wall itself the hand scanner can't penetrate the surface and there's no scanner bounce-back."

"That cannot be," Glenda insisted. *"Even if the material is absorbing the radiation, there should be some part of the spectrum to which it does so to a lesser degree. No material is a perfect black body."*

"Well, this one sure looks like it."

"I can guarantee you it is not. Can you see it? Does it have color? If you can see it then that part of the visual spectrum at least is being reflected. We can begin with that."

"Either way, Glenda, it's going to take a lot more sensitive equipment than this hand-scanner to tell anything. Maybe if you want to come down here yourself?"

"Ja. I will transmit the update then ready some more sensitive equipment. Give me one hour. Professor Hayden out."

The video display winked out.

"Well," Darren said once he'd clicked back to their local channel, "you can't say she's not determined. In the meantime, let's see what clues we can find. Look for any seams, cracks, blemishes, anything that would give us a clue. Akio, try a bigger drill bit or a different spot. Jeremie, you take the scanner and walk around here; see if can find even a small blip of radiation. I at least want a clue. No one goes to all this trouble to invite us here just to leave us hanging."

Dr. Tomoko handed the scanner off to Dr. Claude then started fitting another bit into his drill to begin. He had not put drill to wall, however, when Dr. Claude suddenly stopped his pacing with the scanner and looked at the readout with eyes wide.

"Mon Dieu!"

The unexpected exclamation had all heads snapping in the Frenchman's direction, Dr. Tomoko pausing with his drill poised before the mysterious wall.

"Jeremie?" Darren asked. "What is it?"

For a few seconds, Dr. Claude just stared down at the device in his hand, then gave another exclamation under his breath and a slow shake of his head.

"And it's gone… as quickly as it came."

"Uh, Dr. Claude," Darren ventured, "if you don't mind interjecting a few details so we can all be surprised together?"

"What? Oh, I was just... I was reading nothing as before then suddenly an energy spike."

"How big?" Darren asked.

"Beyond what I can reliably read with this meter. For three seconds, it literally went off my scale, then cut off just as abruptly."

"Colonel Hildure, this is Professor Hayden."

An unusually urgent tone for the German woman, Darren immediately clicked over to the other channel to reply, her face once again appearing in a small corner of his visor.

"I'm here. We just recorded an energy spike down here. Any chance you picked it up over there?"

"Energy spike big enough to power an entire city? I think they'll be seeing it from Earth."

"Then let's get that scanner equipment down here and see what's going on. Maybe we triggered something."

"Right. Command Base out."

Darren had no sooner clicked his radio back off, the video image vanished when he paused to reach a hand to his forehead, nearly staggering on his feet.

"Jeremie, I think I need you for a minute," Darren called out. "I got this sudden headache."

"You aren't the only one," Feng echoed, one hand massaging his forehead.

"Make that three," Akio added.

"All four of us," Dr. Claude stated, looking a little pained as well. "Perhaps something from that energy spike. I can't really... really... rrr–"

Dr. Claude was the first to collapse, then next Dr. Tomoko fell to the ground. After that, darkness overcame Colonels Hildure and Yusheng as well...

Dr. Claude was the first to awaken, one arm to prop himself up with while the other checked his suit's chronometer.

"Looks to be only about ten minutes," he weakly announced. "Perhaps some sort of reaction to whatever was behind that energy spike."

"It's the only explanation," Dr. Tomoko now replied as he too propped himself up. "Colonel Hildure, might I suggest we retreat for a bit until Professor Hayden can get here with the other scanning equipment? Colonel Hildure... Darren?"

Slowly Jeremie and Akio looked around. All four were on the ground where they had collapsed, but Darren and Feng had yet to move. Then as Akio righted himself, from the light of his helmet lamp he could see why. Their spacesuits were there, laying on the ground where they had fallen, but deflated, empty now of the bodies that had once occupied them. Akio staggered back up to his feet, taking a few tentative steps then pulled out a hand-light from his belt for a better look around.

"Colonel Hildure? Colonel Yusheng?"

Nothing in the dimness save the row of lights they had left along their walk. Just himself, Dr. Claude, and the two empty spacesuits. Dr. Claude now staggered up to his feet, then remembering the little scanner still in his hand, gave it a quick glance before reporting to Dr. Tomoko's questioning look.

"Nothing. No sign anywhere. They've just... disappeared."

That last word echoed down the strange alien tunnel as if seeking to deepen the mystery about them.

CHAPTER TWO

AMELIA FRANKLIN

August 19, 2050

"I'm telling you, there's a lot here that just doesn't make any sense."

As the woman spoke, she was gesturing to her screen and an article displayed across it captioned as "Top Secret". A mix of African and Chinese, she was of medium height and slim build, exotic green eyes, finely sculpted facial features, skin a soft-hued black, and with her long dark hair currently tied back. She wore a black designer pantsuit and matching vest overtop, pinned to which was an ID badge that read "Amelia Franklin" and bears the insignia of the CIA.

Hers was one of a dozen desks in the room, each with twin flat-screen monitors, arranged in three rows, the hustle and bustle of Agency life ebbing and flowing around them like water around stones in a river. An office located within the complex at Langley.

Her desk, however, had more than the expected amount of papers and printouts strewn about before her. Studious woman with a suspicious eye, this was not the first time she had added to a growing mound of evidence for a case even she had no name for. The one to whom she was speaking, however, had a somewhat lower opinion of her mound of evidence. A man, like many others in the room, a dark-haired cookie-cutter clone of a man that others might instantly label as "government spy" from his general appearance alone; even down to the dark glasses sticking out of his left vest pocket. To Amelia's observation, he simply gave an eye-roll as he sat down at his neighboring desk to do his own work.

"Amelia, you are *supposed* to be working on the Brownswick case. The Chief wants that case resolved before the weekend."

"Oh, I finished that one a couple of hours ago," she replied offhandedly, her eyes still fixed on what she has scrolling across her screen. "The liquor store's a front for the terrorists' money laundering. I established a paper trail and enough evidence to link it all up. They should have the place raided by now."

"Wait," the man paused, "you *finished?* But I thought we were far from–"

"Never mind that, just have a look here. Another scientist came back after a week-long disappearance. No sign at all of where he went, what he was doing, or where he came back from."

"Probably on vacation. Just give it a rest. Ever since you got pulled from that Doctor Klein missing-persons case–"

"And *three* others after that," she reminded him. "It seems as every time some big-name scientist or political figure goes missing under suspicious circumstances we get pulled from the investigation before we can get anywhere. And then they show up again just as mysteriously. What do you think got me started on this?"

"Listen, you're brilliant, but this paranoia you have about–"

"Bill, we're CIA; we get *paid* to be paranoid, and in this case, I think you should be too. Of course I looked into the possibility of him just taking a trip. Facial recognition searches at every airport, bus station, and train depot within a hundred miles of his last reported sighting before his vanishing act. Nothing. The last image I have of him is this one; I took it from a local security-cam hooked up to the National Surveillance Network."

A press of a key and an image sprang up on her right-hand monitor. A view from above on a dark night of two gentlemen entering an apartment building. One of more elderly appearance, the other a tall muscular looking man covered up in a long coat and hood.

"He entered his apartment with whoever this other person is and never came out."

"So he took a vacation in his room for a week," the man shrugged.

"Bill, the next image of any sort that I can get of him is him walking *out* of a government building about five hundred miles away, and no sign of whoever that was with him."

"So wait," the man chuckled, "are you saying he somehow magically teleported across the state after staying in his room for a week? Amelia, you're really going off the deep end on this one."

The expression she now presented as she returned his answer with a look was as serious as his was mocking and not an eyelash did she bat from his outrageous suggestion.

"After you have eliminated the impossible, what you are left with no matter how improbable–"

"Yeah, don't go quoting Doyle with me, everyone knows that quote."

"Then perhaps everyone should listen to it more often, because this is far from being the first such disappearance. Look…"

A few keystrokes and her other monitor popped up a table with names, dates, and notes.

"…Scientists, politicians, not just from this country but scattered all over the world. In every case gone for about a week with little explanation, then when they return– Well, it's like their whole attitude changed."

The man briefly glanced over to see the list, then scoffed as he pointed in the direction of one of the names.

"That third one down; big wig ambassador. That date you have listed was about when he went into some super-secret conference. Something about terrorism talks. Nothing so mysterious about that."

"In itself, perhaps not. But taken with all the rest, it suggests a pattern. Bill, someone is spiriting these people away and doing something to them, because in every single case, right after their return they all seem to abruptly change their lives. Scientists leave positions they've worked all their lives to achieve, just to go work at… Well, I can't seem to find the security clearance high enough to find that out. Then the more political types, it's like they've suddenly found a new mission. For instance, certain leaders of Russia, China, and India entered into a private conference on the climate."

"There's been a few of those the last few years," he shrugged. "What of it?"

"When they came out it was with a new, and quite honest, resolve to cooperate with one another."

"So?"

"Bill, those three countries *never* cooperate with one another. They never even pretend to. Something got their attention that goes well beyond national boundaries, or maybe someone brainwashed them or something. I'm not sure yet, but I'll find out."

"Everyone needs a hobby," he sighed, turning back to his own work. "Yours is finding out where people spend their vacation time."

"It's more than that, Bill. Haven't you noticed the recent increase in satellite launches? Whatever they're for is so top-secret that I can't find out a thing. Heck, I think they're even above the *Chief's* pay grade."

"The Military's always doing stuff like that. Probably just a bunch of spy satellites."

"In which case, we– being *spies*– would have access, but we don't. And is it just coincidence that the astronauts tending these satellites all happen to have had their own one-week vanishing acts? There's definitely a conspiracy and it all dates back to that Mars landing ten years ago."

"The old Mars mission?" Now he turned from his work, puzzled look for his coworker. "They established a base to, I believe the exact line was, 'research the possibility of colonizing Mars in the future.' A bit of a money-pit if you ask me. A full decade and they still got nothing except a Mars launch every couple of years."

"And that in itself would be the next piece of evidence, because there is no way those few launches could supply enough material and resources to support any kind of base up there. Even assuming they've found a way to mine local minerals to supply their needs, they would have had to ship the equipment to do so over there and those launches wouldn't even have supported *that.* Bill, don't you see? It all connects together."

"Okay, Miss Wonder-Agent, how?"

To this she had nothing but silence and a hesitant expression, which a moment later Bill took as a win.

"Just what I thought. Amelia, you need a break. Maybe this job has made you a bit too paranoid, because you're jumping at everything."

"Bill, there's something there. I… I just can't find what it is yet, but I know it's big. It feels… Well, I'm just not sure."

The other turned away with a shake of his head, resuming his work while Amelia was left once again puzzling things to herself. Her gaze drifted across her screens, then down to the papers on her desk, all labeled as evidence for a case that did not exist.

"Maybe I *am* going too far," she whispered to herself. "But there's something there, I just *know* it."

Another moment of staring blankly at her work, a sigh, then she reached out for the key to blank her screen. A moment before her finger hit the key, however, both screens blanked themselves, replaced by a single message in the left screen furthest from view of Bill's desk.

Report to Director Forester's Office immediately.

Nothing more, then seconds later the message vanished.

"The *Director's* office," she puzzled to herself. "But why not come down through the chain of command? Why not from the Chief and why so secretive? What have I just tripped over?"

She sat there wondering for just a moment longer before standing up. A last look down at the empty monitors before just about to step away when another prompt appeared on the left monitor. It was a progress bar quickly flashing by with the names of files being deleted… all of them from her own private research project. Trained as she was, she gave no outward sign of what she felt at seeing all her work suddenly vanish before her eyes, but inwardly she knew what this meant.

"You're stepping out for a bit?" Bill asked.

"Uh, yeah. It looks like I might be taking a vacation after all… for about a week, would be my guess."

"Then enjoy yourself. Some of us have work to do."

She said not a word more, just stayed long enough to see the progress bar finish itself and vanish before stepping away. She had no doubt that the printouts on her desk would also be gone by the time she returned.

If she returned…

Erica Forester was a mixed white-black woman with severe facial features and hair a dark red, tight afro curls trimmed down to an almost military length. She sat behind a sturdy oak desk dressed in her usual grey pantsuit, in an office on the topmost floor of the CIA building. The door simply read, "Director Forester", though the official annals of the Agency would never say exactly what she was director over. Officially, another was director of the CIA, but within the Agency itself, it was well known that it was she who ran it… and perhaps a bit more.

The office was a study in Spartan luxury, as if its owner didn't mind a few of the more expensive things in life, but only the bare minimum necessary. One plush leather chair for herself, a smaller one for a possible guest. One bookshelf behind her festooned mostly with an assortment of Agency-related manuals and legal books. No personal effects, nothing to connect her with any weak links such as might be found in one's private life; not for the type of business she is in. Finally, the one window looked out over an open courtyard at the center of the surrounding Agency buildings; not even the risk of a direct view to the outside world.

Amelia hid her nervousness behind a professional mask of unconcern. Erica Forester may be unknown to the outside world, but within the Agency she was a legend, known to stare down men twice her slender size. No secretary was there to admit her, the door just opened of its own accord when she stood before it, closing immediately after her.

"Agent Franklin."

Amelia stood before the desk, trying to maintain both composure and eye contact as the Director looked her up and down, but it wasn't easy.

"I have an assignment for you."

"Begging the Director's pardon, but why not send it through my section chief? Why ask for me personally?"

"An obvious question with an obvious answer. You have uniquely qualified yourself of late. Now, your assignment is in China. You will be leading a group there to help safeguard the wedding of one General Feng. You speak some Chinese, right? Good."

"A wedding, ma'am? In China?"

"It's a lot more important than it sounds, Agent Franklin. Elements in the Chinese government believe there may be an attempt on his life, but our contact doesn't know who to trust. As such, we are using the excuse of Feng's longtime American friend and his family attending to send in some of our own agents."

At mention of the name, Amelia's attention perked up just a bit. It could be a coincidence, but she wasn't about to bet on that. Could it actually be Feng Yusheng of the original Mars mission?

"This," Director Forester continued, pulling out a couple of photos from a drawer in her desk, "is a picture of General Feng and his soon to be girlfriend. This other photo is of his friend, Darren Hildure."

Now Amelia's attention was riveted and this time she could not hide her reaction.

"They're the two men from that first Mars mission. Hildure was the commander and Feng his second. I remember seeing pictures of them both from their return, including Feng hugging his girlfriend at the time."

"Soon after which they both disappeared from public life, is that what you were thinking, Agent Franklin?"

"Well, I… that is…"

Truth be told, she wasn't exactly sure what to think at this point, so she opted for silence as she took the photos. The first showed Feng and his girlfriend, the other his American companion.

"How old are these photos?" she asked. "I could use something more recent."

"They were taken last week."

"Last… But Feng's girlfriend looks exactly the same as she did a decade ago. Good genes I guess; some girls get all the luck. The two men don't look any older either, come to think of it."

"Genetics aside, Agent Franklin, you will head up the security team but report to Darren Hildure."

"Yes, Director."

"Only to Hildure. I don't care if some General tries to pull rank or some political buffoon tries to blow smoke up your ass, you are to only take orders from and report any findings to Hildure directly. Do I make myself clear?"

"Yes, Director," Amelia said, snapping to attention.

"Good, now get packing. You leave in a few hours; you'll find the details on your company cell phone. Dismissed."

Amelia nodded, feeling much like she was in the military before her commanding officer than in the CIA– Director Franklin just seemed to have that effect on people– then turned to leave. Before she reached the door, however, Director Forester had one last word for her.

"And Agent Franklin. Do well in this and you just might get that vacation you were talking about earlier."

With all that one statement seemed to imply, Amelia wasn't sure if the promise boded ill or not…

It wasn't long before Amelia found herself getting off a military suborbital jet at the Beijing Capital International Airport in China, behind her other agents and security personnel under her command. The section of airfield she found herself in was empty of all save the technicians tending the plane and one man at the base of the ramp waiting to greet her. A man close to thirty from his looks, tall and muscular, his dark brown hair trimmed short, chin shaved clean and a slight tan to his features. He was currently dressed in a long-sleeved blue and green shirt over a pair of jeans– something that might peg him as any given American tourist– with a friendly smile for her as she walked down the steps.

"Agent Franklin, I take it. I'm Darren Hildure."

"Nice to meet you, Mister Hildure," she replied, reaching out a hand.

"I understand you got this assignment direct from Director Forester?"

"Yes, Mister Hildure. I still find it rather odd, but will prove myself up to the assignment."

"I have no doubt that you will."

He reached out in greeting, his other hand lightly brushing a lock of hair away from the side of his head as he smiled. A knowing smile, confidence in a look held briefly before he released his grip.

"Yes, definitely a good decision. This way, I have some cars waiting. You'll be riding with me while the rest of your team will be in the vans. What equipment did you bring with you?"

"The usual assortment of weapons and spy-craft equipment. As soon as I see the layout of the wedding site then I'll know what more we'll need."

"Good."

Amelia signaled back to her team to start unloading then accompanied Darren across the open stretch towards a hanger before which was parked a long black four-door sedan and two vans, all of which had windows tinted black. Behind her the team began unloading small unmarked crates while Amelia got straight to the point.

"The Director told me to report only to you. Other than that I am in charge of all wedding security."

"In cooperation with our Chinese friends, yes. The problem is, we don't know which of our Chinese friends are really friends."

"How much time do we have to prepare?"

"The wedding's in three weeks, but first we're going to meet with the family of Feng's girlfriend. That will be later this afternoon, so I hope you won't take long to settle in."

"I'm a field agent, Mister Hildure, the last five years I've lived mostly out of a suitcase. I'm ready *now.*"

"Good."

He said not a word more until they reached the sedan, then opened the back door for her. Her team was already packing a few things away into the vans. Besides the driver– an increasingly rare luxury in an age of self-driving vehicles– the sedan held one other person in the back seat; a young Chinese man about Darren's age dressed in similar nondescript clothing.

"Agent Amelia Franklin," Darren said by way of introduction as they both got in, "this is General Feng Yusheng."

"General."

"Please, just call me Feng when no one's around to know the difference; or Mister Yusheng, if you must."

"As you wish, Mister Yusheng. If I didn't know any better, I'd say that you look rather young to be a General anyway. The both of you seem to hold your ages rather well."

For a moment neither man replied, just exchanged a look that seemed to communicate volumes that Amelia could not read. Then Feng broke out into a smile as Darren closed the door while he got seated.

"Good genes, Agent Franklin. This is your first trip to China, so just remember to look before you leap, but by all means, maintain that suspicious demeanor of yours. It should serve you well."

"Thank-you for the advice, General."

She then paused for a moment, flicker of confusion flashing across her face, for she had not mentioned to either one that this is her first trip to China. Maybe they read it in her file.

A minute later the sedan pulled away.

Agent Franklin had little time to enjoy the sights of downtown Beijing as they drove through them; just enough to assess with quick glances possible threats to security, if they were being followed or watched, and anything else that might arise her suspicions. Tall gleaming towers a hundred or more stories up, multitudes of people and vehicles surging through the streets, multi-story electronic billboards flashing colorful holographic ads of the latest in consumer attractions, centuries-old Taoist temples nestled amongst the towering skyscrapers, the distinctive appearance of an occasional American fast-food chain, highways like speeding rivers of light, and above it all the grey cloud of smog that had become a permanent fixture of Beijing and its surrounding environs. The people were dressed in a mix of the new and the old, West meets East, with everything from business suits and the latest in designer trends, to old-style Chinese coil-button jackets or colorful robes and dresses woven with complex patterns. Cars mixed with trollies, bicycles, the occasional rickshaw, driverless taxis, and large auto-busses to clog the highways. Those of the street signs that were also in English were made even more unintelligible by their translation or confusing appearance, but there were a few she managed to catch; signs directing to such places as the Grand Pacific Mall or Joy City.

It was more than enough to keep her occupied trying to determine which of all this could pose a threat to her charges and no time for tourist-like gawking.

Their hotel was one of those many gleaming towers– the Grand Millennium Beijing– their room an elegant suite that encompassed most of one of the upper floors; a side benefit of who her charges happened to be. Once arrived she wasted no time and got straight to work. First, she directed her team in getting set up– making sure all their weapons were ready, unpacking any monitoring equipment and computers– then quickly freshened herself up and changed before meeting again with Feng and Darren in the suite's common area. She had her first question ready as she stepped out with a last brush to straighten out her vest, but Feng was already giving answer before she had a chance to ask it as he and Darren sat down around a table in a sunken part of the room before a large picture window that overlooked the glittering city outside.

"The wedding will be held in the home village of my girlfriend, Dao-ming Yeung, in Heilongjiang Province. It will be very traditional, at her father's insistence, and involves certain things happening over the days preceding the wedding. For one thing, the bride-to-be retreats from her ordinary routine a short time before the wedding to live in seclusion in another part of the house with just a few close friends. During that time, I am not to get close to her."

"That leaves us with a security hole before the wedding even starts," Amelia noted as she sat down to join them. "We'll need a security detail around her as well, in case someone decides to kidnap her to get to you. The wedding, I assume it will be out in the open?"

"Very much so," Feng replied. "Security will be supplied by the Chinese government, given my status as a General, but again there are those suspicions as for who to trust."

"Which is why you're here," Darren put in. "Allegedly you're here for my protection, so the story will be that securing me means having to watch over my good friend Feng here as well."

"I'm more worried about Dao-ming," Feng replied. "You know I can look out for myself, Darren."

"With all due respect, General," Amelia stated, "if the conspiracy lies within your very own government, I doubt if even a respected General is truly safe. I'll have to inspect the wedding site before the wedding. Mister Hildure here said that you are scheduled to meet with your girlfriend's parents later today? I assume that will be at his house, so if Mister Hildure accompanies you as a friend, then that gives me a chance to case the area out. I'll bring two of my team with me to make it look like Mister Hildure's bodyguards."

"Please," Darren put in, "first names only while we're in here. Save all titles for the outside world."

"Very well… Darren. I also want to put a tracking device on you and Feng."

She then pulled out from one pocket a small palm-sized case and clicked it open to reveal what looked like a pair of metallic dust motes. Feng took one look at them then smirked to Darren.

"Don't underestimate them from their size," she explained, "they're hooked up to a worldwide satellite tracking network. Now, say ah."

"Huh?"

Before Darren could elaborate on his question, Amelia plopped one of the devices into his mouth then shut it with a lift of finger to chin. While Darren was swallowing she then turned to Feng.

"The lady does appear to be insistent," Feng grinned. "She just might– Urgf."

She hadn't bothered to wait and jammed the second device into Feng's mouth while he was still talking, then while he was trying to turn his gag reflex into a swallow, Amelia briefly explained.

"These will latch into your stomach lining and remain there for about two to three months before your stomach acid breaks them down." From a top vest pocket she then pulled out a small palm-sized device, flicked it on with her thumb, and looked at the display. "They're working, I'm picking you both up. From this point on I will know where the two of you are no matter where in the world someone might take you, should the worst happen."

"Well," Darren grinned, "that opens up some amusing possibilities."

"Darren, behave," Feng replied. "We have some serious business here."

But then Darren gave his friend another brief look, which had them both smirking for a moment or two. Amelia wasn't sure what the joke was that they both seemed to share, but it was starting to stir her paranoia. Her mission was to look after Feng, but she had a feeling that there was more to it than what she could see…

The village in Heilongjiang Province was the intersection of the traditional and more modern aesthetics; a place that had not forgotten its ancient roots, nor shirked the need of modern conveniences. Stylized curved roofs like rows of king's crowns arranged in terraced steps down the gradual slope of a hillside to a wooded valley below, a covered bridge spanning a small river meandering its way along, the remains of an old stone wall marking final border about the village, here and there an old stone foo-dog decorating its tops as if ancient guardians. All as it might have been a millennia ago, but gone were the old dirt streets, long since paved though still narrow and winding, as if themselves unsure of which way to go. Modern street lights had replaced old hanging lanterns, and there was even a cell tower in the distance, designed to look like a tall stand of bamboo.

The two-story house they approached bore the same old designs as the rest of the village, though built with far more modern materials. Roof of rippling blue ceramic waves frozen in place, tall walls of white plaster; it could have been a local Governor's mansion from days past, save the telltale signs of electricity, phone, and plumbing, with windows that could tint themselves at the turn of a dial. The front yard bore a carefully tended herb garden wrapped decoratively around a concrete driveway in which two cars rested.

One of which was stamped with governmental insignia.

"Someone's beaten us here," Amelia noted as they got out of the sedan, behind them one of the vans with a couple of her security men exiting as well.

"Chinese Intelligence, from the looks of the markings," Feng replied. "Probably Chief Lee Pinyin. He's supposed to be handling security for the wedding."

"Then I hope he doesn't mind if I check *him* out first," Amelia flatly stated as they approached the house.

"I think you will find him to be okay," Feng told her. "I've known him for a few years."

"I'll judge for myself, if you don't mind."

The front door was like a gateway into an ancient world speckled with more reminders of the modern age. The interior was built around a small courtyard open to the sky, populated by arrangements of colorful potted plants, a few hanging decorations hand-sculpted in polished wood, and a single tree near the center growing straight up from the ground. On the far side of the courtyard could be seen a sliding glass door leading into the interior of the house, another path off to the far left leading away to parts unseen. Three individuals were already there, seated on a circular garden bench that wrapped around the tree, all of which now rose at the new entries.

The first was an older Chinese man with neatly combed grey hair, his chin sporting an equally grey goatee and mustache; he was dressed in a suit and tie, expensive Italian shoes, but despite the casual friendly façade and the cane topped by the brass Chinese dragon head that he used, was one that Amelia would peg as the Intelligence Chief. Opposite him stood a man whose age had not yet cost him the dark color of his hair, though looked not quite as fit as the Chief, with close-cut whiskers around his chin, and currently wearing a dark blue old-style Chinese jacket with three strap-buttons down the front. Beside him a far younger woman, in appearance perhaps mid to late twenties, but if she is the same person in the photograph in Agent Franklin's pocket, then she should be in her late thirties by now; a slender woman with long black hair and a dress that mixed the traditional with more modern styles and colors.

This latter had a gentle modest look to her, but the second they entered her face beamed with a radiant smile and she would have no doubt bounded straight over to throw herself at Feng were it not for the presence of the one beside her. Instead, she gave a demure nod in Feng's direction, though Amelia could see she wanted to do far more.

"Agent Franklin," Feng made the introductions, "this is the father of my bride to be, Chang Yeung, and that lovely vision standing beside him is my love Dao-ming."

"I am Chief Lee Pinyin," the older man said with a nod. "Chinese Intelligence. I am in charge of wedding security."

"Agent Amelia Franklin," she replied, reaching out a hand to shake. "I'm here to look after the safety of the American contingent, particularly Mister Hildure here."

"As I was told," Chief Pinyin said as they all paced slowly across the gardened courtyard, Amelia's two security men remaining standing by the entry door. "I was just telling Mister Yeung here that while it is very unusual for Chinese Intelligence to take an interest in the planning of a local wedding, these are very unusual circumstances."

"My son-in-law," Mister Yeung stated, "is very important person. Famed hero. I know what comes with that."

"Then to start, I understand that you want the wedding in this village," Chief Pinyin began. "That is not a problem, and in fact is easier for my people to control than in the middle of a crowded city. I assume all the people in this village will be in attendance, as well as the family of General Feng, so I have been checking everyone out. Mister Hildure, what about the American contingent?"

"Right here."

Darren took out a slip of paper with names on it and passed it to the Chief, though not before Agent Franklin intercepted it for a quick review herself.

"Just me and my parents," Darren assured them both.

"With permission of both Chief Pinyin and Mister Yeung," Agent Franklin put in, "while we're here, I would like to walk around the wedding site and adjoining areas, and anywhere else that will involve such festivities."

"I have no objections," Mister Yeung replied. "Though, Chief Pinyin, I must confess that the guest list is incomplete. I have a son studying at MIT. He has stayed there longer than he should. Will this be a problem with him coming to the wedding?"

"Hmm, yes I remember reading about him in the file," Chief Pinyin mused. "Yes, it could be a problem. He was supposed to join the military after finishing school and he did not. I believe he is twenty-eight? Yes, he is too old to go into training with the eighteen-year-olds, but I have an idea."

"Anything," Mister Yeung replied. "I would not wish my son to be arrested just for desiring to attend his sister's wedding."

"Well, if he is willing to work for me as an Aerodynamic Engineer, with pay, then the Republic of China will erase his shortcomings. After that, if he wishes to return to the United States then he can. This assumes, of course, that he has not gotten into any trouble in America."

"Thank-you, Chief," Mr. Yeung said with a slight inclination of his head. "He is a good boy and would like to visit his home. He is not physically made for service in the army but is a brilliant engineer."

"Then we have an agreement." Chief Pinyin then stepped back, bowing his head in departure. "Mister Yeung, General Feng, ladies. I will see you all later; I have much work to attend to."

Agent Franklin nodded her own head in reply, but not once did her gaze leave the Intelligence Chief as he walked away with his cane and out through the front doors. Moments later they heard his car drive away.

"If there is nothing more," Agent Franklin stood up, "I would like to look around the wedding site."

"Then allow me to lead the tour," Feng offered, as he got to his feet. "Dao-ming, I count the hours until we are united as one."

"I feel like we already are," she replied with a shy smile.

"Sir," Feng then said to her father, "I will be back after I show them around the village."

"Before you leave," Mister Yeung said, standing up as well, "there is something I would like to ask of you."

Agent Franklin kept a careful eye on them as they stepped away across the courtyard, while Dao-ming walked away to tend some of the flowering pots. They switched to speaking in Chinese, but as part of her training that was one of a couple of important languages that Agent Franklin had a passing familiarity with. She strained her ears while trying to look like she was not eavesdropping.

"I mean no disrespect, but you have known Chief Pinyin for a long time, so I would ask. The deal he offered for my son, will he keep to his word?"

"He will," Feng replied. "After his term is up, he will allow him to return to America if he so chooses, but in his heart would hope that he remains with China."

"Then I have a further request. I have heard rumors of a… special project being built. All governments. I realize you cannot confirm its existence, but could you get my son into that project? He is very smart and would be most enthusiastic for something like that."

"Mister Yeung," Feng smiled, "if such a project exists, then I would be most willing to recommend him for it. Assuming, of course, he passes my interview. My friend Darren will be having some business back in the States before the wedding, so I will be flying over to pick him up. I can stop by and interview your son while I'm there."

"That is all I can ask. Thank-you."

Agent Franklin managed to school her features, but all the way out and as they surveyed the site for the wedding, she could not help but think over what she had just heard. Some sort of special project? Involving *all* the world's governments? She had heard nothing of this at all.

What sort of conspiracy had she stumbled into?

Agent Franklin was given her quick tour, after which she decided to return the next day for a more thorough inspection of the village and its denizens, going over her proposed security precautions with her team and Darren, while leaving Feng safely back in the hotel room with a couple of her men. Feng though had his mind on one thing alone, and that was his nearing wedding with Dao-ming. The time would soon come when she would have to seclude herself before the wedding, leaving very few opportunities for them to be together until after the wedding.

It was in this mindset that he checked his messages during his breakfast. He sat back in his assigned bedroom of the hotel's suite, a coffee and Danish on the small end-table beside him as he tapped on the keyboard embedded into the arm of a plush leather chair and watched his messages flash across the video wall before him. One of the messages was from Dao-ming.

"Ah, I wonder what my lovely vixen has to say to me this morning?"

It was an invitation. Dao-ming had invited him for lunch and wanted him to meet her in the parking garage of the village temple.

"Hmm, I wonder why she didn't just call me? I could always– No, that would be spying on my own intended. I'll just trust that she has something special in mind away from the prying eyes of her father, or simply wants to play at being mysterious. Just a simple matter of getting away from Agent Franklin's bodyguards; that shouldn't be too much trouble."

With a smile as he pictured the delight of things to come, he finished off his coffee then clicked off his video wall and stood up…

Shortly before lunch, Feng found himself walking up to the village temple parking garage, glancing around for Dao-ming's car. Into the shadowy recesses of the garage he went, and it wasn't until he had walked fully out of sight of the road that he saw her standing by one of the parking stalls.

"Dao-ming," he waved.

She waved back, then before he could take another step further the world went black.

Agent Franklin had been spending most of the morning with her security team driving and walking around the village where Dao-ming's family lived, canvasing not just the wedding site, but anywhere nearby, any structure tall enough for a possible sniper to get a good shot from. Every villager that walked on by she would eye with just as much suspicion as they would her and her team. Many of the people living anywhere near the wedding site she would interview personally, while Darren said he would be at the other side of the village engaging in what he called his own way of investigating.

Strange, though, that she never caught sight of him the entire morning. At any rate, it was enough to keep her quite busy until well past Noon.

Then, while finally finishing up her initial assessment of the park where the wedding was to be held and what security measures the event would need, she suddenly stopped. For no reason that she could fathom, an odd feeling came over her; a sudden concern for General Feng. On instinct, she pulled out her little tracking device and noted the two readouts displayed. Feng's was somewhere well outside of the village, deep in the woods.

"Why do I have a really *bad* feeling about this? You," she said, pointing to two of her security men, "grab me a car and come with me. I think Feng's in trouble."

She soon found herself in a police car with two of her security men, drive-mode set to manual as she raced across the village and out into the surrounding woods until the road gave out and nothing but thick clusters of trees lay before her. At that point she pulled over and started going it on foot, following wherever her tracking device showed her with a rapid pace through such uneven terrain as might impress the two men with her. It wasn't long after that before she came to a clump of trees and what looked like a mound of freshly dug earth.

"*No,"* she gasped, then to the two men with her, "Get some shovels, quick!"

While the other two went back to the vehicle to find something to dig with, she ran over to the mound and started into digging with her hands. She had not finished her first scoop of earth, though, when the ground beneath her rumbled; not from a quake, but just the dirt itself immediately around the mound suddenly bulge. She immediately leaped back, gun drawn, then saw it move again. Like something trying to push itself up from beneath the ground.

On the third try, the dirt suddenly exploded, leaving a small hole behind it. Another such little explosion, and then a third and she finally saw a single fist sticking straight up, splinters of wood still clinging to the knuckles.

"My God, they buried him alive! But how–"

Then a final explosion of earth and she could see it all plain. It was General Feng, at the bottom of a shallow grave, in a cheap wooden casket. But as to how he had moved the earth off from above himself she had no clue, for his other arm was still strapped down to the base of the coffin, as were both his legs, while the broken remains of the strap for his one free hand lay beside him.

"That's impossible!"

Impossible or not, she had one duty now before her. As her two men returned with a couple of small shovels, she grabbed a knife from the belt of one of them and jumped down into the hole to cut the gasping Feng free. Feng's first sight as his eyes fluttered open was of the young agent cutting him free.

"Oh good," he gasped, "you heard me. Chief Lee's on his way, but with Darren popped off across town on something, you were nearer. Just wasn't sure if…"

His eyes closed again as he fell into a deep sleep.

Feng awoke in a hospital bed, a room all to himself, cleaned and wearing a white gown with an IV connected into his right arm. Blinds were drawn across the one window, a man standing guard just outside the door, the television on the wall currently turned off. Sitting beside him was Agent Franklin, poised to leap to her feet the instant she saw him wake up. She stepped over, looking at him curiously, and from the tired grin on his face had a disturbing feeling that he somehow knew what was on her mind.

"I can't explain how you threw all that earth off of you, nor how you managed to punch your way out of a coffin with just one free hand, but as incredible as that is, even more so would be the doctor's report. The hair on the back of your head was caked with blood, as if you had just been knocked on the head."

"I was. They caught me when I had my attention on my girlfriend; I was meeting her in the temple parking garage. How is she, by the way?"

"Worried about where you've been. She'd never left her house, so whoever it was you saw was not her. But getting back to my point, the doctors found plenty of blood but no head wound from being struck. Not so much as a scratch."

"I heal quickly," he grinned.

"Then there was the poison," she continued, stepping over close to his bedside, lowering her voice for just the two of them alone. "According to one Doctor Jin Yuwei, your body was full of it. Should have killed you deader than what I saw."

"Poison… I guess they wanted to make sure. Probably why I felt so weak. Were you able to trace its origin?"

"Made from a plant in Costa Rica and not available here in China."

"That reaches a bit farther abroad than we'd thought. I suppose there's more?"

"Yes," she nodded. "Because when the doctor ran his tests, he was able to examine your DNA, and do you know what he found?"

"A few things never found in Human blood before?"

"There were some technical terms, but something like that. He wanted to call in a whole roster of colleagues to work with him on it."

"So, what did you do, Agent Franklin?"

"Shut him down until Chief Pinyin could get here to slap him with your country's equivalent of an Official Secrets Act notice. I know a Top-Secret when I see one, even if I'm not in on it. Then there's the fact that Mister Hildure had somehow found himself all the way in Beijing when I went looking for you, instead of the other side of that village where I left him. Feng, what is going on?"

"Looks like Darren was right to recommend that Forester assign you," he chuckled weakly. "I'd say you're definitely qualified for the next trip to Mars."

"My next *what?*"

"Easy Amelia; it's nothing like what you might fear, though it does involve that one-week vacation you've been thinking about. As of this moment consider your security clearance increased a few notches. Now pull up a chair while I tell you what happened on Mars about ten years ago..."

CHAPTER THREE

FLASHBACK

August 4, 2040... Ten years earlier.

We were exploring some caves looking for the feasibility of using them as habitation; perfect for protection against radiation and easier to oxygenate than an entire planet. At least that was the official report. In truth, some years before that a single burst transmission had been received from Mars. A first mission failed before it had even a chance to investigate, but we'd found something. A cave, artificially carved, though not with tools or heat. Focused sonics was our guess. Anyway, at one point the bottom of it started to look like a road, but it ended up at a blank wall. Nothing we had with us could scan past that wall, or even scratch it, much as we tried. We were just sending out for some better equipment when a sudden surge of energy was recorded by our equipment, accompanied by a rather astounding headache.

Sometime after that, Darren and I woke up elsewhere and without our spacesuits on. Something about them being a bulky nuisance according to Observer, but I'm getting ahead of myself.

We were lying on our backs on a large table, and there to greet us was some sort of alien robot. Roughly humanoid in appearance, but the eyes were clearly artificial. Its face was sculpted to look human enough, but it didn't really need to move its mouth to speak; I think that was just for aesthetics. Its skin though; covered in some sort of light blue polymer to look like skin, at least until you touched it.

Darren and I were both trained for the unexpected, especially considering we'd entered in this mission knowing that intelligent life must be behind it, but when you see a robot you expect a robotic voice, not the normal flow of speech with an American accent. It greeted us in pleasant enough tones...

"Good morning Commander Colonel Darren Hildure and Colonel Feng Yusheng. I am pleased to have you as my guest."

"A... A robot?" Darren asked.

"That would be your correct term for me, though rather more sophisticated than what you are used to. I am designated as Observation and Contact Unit Number Two Seven Zero Five."

"Uh, that's a bit of a mouthful," Darren remarked. "Do you mind if we shorten that a bit? Say... just call you Observer?"

"As you wish," the robot replied. "Be that as it may, what I have to tell you concerns much of both your world's history and that of the rest of the galaxy. And, I have observed much of your world's history first hand."

"First hand?" Feng asked. "Wouldn't that make you rather old?"

"I am eight thousand five hundred of your years, four months, three days, and going on twenty-two minutes since I came online. I have been on Mars for about that same length of time. Now, there is much I have to tell you that you must listen to."

"And if we refuse?" Feng asked. "We could just force our way out of this place."

"Your profile suggests that you will not, Colonel Yusheng. You came all this distance to find an answer; you aren't about to turn away from it now."

"He's got you there, Feng," Darren grinned. "So what's going on? Why the invite signal?"

Observer waited until both were sitting up and had a brief moment to look around before he continued. They were in a cavern-like room, rounded out as smooth as had been the tunnel. Scattered about were various panels of what they guessed to be controls, though they looked like polished obsidian with colored designs displayed across them, while overhead light came down from brightly glowing patches in the ceiling. As far as exits, behind them was what looked like the inside of the strange wall they had encountered in the tunnel, while at the far end of the room were two open passages carved in the same manner, though sized more like normal hallways.

"I was actually expecting closer to ten people to initially train, but I can start with two."

"Expecting?" Feng asked. "How could you know what to expect?"

"Probabilities calculated long ago," Observer answered. "My makers approximated how many people Earth would send on its first mission to Mars once I would have sent the invitation signal, and set up the facilities accordingly. Of course, I have had plenty of time to work on expanding them while maintaining my stealth, but I will explain more on that later. I will tell you as much as I can about the purpose of this facility, but for anything more I am afraid that you will have to undergo an indoctrination period. That will take approximately twenty-four hours, during which time you will be fed as much technical information as your brains can hold, as well as be physically improved."

"Wait, slow down," Darren cut in. "Let's start with the reason why we're all here to begin with. Why have you been watching Earth and why do you need to gift us with all this sudden knowledge?"

"In brief," Observer began, "there is a crisis in the galaxy that involves every intelligent species, including yours. My creators were at your level of development some four hundred and fifty thousand years ago and are far from being the only other sentient life forms in this galaxy. In fact, there are some twenty thousand intelligent races in this galaxy alone that are capable of interstellar travel. At least of the ones that we know of."

"Wow," Darren grinned, "sounds kind of crowded. You sure there's anywhere left for us to explore?"

"How can you know this?" Feng asked. "What I mean is, how can you traverse such vast distances to know?"

"My makers have the capability to travel thirty-thousand light-years in a single jump, after which the drive needs to rest for one hour before the next jump. After one hundred and twenty thousand light-years of such travel, the negative-matter drive system needs to be replaced."

"Thirty-thousand– In a single jump? It boggles the mind," Feng said, a new wonder filling his eyes. "But, there's a catch, isn't there?"

"He's right," Darren echoed. "You aren't here just to invite us into the galactic travel club."

"You are both as astute as my reports to my creators have made your species out to be. Yours is the only race in this galaxy known to be ninety-nine point nine-nine percent compatible, both physically and mentally, with my creators' race."

"We're just a few thousand years behind them is all," Darren grinned.

"Exactly so, Commander Hildure."

"And why is that so important?" Feng now asked.

"Two reasons, Colonel Yusheng."

"First, it's just Darren and Feng," Darren stated.

"As you wish. To begin with, there is a race out there we call the Zelos. They are much like the swarming insect you call the locust, in both appearance and tendencies. They stand approximately one and a half of your meters tall, are very tough, and survive in a mix of carbon dioxide and nitro-oxide. Individually they are unorganized and not very intelligent, but communally they become very intelligent and highly organized. As far as we can determine, they communicate by a form of telepathy that reaches no more than one kilometer away. Ship to ship their communication is likewise telepathic but can apparently be extended over thousands of light-years."

"You said they're like locusts in tendencies as well," Darren realized. "What do you mean by that?"

"The only times they have been observed is in the raiding of planets. They only seem to raid worlds inhabited by sentient species and they leave nothing alive in their wake. They have also been observed pillaging such worlds for their resources, but the main goal appears to be destruction of life. The reason for that is not known."

"With twenty thousand races in one galaxy," Feng points out, "why don't you just chase them down and destroy them?"

"Many would like to," Observer replied, "but no one knows where their homeworld is."

"Um, here's a disturbing observation," Darren interjected, "you said they attack worlds inhabited by intelligent species... Like Earth."

"Like Earth," Observer confirmed. "By current calculations based on the attack patterns of the Zelos, they will reach your Earth in approximately one hundred and fifty years, perhaps less; where the Zelos are concerned, predictions are not too reliable. My mission was to wait until you had achieved the status of interplanetary travel to contact you. With the impending Zelos threat, once you had established a regular base on your Moon, I could wait no longer. Now I must bring you up to a level where you may be able to defend yourselves against the Zelos."

"Defending ourselves against a race that can exterminate planets," Darren pondered. "Sounds like a tall order."

"Or a lie," Feng suggested.

"Gentlemen, if you will observe."

The lights suddenly dimmed as projected in the air above them came a view of space, closing in on one planet in particular. The bright marks of explosions decorated the planet like gleaming lures, an ornament twinkling in space. But then the view zoomed in and things took on a far less pleasant demeanor. Through the clouds now came sights of burning cities and alien craft tumbling out of the sky as they were chased down by swarms of smaller ships. The view held for a moment before abruptly cutting off. The lights in the room rose once again.

"The craft that captured that image was destroyed by the Zelos at that point. They always attack with three large ships, each of which holds many of those smaller attack craft just as you saw. The world that you just saw victimized was far more developed than your Earth currently is."

"Okay… so we know who the bad guys are," Darren sighed, "and you chose us because we're the most compatible with your creators' race so it's easier to teach us. Got it."

"That would be part of the reason, Darren," Observer corrected. "There is a race out there more advanced than my creators, but one we know nothing about. It is they who bequeathed a gift to us with the obligation to use it to help your race once you were ready. Your race is ready and the two of you are amongst the brightest your species has to offer."

"I'll agree with that," Darren shrugged.

"Speaking as the more intelligent of us," Feng grinned, "seeing as how I was a year younger than you when I got my doctorate."

"Same year," Darren reminded him. "That still puts us in a tie."

"The point I wish to make," Observer continued, "is that you were both teenagers when you finished your education. A feat deemed quite improbable for your species a mere hundred years ago, and the reason lies with my creators."

"What," Darren quipped, "they came in the dead of night and impregnated our mothers?"

"Not quite. Twenty-three thousand years ago an expedition from the region of space you would call Sagittarius discovered your world and organized this base on Mars as a supply depot. Close enough to observe, far enough away to not get in the way of your development. Due to your similarity to my creators the Sagittarians– Satarans, to use their own name for themselves– a science team was organized to study you, then ten thousand years ago some changes were inserted into the DNA of five hundred male and five hundred female babies, along with a marker that may be transferred from mother to offspring. My instrumentation allows me to detect this marker from up to one hundred meters away."

"And we each have the marker," Feng stated.

"Affirmative. By a thousand years later, the descendants of those creatures developed into a people we called Atlantra. They inhabited an island in your Gulf of Mexico and were quite advanced for your world in all fields of study. Unfortunately five hundred years later a pending volcanic threat was discovered by our observing science team. They transmitted a request to move those people safely off their island, but unfortunately policy had changed by then; they were not allowed to interfere and the civilization of Atlantra was lost."

"But a few of them escaped to breed with the rest of the population," Darren finished for the robot. "Yeah, I think we get the story."

"The policy became that we could still observe, but no interference or contact until such time as your world has a one-planet government, achieves the beginning of space travel, and asks for our help. I have been set here to watch you the entire time, awaiting such a time. You have now come to the point where I may offer out the invitation after explaining the peril you are in. Our learning enhancer will work best with those of your kind with the special DNA marker, but for the rest they will only be able to bridge approximately two thousand years of evolution. My question now is–"

"Yes," Darren and Feng said nearly in unison.

"The chance to learn so much?" Darren elaborated. "Of course we'll take it. Consider the request asked."

"I am afraid you forget," Observer reminded him, "you have not yet a one-world government."

"The way everyone's always bickering," Feng sighed, "that may not come in our lifetimes. Only our mission brought this international team together."

"Do not be so quick to assume," Observer told them. "The learning machine is set up to take twelve at a time. The enhancer and rejuvenation machine can seat two and is what was gifted us by that unknown race; it will enhance your physiology so that you will stay young for quite a lot longer; long enough to see this project through."

"Exactly what is the nature of this machine and the people that gave it to you?" Feng asked.

"All we know is that approximately ten thousand years ago a robot appeared at the home planet of my creators with instructions to build exactly two of these rejuvenation machines; one for our home planet, and one that was to be housed here on Mars to await such time as when the descendants of those with our DNA markers made their way out into space. Only when this was agreed to would it construct the one for my creators' homeworld. Nothing more would the robot say, either about where it came from or the details of the device. That only served to renew interest in your world."

"So we have some mysterious benefactors out there," Darren stated, "but how does that help us if we can't get access to it until Earth is united?"

"Since you are my first contacts," Observer explained, "and possessors of the DNA marker, I am now empowered to treat the two of you as ambassadors of your planet and am allowed to assist you in some limited ways. Including convincing others as to the importance of your mission and a united Earth."

"Then I suggest we start with the rest of my crew," Darren suggested. "Maybe between all of us we can convince Command once we get back to Earth. But we're still talking a couple of months before we can do that."

"No need to wait, Commander. Once you and your crew have been enhanced, I have equipment in this facility that can teleport you directly back to Earth."

So casually said by the robot, but neither man there missed its import.

"Wait," Feng said with very curious attention, "did you say *teleport?*"

The energy spike turned out to be Observer fully powering up his facility, after which he'd teleported us straight out of our spacesuits. He said we wouldn't need them and they'd just get in the way. At any rate, Observer put us both into what we ended up calling the 'Evolution Chair', then a day later sat us both under this cap of electrodes hooked up to his learning machine. I have a hunch you'll be seeing the entire setup soon enough. Anyway, when we came out of it we were both not only stronger and healthier– not to mention much longer lived, which is why we still look as young as we did then– but gifted with certain other abilities; some of the side effects that Observer told us we might have just before he threw the switch. For instance, the both of us have telepathy, I'm now a telekinetic, and Darren can teleport. That's how I got out of that grave, Agent Franklin; my telekinesis. Though I wouldn't have made it very far after that if you hadn't been there to get me to the hospital; for all I know my kidnappers may still have been in the area. Darren had teleported back to Beijing to double check on Chief Pinyin's background just in case; too far away for me to contact in my weakened condition, so I am glad that you heeded my telepathic call, weak though it was.

Well, by the time we made it back to base we'd both been gone for three Earth-days, and everyone from our crew to Earth Command was quite frantic. Darren teleported the both of us right into the middle of our base where, after reviving a stunned Andrii and being carefully prodded by Glenda, we explained everything that Observer had told us and a little of what we'd learned from the enhancer. Soon after that, we managed to talk them each into undergoing the same treatment. The learning machine is set up for twelve people, so that didn't take much time, but there's only one Evolution Chair, and while it can process two at a time, it still takes a full twenty-four hours a cycle. All we told Earth Command during that time was some pretty standard progress reports, and that Darren and I had simply slipped and fallen.

About a week later, though, Earth command had quite a surprise when Observer teleported us all right into the middle of the command center. Much of our time afterwards was spent in giving the sales pitch to certain key world leaders and deciding how to work this. One thing we were quite clear on and that is if Earth does not unite then it *will* die at the hands of the Zelos. Observer's creators are far too busy trying to find clues to the Zelos homeworld to reach out and directly help every single little world like our own, which is why they have to work things this way. Twenty thousand space-faring civilizations, how many more little backwaters like ours do you think are out there begging to be saved from the Zelos? Do the math; they can assist us only so far.

During his eight thousand years, however, Observer was not idle. There were already some basic production facilities ready on Mars, he just started expanding them. Of course he could not know what manner of designs we Earthers might come up with, so he opted for a variety of different kinds of production facilities and used only the materials to be found beneath Mars to construct them as well as harvesting a few asteroids behind our backs. Those lava tubes? Many of them he dug out with his other construction and harvesting bots. Of course he did it in as much secrecy as possible so as not to be discovered by the Zelos, which limited how much he could get done, but it's still a pretty good start.

The early meetings were a bit chaotic at first, but we settled upon a standard plan to convince everyone real fast. We'd meet with someone then have Observer teleport us straight to Mars. After they got over their shock, they were convinced. Brought in a few scientists that way as well. I understand that you caught Darren on video doing just that with one of our newer climatologists.

The return of our craft from Mars was for public show, and of course we didn't display any of the upgrades Observer helped us give it, but you'll find out more on that later. Since then we have been operating outside of public awareness to try and unite Earth and get it ready for some pretty impossible odds. All those one-week vacations you discovered was us giving either a world leader or key scientist the whole Mars tour and in some cases time in the Evolution Chair and learning enhancer. As our operations expand, both on Mars and down here with talks of unifying all the countries, we bring in more people for those vacations, as you put it.

Naturally, it was quite early on that I brought my lovely Dao-ming up to Mars, which is why she too remains just as young as before. She is a brilliant research scientist in her own right, so Observer had no qualms about her.

After a time, Observer asked us to come up with a list of what key things that Earth needs most to survive and develop as a united world. One of those things was some sort of weather control system… Yes, Agent Franklin, those were not spy satellites. The system hasn't been fully activated yet, though; that won't be done until we're ready for full public disclosure. We just want to make sure we're as ready as we can be before panicking seven billion people. The rest of the things on the list are what you'd expect; clean power supply, cure all known diseases, the ability to predict or control such natural disasters as earthquakes and the like, general waste cleanup, that sort of thing. Some of the scientists we brought on board have been working on those projects with help from what information Observer's learning enhancer can provide.

As for myself and Darren, once we got things going on their own, the bulk of the last ten years we have been involved in the design and construction of Earth's first space-going battleship up around Mars. We decided that we can't possibly outstrip the Zelos in terms of sheer numbers, so we're going for what we hope is a superior design. Quality over Quantity. It's coming along pretty nicely.

But not everyone is on board with a united Earth. The last few years we've been catching rumors of some big industrial leaders who are very much against unifying the planet and may be willing to do something drastic… including trying to kill or kidnap me during my own wedding. After a few final high-level secret meetings, there is a big world conference coming up during which a series of gradual information releases concerning Mars and the Zelos is planned, at which point the conspirators may decide to operate a lot more openly. That's why we've been looking for qualified people such as yourself. It began with key politicians and some rather brilliant scientists, then a few needed soldiers, and now time for other types of specialists like brilliant CIA operatives who aren't afraid to poke their noses into dangerous territory.

The conspirators have been covering their tracks rather well, I might add. The only way we managed to catch wind of anything going on against us was when Darren and I happened to pick up a few stray thoughts at a party, but it was too crowded to tell who they came from. Well, that's the highlights, do you have any questions?

"…Wait. You can read minds?!"

CHAPTER FOUR

INVESTIGATION BEGUN

August 20, 2050.

Feng was out of the hospital in what Agent Franklin viewed as record time, but then again she was still processing all that Feng had told her, so perhaps she shouldn't have been too surprised.

"Not so much as a limp," Amelia marveled.

Feng was exiting the hospital with Amelia to one side, Darren the other, and a pack of agents both seen and unseen surrounding them. It was midmorning, the glittering streets of Beijing were awake and quite active and mostly ignorant of the events unfolding within them. Before them a black sedan awaited their use by the street curb, flanked front and back by a pair of what looked like security vans, while a couple of American soldiers stood to either side of the distance between them and their ride.

"You'll get used to it," Feng shrugged. "Darren, I gave her the entire story."

"And yet you didn't think him crazy," Darren said to Agent Franklin. "You're pretty open-minded; that's a good trait to have."

"For a brief moment I might have considered that the knock on his head had jostled around a few brain cells," she admitted, "except that even a couple of scans showed no damage or scarring whatsoever. That, and the fact that everything he says fits within my own prior investigations."

"Yeah, about that," Darren put in, "sorry we had to erase all trace of what you'd compiled."

"No, I get it," she told him. "I know the answer now and it's something that you have to be careful in revealing. But tell me, has anyone else gotten that far on their own before?"

"That we know of," Darren replied, "no. It is quite possible, though, that whoever is going after Feng may have figured something out, or just simply does not want a united world for more selfish reasons."

As they came to a pause before the central sedan, Agent Franklin's gaze swiftly taking in the surrounding street and environs, the pulse of passing traffic, from out of the other vehicle in front of it stepped Chief Lee Pinyin leaning slightly on his dragon-headed cane, a couple of his own men behind him. He bowed his head in greeting, to which Feng replied in kind, then spoke.

"I am very happy to see that your trials have left you undamaged, General Feng."

"Not that someone didn't try very hard," Feng stated. "You're my escort, I take it?"

"To see you safely to wherever you must go. I do not wish to see you buried once again. And I must congratulate Agent Franklin on locating you so swiftly. I take it, Agent Franklin, that you will be having elements of your own security team accompanying the General now?"

"Not that you'll see them," she replied. "For my own security reasons I must now ask; Chief Pinyin, how many people do you currently have stationed around here?"

"Three in the front car, three in the back one, and three spotters across the street," he replied. "Why?"

"Because there's a fourth spotter," she said with a slight gesture of her head. "Across the street by the herbal shop showing a decided interest in his fingernail trimmings. He's not one of yours?"

"Why... no," Chief Pinyin said after a slow glance over. "I shall have him picked up immediately."

"No, don't," Feng told him. "I want to investigate my own kidnapping and he may be my first lead. Leave him to me."

"As the General wishes," the Chief consented.

"It's not as *I* wish," Agent Franklin disagreed. "You've already had one attempt on your life, the minute they confirm that you're still alive, there will be others."

"Agent Franklin–" Feng began.

"All things considered," she continued, "I realize I couldn't stop you if you really tried, but there *will* be two of my men shadowing you at all times, and remember I have my own way of tracking you."

"I shall endeavor not to forget," Feng replied with a slight grin. "Chief Pinyin, you will escort me across town as my driver will direct. We won't be going too fast; after all, someone went through a lot of trouble to put a watch on me, and I would not wish their efforts to have been in vain."

"I quite understand," Chief Pinyin said with a slight incline of his head.

A nod and he was away, back to the front escort van, while Feng led the way into the central black sedan. Agent Franklin made sure that Feng was seated between herself and Darren, then a last glance out the window at the one trimming his fingernails and they were off.

"I'd still rather you leave the investigation to me," she then said.

"Agent Franklin," Feng gently smiled, "you are quite the headstrong and determined young lady, and extremely capable, but as you will remember from what I told you, I have ways of gaining information that are currently beyond your capabilities."

"Telepathy, I know. But never underestimate basic investigative capabilities."

"I do not," Feng told her, "which is why I think you should be taking that vacation we talked about; it will greatly enhance those investigative capabilities of yours. Darren, she's ready for Mars."

"I agree."

"Wait," she protested, "I'm supposed to see to your security from now until after the wedding, Feng. They tried to kill you once, and they'll–"

"Which is why we need to see that you're properly qualified to do your job," Darren explained. "Feng and I can read minds, he's a telekinetic and I'm a teleporter, and yet these people *still* managed to get around us and bury him. If they'd known his full capabilities then they probably would have chopped off his head before burying him. These are excessively dangerous people, Amelia, and we need to make sure that you're equally dangerous. Believe me, it will be worth the trip, and you'll still be back in plenty of time to set up security around the wedding."

"But I–"

"I'm also your direct superior, if you'll recall. This is not a request."

She sighed then replied with a nod. Darren continued.

"Feng, how do you want to work this?"

"I'll make sure to find myself rather public so they can get a good look at me. The first one with thoughts of 'oh my God, what's he doing still alive' is the one I start tracking. Don't worry, I'm aware of them now, they won't get the drop on me again. Guess I was too occupied with the thought of meeting Dao-ming behind her father's back before the wedding. How is she doing, by the way?"

"Still being looked after by my security detail," Amelia promised. "I have a female agent disguised as one of her friends staying with her."

"That should have been my first clue that something was off, now that I think about it," Feng said with a slight chuckle. "The woman who I thought was Dao-ming wasn't accompanied by your security."

"They had orders to follow her wherever she went," Amelia explained, "*not* necessarily to follow her father's orders about where she can and cannot go. They would have been around no matter where you two tried to sneak off to."

"Just the sort of person we were looking for," Darren stated. "Okay, are you ready?"

"As I'll ever be," she shrugged. "How's this going to work? Is there a shuttle or something we have to take?"

Darren just grinned and reached out for her hand, then called out into the air, "Observer!"

A moment later both were gone, leaving Feng alone in the back seat of the sedan to lean back and remark to himself.

"That should quiet the good agent up for a while," he grinned. "I wonder what her reaction will be when she has her first look at the spaceship..."

Somewhere in the street behind him, the fingernail-clipping man had hopped into a car of his own and begun to discreetly follow the security force flanking the General's black sedan.

"Welcome to Mars, Agent Franklin. I am Observation and Contact Unit Number Two Seven Zero Five, but you may call me Observer."

It is one thing to hear about something, but quite another to actually see it. The cavern was exactly as Feng had told her, as was the robot before her with the perfect diction.

"How– We really teleported? This is really Mars and not some telepathic trick?"

"All very real, Agent Franklin. I have your place reserved at the learning enhancer and you are next in line for the Evolution Chair."

"Let me give her the tour first, Observer. Give her a chance to get the shock out of her system before she gets her brain rewired."

"Rewired?" Amelia said with a trace of some concern.

"Just an expression," Darren grinned. "Observer, tour first."

"As you wish, Darren. You may also view the progress of your vessel while you are here."

"That's right," Amelia realized. "Feng said something about a spaceship, but I was too busy processing a lot of other things. Like the Zelos."

"A very real threat, Agent Franklin," Observer remarked. "Which is why I was assigned to watch over your world. We have no way of telling exactly where they will strike save that they always attack worlds inhabited with a sentient population."

"I'll show you the easy stuff first," Darren told her with a smile. "By your leave, Amelia?"

He put out an elbow for her to take, an act of gallantry which from her point of view seemed more alien than the robot, but after realizing how much more than what was in this room there was for her to see, she opted for holding close to Darren just in case. He walked her across the room towards one of the two existing halls and into another room also carved from the native rock and lit from glowing panels in the ceiling. The first thing she saw was a circle of twelve chairs, each of which was topped by a metal helmet, from which cabling ran to a central port in the ceiling above. Off to one side of this arrangement stood a control panel of polished obsidian and racing lights, with a very large display screen built into the wall.

"Looks like a bunch of high-tech salon hairdryers," she remarked.

"That's the learning enhancer," Darren told her. "Basically a mind-computer interface that allows direct input into the human mind. It also does some other bits of rewiring, which in people with the correct DNA marker can sometimes have the effect of granting such abilities as telepathy and possibly a couple of other things. The thing beyond that is the Evolution Chair."

The device in question looked rather like two tanning beds placed head to head, the top lid of each bed currently flipped open to reveal a blue inner lining with tiny points of light winking and flashing across its surface. There were no dials or controls that she could see, and the interior of each half looked big enough to hold someone up to eight feet in height.

"Looks more like a coffin," she noted. "Twin coffins."

"Agreed, but Evolution *Coffin* just doesn't have quite the same ring to it. It's entirely automatic. You get in, it closes down then scans you. If you haven't been enhanced before then that's what it does. If you have been, then it scans for any injuries or effects of aging, and fixes it. The enhancements take a full day, repairing injuries a bit less depending on their extent. While you're in either it or the learning machine, you will have no sense of the passage of time. Just one minute you enter, the next it's done, only it's been a full day outside. So, overwhelmed yet?"

She took a few steps in, lightly fingered the control panel for the learning machine, eyed the Evolution Chair, then turned on heel back to Darren.

"Quite advanced, and rather astounding, but all within the realm of possibility."

"Hmm, looks like I'll just have to try harder. Okay, let me show you what's down the other corridor."

They left that chamber for the other exit from the main room. This corridor was lit as had been the previous rooms and carved out of the same red rock just as the other chambers had been; smooth to the touch yet not from any amount of melting or chiseling. It led a long walk down, to what Amelia guessed to be a very large chamber at the end, if to judge from the feel of a slight breeze gently wafting from it across her face. About midway, Darren paused and reached out a hand to what looked like any other section of smooth stone wall, save for a slight discoloration.

"This section here is like a window. At a touch it can become transparent, though from the outside it will still look like rock. I just wanted to show you something."

A touch of his hand upon the wall and the discolored section faded into transparency. Still nothing much more astounding than the windows of tunable transparency common enough on Earth, but it was what she saw that riveted her attention. The red cliffs and empty sands stretching off to a truncated horizon, a distant crater, bright red sky, and in the near distance an extensive single-story domed structure built into the side of one of the icy cliffs, a couple of space-suited figures walking around just outside of it.

"Mars," she gasped. "We really are on Mars."

"Looks like we're getting close to being overwhelmed," Darren grinned. "But don't go on me yet, there's still the big surprise to see."

Another touch of the panel and it faded back into the appearance of slightly discolored rock, then Amelia felt a gentle tug pulling her away.

"S-sorry," she said after a moment, "it's just… I'm okay now. Mars. And Observer teleported us here?"

"I can teleport around the planet from what his machines unleashed within me, but interplanetary travel may take a bit more practice," he explained as they continued their walk. "Fortunately, Observer has devices around here that can reach across the solar system. Only a couple of people at a time though, which is why my old ship the Omega Centauri was refitted with some help from Observer. It can make the trip in about three days now, which is how we get larger amounts of supplies back and forth. We've been working on various design improvements, of course, and the Centauri is always the first to get them and test them out, but everything we've been doing here has been ultimately focusing on what you'll be seeing in the cavern up ahead."

"The ship."

"Battleship, technically. As Feng may have told you, we can't possibly hope to match the Zelos in sheer numbers in the time we may have until their arrival."

"I thought Feng said that we have a hundred and fifty years?"

"Well, first that was ten years ago, and second it was also a very rough estimate. They really don't know much about the Zelos, so we could have another hundred and forty years, or just ten. That's why it was decided to go the route we did; quality instead of quantity. There were a lot of strategy meetings in the early days before this decision was made, and fortunately, Observer kept increasing the construction facilities around here in his spare time. Which he apparently had a lot of."

"If it's all so massive, then how come the initial radar scans didn't picked them up?"

"That's the funny part," he grinned, "we actually did. Sure, there were the parts protected from our scans; that was the control section we just left. But the construction facility is mostly empty cavern buried under a lot of rock. The radar simply didn't have the penetration power to reveal any more than big empty places. Ah, we're about there. Are you ready?"

"I've just seen the view from Mars, Darren, I think I can manage anything else you can throw at me."

"Ah, they always say that, and I still love it every time."

Their passage had reached a dead end; a smooth wall of metal with the texture of stone. No controls could she see about them, nor a way of getting past. And yet, Darren reached out and at a simple touch upon its surface, the entire wall opened. Suddenly curved lines stretched across it, splitting it into four curved sections which then irises open to reveal a balcony from which they could see what lay beyond.

It was a single large cavern, walls worked smooth but stretching farther across than anyplace she had even seen pictures of. Perhaps a full mile, she would guess, all of it lit by massive floodlights strewn about ceiling and walls. Here and there along the walls were embedded various robotic or equipment stations, mammoth cranes fixed into the ceiling high above, and what looked like four-armed industrial robots with tools for hands that she guessed to be construction bots zipping through the air on one task or another. As slowly Darren led her to the edge of the balcony and the waist-high stone railing around it, more of the cavern came into view and it was here that Agent Franklin's jaw truly dropped open.

A hundred construction bots flying about, the far end of the cavern lined with large vats smelting raw ore being brought in from other farther entries into the cavern, men working without need of spacesuits, with a vast array of technological equipment well beyond her knowing, but everything centered about one single, very large, construction.

The battleship, as it no doubt was, was unlike what Agent Franklin might have imagined a spaceship to be. Still taking shape, but its general framework was clear to make out, for it was a single spherical shape, over fifteen hundred feet across. It hovered there a few yards above the ground, held in place apparently by beams of focused light shooting down from some of the installations in the ceiling above. A floating monster, waiting to be born.

"*Now* you're overwhelmed," Darren beamed.

Amelia could do little more than give a very slow nod in reply.

The day after Feng left the hospital there was a high-level meeting scheduled in the Ministry building. Little more than a series of interlinked conference rooms spaced around a central lounge, red and gold drapes bordering the occasional window looking out upon the rest of the city from several stories up.

Most there were in the know about Mars, but all of them either high up in the Chinese government, key scientists, or even a few financial movers and shakers; perhaps a hundred in all. If there was a conspirator, Feng had no doubt they would have a presence at that meeting. The main purpose was to discuss details of the final merger of governments, then a couple of more restricted meetings concerning the weather satellites, clean power systems, disease control, and other such advances being developed by people who had been to Mars. That, and an update on the battleship.

Feng made a point of making himself quite visible during this secretive conference, his mind scanning out to pick up any stray thoughts concerning him; any clue as to who had engineered his kidnapping and attempt on his life.

His waiting finally paid off. Early into the afternoon, he caught a feeling of shock from one of the functionaries. That was all he needed and a glance over confirmed it. It was a chubby man talking discreetly to one that Feng recognized as the man with the fingernail clipper. They spoke in hushed tones, the one discreetly indicating Feng to the chubby man when they thought he wasn't looking, or within hearing range.

Fortunately for Feng, his hearing had been one of the things enhanced by Observer's machines.

"That *is* him. But he's dead?! I'll have to report this immediately."

Later on, the chubby man passed closer to Feng when everyone was mingling in the lounge between meetings, no doubt to get a closer look. He schooled his features quite well, but not his thoughts. Feng got a quick flash of an image from his mind; that of a man and an apartment building. A place he would be reporting to.

Feng lingered around the conference, but always kept an eye out on the chubby man, or in a lot of cases more of a mind's eye. When the day's talks came to a conclusion and people started departing for the evening, Feng made sure to carefully follow the chubby man to wherever it was that he would go, even while being aware that Agent Franklin's security detail was, in turn, keeping an eye on *him.* With his own car set to manual-drive, Feng kept himself ever out of sight, but never out of range of his thoughts as he followed the chubby man's vehicle across town.

Once at a busy intersection he nearly lost him, the chubby man's thoughts being but one of hundreds driving or walking about. Fortunately a stray thought of urgency connected with the name 'Feng', soon found him his quarry and he was back on the trail. Along narrow streets where avenues crowded with food vendors and pushcarts selling tourist-bound trifles lay within easy reach of high-rise marvels and brightly-glowing billboards with animated displays, down wider concrete rivers stabbing through the heart of the city, and finally across to one of the older residential sections.

The man finally pulled into an apartment building underground parking lot, where Feng chose a place a few spaces away to park, making sure to keep his own face out of view behind tinted windows. Feng didn't leave his vehicle; he didn't need to. Instead, his thoughts followed the chubby man as he left his car for the elevator and rode it up a few floors, then out, down a hallway, and finally up to a door. It was a bit of a strain keeping focused on just the chubby man, trying to tune out other thoughts coming at him from intervening and nearby apartments, but Feng had been practicing this for the last ten years. He stretched out his seat, lay back, and closed his eyes as he focused on the chubby man, hearing what he heard.

The door opened and there facing the chubby man was a slightly older skinny man with a balding head and angry looking features.

"What are you doing here!"

"It's important, Mister Yang," the chubby man spoke. "General Feng, I saw him."

"Saw him? How, in the morgue? Did they find his grave?"

"No, I mean I saw him. *Alive.*"

"That's impossible! I buried him myself."

"I stood as close to him as I am to you. It's Feng, and he's at the conference."

"It can't be. I'll have to see for myself. Okay, go before anyone sees you here. I have a call to make."

The chubby man left, but Feng kept his thoughts on those of this Mr. Yang in his apartment. There was a pause as the man closed his door then took out his cell phone. A moment later Yang was talking again, but of course Feng could only pick up the thoughts of Mr. Yang, not who he was speaking with.

"Sir, General Feng is still alive... Yes, I did the job myself, and buried him deep in the woods. I guess someone found and revived him, but... No sir. I'd injected him with the poison, even had him tied down inside the coffin. I have no idea... Yes sir. I will go to the conference tomorrow and see for myself... Of course, sir."

Feng let out a deep exhale of breath as he came back into himself, his thoughts once again solely his own.

"So, this Mister Yang reports to someone. I'll just have to make a point of attending that conference tomorrow so he can find me..."

Agent Franklin leaned back in the chair as one of Observer's robots carefully placed the helmet down over her head. A med-bot in function, metallic humanoid design though lacking the finesse in design that allowed Observer to more easily function with people, and its hands sporting an assortment of built-in retractable medical paraphernalia such as needles and scalpels. One of many various types of robotic devices that Observer controlled to help carry out his dictates around the facility.

"What's this going to feel like," she asked of the robot.

"Why, like nothing Agent Franklin," the robot answered. "We are merely going to turn your brain off long enough to upload some new data."

"Wait! What do you mean you're going to–"

Flicker.

"–turn my brain off for– What the heck?"

One instant the robot was standing to her right side lowering down the helmet, the next he was to her left lifting it back up again.

"Upload completed, Agent Franklin. Are you ready for the rejuvenation process?"

"Wait, completed? What just happened? It's like everything just… jumped."

"Your mental functions have been suspended for a full twenty-four hours, Agent Franklin. I suggest you check your memory banks to confirm the new data you have received."

"Memory banks? I can see you're not as well programmed for Human niceties as Observer."

Nonetheless, she eased herself carefully up from the chair, her thoughts running a myriad of subjects she had not been aware that she knew of. Her understanding of Chinese was suddenly a lot more complete, as was her Russian, but where did this knowledge of Portuguese come from? And the military history of the Roman Empire, not to mention the complete works of Machiavelli?

"What the heck is in my brain?"

She thought briefly of Darren as she got to her feet, then a moment later another's thoughts unexpectedly forced their way into her mind.

You called, Amelia?

"What? Who said that? Did I just hear that in my mind?"

Just answering your telepathic call. How's it feel?

"Wait, you mean I just sent a– How?"

Side effect of the learning enhancer. It opens up your brain to put some stuff in, and at the same time allows a few things to get out. You must be one of the few with the DNA marker, because so far only Feng and I have telepathy. Once you get the treatment in the Evolution Chair you might also see something else manifest besides the usual perfect health that the Chair gives you. I must say, though, that I'm curious as to what that might be.

"This is going to take some getting used to. But what if I don't want to send out a call? How do I–"

I'll show you how to control it once you're out of the Chair. Took me and Feng a bit of experimentation before we got the hang of it. Basically, if you think really urgent thoughts about a person, then you can form a connection to his mind. Now, I've got some work to do over here with the ship, so you just let Observer's robots ease you into the Chair and we'll talk later.

"Yeah, you bet we will."

She strolled absently over to what still looked like a high-tech double tanning bed, then paused with a look back at the robot who had overseen her connection to the learning enhancer.

"How does this work?"

"It is entirely automatic, Agent Franklin," the robot replied as it walked over. "You merely get down inside then the mechanism senses your presence and commences with its operations. I suggest you undress first, though, lest the material of your clothing restricts any muscular expansion or reworking of your body."

"Makes sense. Where do I change?"

"Right here will be fine, Agent Franklin. I will watch over you."

"Right in front of–"

Then it occurred to her. While this med-bot was humanoid in general design and spoke well enough, it had no skin covering like Observer and nothing in the way of a mouth to even pretend the act of Human speech. Just a round red speaker port where a mouth would be.

"That's right; you have all the emotional content of a teapot. Well, here goes."

She stripped down then slipped herself into one of the two beds of the device. Nearly immediately the lid began to ease down over top of her, the lights in the inner membranes to raising faster than before. Once she was completely sealed in, then it was as if she was suspended in a world of blue with stars shooting about her body, tingling her from head to toe.

"Wow, this is definitely worth the trip. Feels like I'm being massaged by a hundred tiny–"

Her thoughts held suspended at that moment, her mind once again in stasis as the machine began its job of reworking her body.

"General Feng, what an honor to meet such a renowned astronaut. My name is Mister Yang."

One of many faces on the second day of the secretive conference, he would have been lost in the crowd had not Feng recognized his thought patterns from the night before. He greeted Feng just as he was stepping out of one of the conference rooms into the central lounge.

"Nice to meet you, Mister Yang. Which office do you work for around here, if I may ask?"

"Oh, I am a very unimportant functionary merely enamored with your presence. Here, let me freshen up your drink."

Mr. Yang took Feng's glass and walked away to the bar, though Feng noted that the gentleman was careful to grab it by the very top, away from where Feng had been holding onto the glass by. He was also careful to see that Mr. Yang handed the glass not to the bartender but the chubby man from the day before, dropping it quickly into a purse as he passed him by.

"Confirming my fingerprints," Feng said to himself. "Then he's going to tell the results to… Li. Mister Li Zheng, if I read his mind correctly. Hmm, not a name I know of which means I probably haven't hit the big guy yet."

Mr. Yang returned with a fresh glass and polite smile, after which he made small talk with Feng for several minutes. At least until the man caught something out of the corner of his eye and politely dismissed himself. Feng tracked him visually, and when that failed he did so mentally. Mr. Feng met with the chubby man in one of the unused conference rooms ringed around the lounge, speaking in hushed tones.

"The fingerprints match," the chubby man said. "That *is* General Feng Yusheng."

"Then I have to tell Mister Li, though he won't like it. Okay, go. I'll stay another hour to make it look good then be off to Mister Li's."

Feng hid any reaction he might have had at his discovery behind a sip of his drink, then saw a far more familiar face come up to him. Chief Lee Pinyin.

"General Feng, how goes the conference?"

"Well, if you mean have I managed to lose Agent Franklin's attendants yet, no; they're still around here somewhere."

However, he then continued in a telepathic transmission to the Chief, *I've uncovered a few things we should talk about. Soon.*

Not telepathic himself, but apparently well aware of Feng's own capabilities, the Chief didn't miss a beat as he verbally replied.

"You know, you and your girlfriend should come over to my house for dinner tonight. One last date before you're both married. My wife's a fantastic cook."

"I think I'll take you up on your offer, Chief. We will see you tonight. Myself, Dao-ming… and the squad of bodyguards constantly about me."

He said this with a discreet glance around at certain men in suits trying to look like they were part of the furnishings while keeping an eye out for their assignment. Chief Pinyin chuckled a bit before downing his own drink, though there was nothing amusing in what they would be discussing later that evening.

"Lee, you know Dao-ming."

"It has been too long, Chief Pinyin."

"Please, we're in my home now. Just call me Lee. My wife May is setting the table."

The Chief's house was located in one of the many suburbs of Beijing, a spacious and modern home adorned with the expected traditional Chinese accents. The front doorframe looked to take its inspiration from some Buddhist temple's gates, hanging over top of it a small carving in red and gold of a money pouch for good fortune. The floors were paved in bamboo tiles, the walls of the anteroom hung with a mix of Mandarin symbols and framed pictures of loved ones before they had grown up.

From the anteroom through an arch festooned with a couple more ornamental knickknacks inscribed with a dialect Feng did not recognize, they came to the dining room. The right-hand wall held a picture window looking out to a small garden outside, red curtains currently drawn closed, the wall opposite painted with a mural of a stylized landscape populated with creatures out of Chinese mythology, while the far end of the left-hand wall bore a small entry covered by a beaded curtain through which an elderly lady about Chief Pinyin's age was just bringing in the first of several dishes of food for the waiting place settings arranged about the dining table.

It was the dining table that was the centerpiece of the room, however. A large cherry wood Queen Anne table, floral mother of pearl designs wrapping delicately about its sides, legs carved to look like slender dragons of myth. The light fixture hanging above it was a mobile of red paper lanterns strung together by short metal rods, though lit from within by very modern bulbs.

"You have a very nice home," Dao-ming pleasantly remarked as Chief Pinyin's wife put the first of the dishes down onto the center of the table.

"Thank-you," she replied with a smile. "Now please sit down, there is much food to be shared."

The evening began with pleasant talk of the upcoming wedding, and even more pleasant tasting of the meal that the Chief's wife had prepared for them. When it came to the seating arrangement, however, Mrs. Pinyin made a point of sitting between Feng and Dao-ming.

"I understand your father is very traditional," Mrs. Pinyin explained to the young couple, "and he would still want you to stay separated in the days leading up to your wedding. This is the least I can do to see his wishes honored."

The reply got a lilt of laughter from Dao-ming and a smirk from Feng.

"Well then," Feng promised, "I shall just have to make up for it when the time comes."

To Feng's other side sat Chief Pinyin, but it would not be until after the meal when they would depart for the Chief's study to talk more serious business. A feast of several courses drawn from the common bowls at the center of the table was before them, giving them a reason to share their lives, their joys and hopes at least for the evening, and forget for a short time the troubles of the world outside and talk only of the coming joys of wedded bliss.

When the meal finally ended, and Dao-ming was helping Chief Pinyin's wife to clean up the table and help prepare the dessert– training for her pending role as a housewife, the older lady told them– Feng accompanied Chief Pinyin into his study to discuss certain other matters.

"So," Chief Pinyin said as he closed the door behind himself, "what is it that you have uncovered?"

"Do you know of a Li Zheng?"

"Member of the Standing Committee," the Chief replied, stepping with his cane in hand across the carpeted room to a plush looking chair situated before a small fireplace with a mahogany mantle. "That goes pretty high up."

Feng remained standing, glancing briefly about the room before replying. Shelves of old books, here and there a desk-top wooden carving of some beast out of Chinese mythology to act as decorative bookends, the dim lighting given from an old ceiling lamp modeled after a more ancient design, the curtains drawn closed over the room's window to afford them complete privacy. It looked secure enough for him to continue.

"It might go even higher; I won't know until I meet the man and read his thoughts."

"You know, Feng, you scare me sometimes with your abilities. So much you have discovered by just being near them. It must feel amazing."

"That and scary," Feng admitted. "When I meet someone new I usually give them a quick surface scan to make sure they don't mean me any harm, but then it takes a little more effort to actually tune out their thoughts. The first time I walked into a crowded city with this ability was nearly maddening. Darren and I had to practice quite a bit to get it under control. After a while, though, it's like being in a crowd of people all talking at once; you hear it but ignore everyone except the ones shouting."

"Shouting? You mean like if someone is highly agitated or emotional?"

"Exactly. From someone who's very emotional I can't help but pick up their one concern, but nothing other than that. At the other end of things are the few that can control their thoughts to some degree. I had the privilege to meet a couple of Tibetan monks once; neither I nor Darren could get a thing off them. It was like trying to mind read a pool of water."

"It sounds like you had a most educational experience," the Chief chuckled. "But regards Li Zheng, I suggest you find a reason to be around him. I want to know exactly how high up this goes before I start arresting people."

"What about probable cause or physical evidence?"

"You have been spending too much time with your American friend, General. This is China; sufficient people in the know about certain things are aware enough of your abilities to consider that probable enough. Not as many of them are aware of Dao-ming's trip to Mars, so if someone ever decides to kidnap her instead then that will narrow our list of suspects. By the way, I hear that she has been making some very outstanding contributions in biomedical medicine these last few years."

"She is determined to figure out how the rejuvenation machine on Mars works, or at least duplicate a few of its effects."

"In that I wish her luck. Now, if you have not yet fully planned your honeymoon, might I suggest starting with the old Shaolin temple?"

"Lee," Feng grinned, "I do not plan on being a monk over my honeymoon."

"I would hope not, my friend, but it was to the river next to it that I had in mind. Ask for Wong to show you the boat, then go up river until it turns parallel to the coast then on for another fifteen kilometers from there. At that point you will see a hotel made to look like a Shaolin temple. A very nice place with a good view of the ocean."

"That good a hotel to be worth the trip? So close to the ocean I could just go directly that way."

"Feng, you'll be traveling over fifteen kilometers by river through some very beautiful countryside; the destination is not the point of such a trip, but the journey. Now let's get back in there and rejoin the women. My wife May will have dessert ready by now."

"Almond cake?" Feng asked, trying not to sound dejected.

"Goodness no," the Chief said, pushing himself up to his feet with the help of his cane. "If you want a good dessert you go to the experts. She's trying her hand at tiramisu. I'm eager to see how it came out."

The next day Feng spent hunting down the office of one Le Zheng. He found it in another government building next to the Ministry building, so using his rank and the need for some official errand as a cover, Feng had no trouble getting in. The problem would be in spying on Le Zheng without his knowing. Fortunately there was an empty office next to Zheng's that he could use, after hanging a sign he swiped from the cleaning crew to hang on the door. The sign read, "Closed for cleaning."

The thoughts he caught from the room next door were frantic, but they were Zheng's. He then pressed his ear as close to the wall as he could, hoping his enhanced hearing would allow him to hear at least a little of the other side of Zheng's conversation.

Two things were in Feng's favor that day: thin walls from cheap government construction, and Zheng using a speaker phone so he could busy about his office feeding things into a shredder as he talked.

"This is very disturbing what you tell me, Zheng. Feng is supposed to be dead."

"Apparently his abilities have grown greater than we thought, sir. Next time I will see his head chopped off and fed into a meat grinder."

"It is too late for such measures, you fool. I have just read the latest reports at the conference, and it seems as most of the technological wonders we have been receiving from Mars have come directly from Feng and his American friend, and what's more now far too many people know of this fact. That makes them both too valuable to kill, particularly with full disclosure close at hand. No, we need to cover our tracks and think of something else. What about the ones you sent to kill Feng?"

"Dealt with, sir. Mister Yang and his chubby associate will have fallen victim to a certain poison of mine by now."

"Good. And neither one knows who I am?"

"Not even that you exist, sir."

"Also, good. I have some things to do before a final big conference a couple of days from now, you will wait in your room until you hear from me. Do not move for anything."

"Of course not, sir. I will wait just as you say."

The sound of a phone clicking off was the only thing Feng heard next, followed by the soft pad of pacing footsteps. But of a name to connect with the voice at the other end of the call, Feng had picked up nothing from the mind of Le Zheng. The man had been trained well in the disciplining of his mind; not surprising if they indeed were aware of his mind reading abilities. But the only ones that knew *that* were in the top echelons of the Chinese government itself! How far did this conspiracy go?

Then he heard another sound, a disturbing sound that had him rushing back to the wall pressing his ear close. It was gagging, followed by a thud.

Feng raced out of the room and into the office next door, crashing his way through the locked door to find what he feared most. His last solid lead was on the floor, eyes bulged wide with terror, skin a light shade of blue.

"Dead," Feng stated, then glanced quickly around. "But no open windows and the door was locked from the inside… How did they get to him? I'm guessing it wasn't poison this time, but then… what?"

An autopsy would later confirm his suspicions, but leave him even more in the dark than before. Le Zheng had suffered a heart attack that had somehow caused the vessels and muscles around his throat to violently constrict, choking him to death within seconds. That itself would open up more questions than Feng had yet found answers for.

"No, Lee, no sign of who he was speaking to."

Feng was in Chief Pinyin's office back in the Ministry building, just the two of them with Feng's ever-present security assignment standing just outside the door. Blinds were drawn closed across the window, nothing between them but the Chief's desk as they sat down facing one another.

"And you caught no thoughts in Zheng's mind as to who he was talking to?"

"Someone briefed him very well on what to expect of me. My only clue is the other voice said that he would be at a final big conference in two days, but the one I was going to ended today and I know of no other."

"Hmm... I might, though it's not exactly a conference. More in the way of a glorified dedication ceremony out in the Gobi Desert."

"The Gobi Desert? What's out there?"

"You haven't heard?" Chief Pinyin said with a mildly surprised look. "You have been spending too much time with that ship of yours on Mars. That's where they're going to build that new factory with the help of your robotic friend; at least as soon as we have a unified Earth so that he is free to assist us in far more grand ways."

"That's right! It's going to be a combination weather control station and weapons factory. I think someone also wanted to add a massive power plant. Just so much empty space around there, really nothing in the way of ecology for people to worry about, you can build just about anything if you'd had the reason to and no one would care. It's worth a shot. See if you can get me a flight near there, I'm going to attend that meeting."

"But how will you know who you're looking for?"

"Simple. I heard his voice from the speakerphone through the wall."

"Simple for those of you with enhanced abilities, maybe," Chief Pinyin grinned, "but the rest of us don't have such fortune. I will find you a military flight going in that direction."

"Thanks, Lee, but no mentioning my name. I don't want whoever this is to know I'm coming."

It would be later that night when a figure wrapped in a coat with his hat pulled down over his face would board a military plane bound for a distant desert airfield.

Amelia Franklin awoke as if from a long slumber as the lid opened above her. She reached out her arms for a stretch, stuck out her legs, yawned, then noticed something different.

"When did my legs get so toned? And my arms? I look like I've been working out for at least six months straight."

"Merely the effects of the chamber fully optimizing your body, Agent Franklin."

She nearly bumped her head as she sat bolt upright, one hand trying to cover her bare front while the other searched for a weapon nowhere in reach. But the room was empty; nothing in it except for the med-bot that had tended her earlier.

"Oh, it's just you."

"I shall never understand why humans have this problem with the revealing of their skin. Maybe I should find some clothing to drape over myself and see what the difference might be."

"You're fine as is; in fact, I think you'd look rather silly with clothing."

"Then why is it that Humans do not look silly with their garments on?"

"It... It's a cultural thing. Now, where are my clothes?"

"Exactly where you dropped them one Earth day ago, Agent Franklin."

She looked down and there they were, just as she had left them. Hopping up to her feet she dressed quickly then combed back her hair.

"I don't suppose you have a mirror around here... No, I suppose not. Where's Commander Hildure?"

"Still overseeing certain elements of the vessel under construction. If you wish, you now have the capability to call to him direct, mind to mind."

"That's right, I forgot."

"More likely that you have not had the chance to get used to it, Agent Franklin. Might I suggest a walk around the facilities to accommodate yourself to what your new body feels like?"

"A good idea. Maybe I can even find a rec room of some sort to get the feel with a few katas."

Before leaving the room, though, she reached out with her mind searching for Darren. It didn't take long for her to touch upon it.

Sleeping Beauty's awakened, I take it?

And feeling ready for a good workout to test things out. Is there a rec room around here someplace?

There's one in the main base. It's connected up into the tunnels so you wouldn't need a spacesuit, but the way these tunnels twist about, you'd be going for a four-mile run.

That's quite a bit of running.

Not as much as you think, Amelia. You're in an enhanced body on a planet with half the gravity you're used to. It shouldn't take you long.

I guess you may be right. Okay, I'll go for a little test workout then meet you later in the cafeteria for dinner.

Will do.

She then broke the mental connection and walked across the room, but when she got to the edge of the main room where Observer was, she paused and grew a nearly evil grin. Facing towards the other exiting tunnel, she bent into a crouch, then burst off, running as fast as she could. A blur that would easily qualify her for the Olympics as she pressed herself to find her new limits.

Observer spared only a glance to make sure she had not bumped anything on her way out then gave the mechanical equivalent of a sigh.

"That is the first thing they always try when they leave the chamber. Next will be seeing how high she can now jump. I wonder if I shall have to have the ceiling cleaned again?"

Somewhere deep in the cavernous bowels of Mars, a black-haired streak was seen bolting across the main construction chamber on her way to the base and paid no heed by any there. They had seen it before.

The meeting was being held at the Inner Mongolian Hotel; a state-run facility at the edge of the Gobi Desert constructed for just such secret out-of-the-way meetings, and as barren in design as the empty stretches of desert before it. It had been built for a function, nothing more, and stood at the edge of the one city of any real size that Mongolia seemed to possess. The only view the bay windows of the assembly room afforded was of endless stretches of dead desert with the occasional herd of yak in the distance.

Feng kept to the back of the crowds, which consisted mainly of scientists and assorted dignitaries from around the world. The first to take the podium after the initial, and rather boring, introductions, was he who would be the main speaker.

Feng had been spending the time walking around, listening to any voice he came across, but thus far none had come close to sounding like the voice from the other end of Le Zheng's phone call. A few dozen people present, but when all seem intent on talking at once, it becomes rather difficult to single out that one voice he had only heard once through a thin office wall. Then came the voice of the one at the podium blaring out from the speaker system to make his job even harder.

"Ladies and gentlemen, our main speaker and leader of this conference, will be our most esteemed Minister of Construction and Planning, Wang Wei Huang. He will explain in detail what has been planned for in regards to the proposed facilities. Everyone, I give you Minister Wang Wei Huang."

The expected applause greeted the man now taking the podium, but Feng had no ear for it, only for the tone of the voice he still sought. On the stage came a man in his forties of average build, neatly combed black hair, dressed in a dark blue suit and tie, and nothing in the least remarkable about him. He was a politician, a legal functionary, if indeed a very high placed one. He took the podium from the other, waiting until the applause had subsided before speaking into the microphone.

"Thank-you, Amago Haruhisa, for allowing me this time to speak. My preference is still with placing the facility in the Taklamakan Desert, but I will concede to the decision of this assembly. Here we will build such devices that will forever rid the Earth of dead deserts and protect our coastal cities from flooding. We will construct a clean power plant that will supply significant parts of northern China, Mongolia, and southern Russia. And we will build a factory that will assist in our world's defense in conjunction with Earth's first combat spaceship. I am told that it will take nearly a full decade to construct even with all the international cooperation and possible assistance from Observer, but it will be well worth the effort. So with this in mind, let us launch our final organizational meeting and commence with the ground-breaking ceremony."

His words earned another round of applause, but Feng had long since frozen into place, staring now at the man on the podium. For Wang Wei Huang, High Minister of Construction and Planning, was the very same voice he had heard talking to Le Zheng. While the Minister was taking his final bow, Feng backed away a few feet, reaching a hand to his ear under the pretense of scratching something but to both cover his face from view and activate the comm-link implanted into his ear.

"Lee, I found our main conspirator but you aren't going to like it..."

The conference came to an end a day later, and after making the expected appearances at various parties, Minister Huang flew back to his estate outside Beijing. A well-groomed place in the country, bordering on a lake, a fine house whose three stories were built like terraces into the hillside, topped with a roof of sweeping oriental design and colored a blue to match the lake below it. He came in at a quick pace, saying not a thing until he was inside and thumbed a switch by the door. No light came on in response, though he seemed visibly relieved.

At least until the voice called out from the shadows across his well-appointed front room.

"Is *that* what that switch does? I would never have thought to use oscillating electromagnetic fields to scramble any attempts at telepathy. Good job."

He spun quickly around looking for the voice. To his right a closed closet door, further up to his left a hallway stretching on into the interior of his home, the room itself populated by an expensive looking rosewood couch carved with imperial dragon designs, designer end tables, and a smattering of art pieces hanging from the walls. The far end of the room ended with a large picture window looking down at the lake beyond, where the Moon's first light was just sliding across its surface. Next to this window the other now stepped out into full view, the lights snapping on as he did so.

"General Feng. It… is good to see you, but why do you break into my house like this?"

"Just wanted a closer look at the guy that wants me dead," Feng shrugged. "I'd wondered why that might be, so before coming here I had a friend in Intelligence look into a few things. Like the fact that you had been campaigning so hard to have things built on lands in the Taklamakan Desert that you just happened to own significant interests in. Or the fact that with a single world government you could lose quite a bit of money when the international arms market dries up. Quite the self-serving little public servant *you* turned out to be."

The Minister's face went from shock to deadly in a moment, eyes narrowing as he focused his gaze on the General and raised an open fist in his direction.

"I was hoping not to have to dirty my hands personally with your death," he said, taking a step forward, "but since you are an intruder and I have no way of knowing who it was lurking in the shadows…"

As the Minister's voice trailed off, Feng could feel the pressure building. Around his heart and his neck, like an icy grip clutching tighter and tighter as the Minister slowly closed his fist. He found himself gagging, tried reaching out with his mind as his legs started to buckle but could latch onto nothing.

"I think you will find my electronic countermeasures also sufficient for your telekinetic abilities, General Feng. In fact, the only psychic frequency they are tuned to ignore is my own. Everyone else, however– Urack!"

It came from behind him; the closet door he was still standing beside suddenly slammed open, crashing into his back and sprawling him across the ground. Immediately the pressure constricting around Feng released. It was not telekinesis that had opened the door, however, but the hand of one Darren Hildure who'd been waiting in the closet and now stepped out with a grin on his face.

"Got your message, hope I'm not late."

"No," Feng replied with a gasp for his breath, "right on time. I realize you like dramatic entrances, but perhaps next time not quite as last minute?"

The Minister rolled up to his feet, caught now between Darren and Feng.

"Surrender, Minister," Feng urged. "You cannot attack us both psychically like that, and you are no match for us physically."

"Perhaps not," the man admitted, "but you will still both leave here as corpses."

A flick of his wrist and a miniature pistol snapped out of his right sleeve and into his palm. He quickly aimed the pistol in Darren's direction and an open hand at Feng.

"A bullet for one and a coronary for the other," he promised with a grin. "Apparently one of my intruders had a health problem."

"HEEEEYA!"

One foot dropped down across the hand holding onto the small pistol, breaking the arm in the process, while the other came around in a spinning kick that launched the Minister fully across the room, crashing into a small rosewood stand with a very expensive looking porcelain vase on it. He hit the wall with an oomph, smashing through table and vase, then slumping to the ground.

From behind where the Minister had stood, stepping out from the hallway that he'd had his back faced towards, stood a young woman whose long black hair was currently tied up into a bun. An American and looking quite pleased with herself.

"Nope, it's not just the lesser Martian gravity," Agent Franklin decided, "my kicks really are stronger now."

"I take it you have completed your duties on Mars," Feng interjected.

"Lovely vacation," she replied, "now time to get back to work."

Darren flicked off the switch that they'd seen the Minister activate on his way in, then followed behind Agent Franklin over to his prone body, where she made a point of stepping between the Minister and Feng just in case, before turning him over for a quick glance.

"One broken arm, two ribs, and a femur. I broke his femur? Color me impressed, that takes some doing."

"You can tell all that at a glance?" Feng asked.

"I can now."

"So this is the head conspirator," Darren mused. "He's broken, but it looks like he'll live for trial."

"And then be executed," Feng sighed. "Seems like such a waste."

"His life?" Amelia asked.

"No, the trial," Feng corrected. "But we can't simply kill him right here."

"He could have fallen off his balcony," Amelia shrugged.

"I think Agent Franklin has the right spirit of things," Darren grinned. "But no, someone will be wanting a trial, if for nothing else to see if he had any more people in his network. Come on, let's get him up and packed away."

"Maybe I should delve a bit into his mind a bit right here and see what he may know," Feng suggested. "Just in case."

"Let's straighten him out on a couch or something first," Darren told him. "We don't want him dying from a broken piece of pottery sticking into his back before we have anything, now do we."

Just as they were starting to move him, the Minister began to groan, his eyes to flicker. He looked up and directly at the three above him, but there was something about his gaze. Like he was looking past them. Or at something else.

"Master. I failed you..."

"Did he say *master?"* Feng asked with a quizzical look, now quickly narrowing his gaze at the one before them.

"...I tried but... Yes, I understand. But I really tried, please believe–"

His eyes suddenly fixed into a stare they would never leave, his breath abruptly halting, and from his ears then came twin trickles of blood.

"Dead," Feng sighed. "Anyone have any idea how?"

"I sensed something," Darren said almost immediately, "but it was too quick."

"Like a sort of stabbing energy?" Agent Franklin asked.

"She catches on quick," Feng decided. "Yes. Apparently there is someone beyond Minister Huang. Someone with the ability to reach out and snap his mind like a twig. The puzzling part is, that the only way the Minister or anyone else could have gotten such abilities is if they went through the treatment on Mars."

"Observer gave me a complete psyche scan before hooking me into the learning enhancer or the Evolution Chair," Agent Franklin stated. "He says he does that with all candidates."

"It doesn't make sense," Darren agreed.

"I did get a name out of his mind just before he died, though," Feng told them.

"The name of his master?" Agent Franklin asked.

"I think not," Feng said with a shake of his head, "more like another contact in his conspiracy, but it *is* a lead. A Sir Roberts out of England."

"I'll follow up on that one then," Darren decided. "But it still leaves us with a question. How does one get through the enhancement process hiding any malevolent faults from Observer? Given that another could have somehow brainwashed the Minister here after the fact, that still leaves us with at least one person out there that's a psychic loose cannon."

"Add in the fact that you guys have been sending people up to Mars for a full decade," Agent Franklin reminded them, "and I imagine it makes for quite a number of suspects."

"It does indeed, Amelia," Darren quietly agreed. "It does indeed."

The question would linger well after the Moon rose higher into the sky and remain unanswered as Agent Franklin's security squad stormed in to take the body and do a complete search of the house.

CHAPTER FIVE

SIR ROBERTS

August 26, 2050.

The plane shot through the skies like the Thunderbird of ancient legend, a silvery beast in flight. A small craft, more in the private-jet category; just the perfect size for ferrying important human cargo about without any curious eyes around to see. In this case three important passengers of note: Darren, Feng, and Agent Franklin.

Through the window they could see the scattering of clouds far below, the ocean's blue farther still. No sign yet of land, but it would not be long. No one around to hear them speak save a single stewardess, and even she had a higher security clearance than most field agents, trained to know when not to hear something.

The seats were plush, a soft blue to match the carpeting, between where they sat a short table currently with a holographic display hovering above it, one showing a map of New York City. The cup-holders built into the chairs had a drink each, though in Feng's case it was hot tea, while Agent Franklin's held juice. She was dressed in her usual dark pantsuit, Feng in the latest trend in jeans and casual wear, but Darren looked far more formal. Business suit and tie, with a pair of glasses and a blond wig he was currently straightening into place.

"Looks good," Feng critiqued. "You don't look a thing like yourself."

"No," Agent Franklin blandly agreed, "you look better."

"Thanks," Darren began, "the idea is for no one to recognize– Wait, was that a shot? Did she just take a shot at me?"

"I think our little girl is growing up," Feng grinned. "She's getting more comfortable around us."

"Maybe a bit too comfortable."

"Sorry, Colonel Hildure," Agent Franklin levelly returned, "would you rather I say you look uglier than before?"

"Hmm, not sure if that's much better," Darren admitted. "Okay, so you've gotten better; if from thought-reading alone, I can't tell if you're joking or not."

"Definitely an improvement, Amelia," Feng agreed.

Only now did Agent Franklin break from her expressionless features into a slight smile, relaxing back into her lounge chair.

"I've been working at it ever since Minister Huang's house. If he had abilities given him from Mars and someone was able to influence *his* mind, then I could end up being a liability if I'm not careful."

"You're still better than an agent without the treatment," Feng said. "Is the telepathy any better?"

"Seems I can only make contact with the two of you," she replied, "and I can't read minds."

"You can only contact other telepaths," Darren noted. "Good to know your limits ahead of time. And that thing with the health sense? Can you–"

"Affect cures?" she finished for him. "No."

"At least not yet," Feng amended. "Give yourself time to see what you may be capable of. It took me and Darren quite a bit of practice before we had everything under control."

"Though I remember the fun we had practicing," Daren grinned. "The first time Observer teleported us back to Earth, before our more visible return flight, I tested out my teleporting abilities on Forester. Came walking right out of the closet in her office."

"*Director* Forester?" Amelia said with widening eyes. "You popped into the middle of the Director's office?"

"Well, first you should know that she's not exactly the director of the CIA. More like, all of Western Intelligence. A good chunk of the western nations got together for more than just the Mars project and Erica found herself top of the intelligence heap. Her real office is in a bunker in Geneva Switzerland. Anyway, one might expect to see a person pretty freaked out when a guy comes walking out of your office closet who's supposed to be an entire planetary orbital away."

"I take it she wasn't?" Amelia asked.

"She had a gun to my face before I could say hello," Darren sighed. "I swear, I have yet to see what it takes to phase that lady. My little unexpected appearing act was what sold her on the reality of our claims, not to mention the others on the Committee when we gave them the same show. Once we had the political types in on the game, then it was time to start recruiting more scientific minds. My crew stayed mostly up on Mars looking through the alien facilities once they'd had the same treatment, and as amazing as that all made them feel, it was Doctor Claude who pointed out that as physically and mentally advanced as we'd been made, how much more evolved must the Satarans then be."

"And from there, the Zelos," Amelia followed up, "since they've been giving the Satarans so much trouble."

"Exactly," Darren told her. "That's what decided us on the spherical design for our first battleship."

"I'm not sure I follow," she admitted.

"The Sagittarian ships are shaped more like a cigar," Feng explained, "which is great for them but hasn't helped them stop the Zelos, so we decided to do something a little different."

"After some brainstorming, we came up with the idea of a large sphere. More exterior surface area for weapon emplacements, you can place them all around the craft so there's no rear to take advantage of, not to mention it would be able to spin around in place to immediately present a different weapons battery to a foe. It may be lacking certain advantages of the Sagittarian design, but it also lacks all their weaknesses.

At least it should; we'll know more when we finally have a chance to test it once it's finished."

"It looked formidable enough when *I* saw it," Amelia shrugged. "But what about the physical treatment from the Evolution Chair? Observer said it rejuvenates, but how long does that last?"

"About a century before you have to go back for a booster shot," Darren replied. "Any one of us should be good for about ten such treatments before our cells get just too worn out to replenish."

"So... we could live for a *thousand* years? No wonder you two look so good, not to mention Dao-ming."

"Yes," Feng said with a grin, "I get to enjoy her lovely visage for the next millennium."

"To be able to live so long," Amelia said in disbelief. "And yet... have you ever wondered who you might be leaving behind? How many friends and family you'll watch die of old age?"

"My dad took the treatment," Darren put in. "He has some skills the Mars project finds useful, not to mention I insisted. Unfortunately my Mom wouldn't take it. Said she didn't want to start all over again with life, so she'll live out the remainder of a normal life."

"Well, that's..." Amelia began hesitantly, "well, kind of mixed feelings I guess."

"Don't worry about it," Darren said with a dismissive wave of his hand, "I've had a decade to deal with it. But maybe with another decade I'll be able to figure out how Feng here managed to make General. You know, I was your superior on that first mission but I didn't make General."

"Maybe if you become a Chinese citizen," Feng suggested, "they make you General too. I can put in a good word?"

"No," Darren replied, "then they'd think I was kidnapped or brainwashed or something, and someone would start launching missiles. Besides, MSG gives me heartburn."

The two men finally broke out into grins, leaving Amelia to wonder if they would be able to keep up such bantering as the centuries wore on.

"Back to the telepathy," she pressed, "I'd like a few more details on how it works, what are its limits. For instance, how far can you two pick up thoughts or transmit?"

"Well first, you just mentioned two different things," Darren replied. "There's mind reading and telepathy; the two are a little different from one another."

"How so?"

"Imagine it like a radio, since the brain is basically electrical by nature," Feng explained. "Radios can send or receive; two different but related functions. The reading of someone's thoughts is basically the ability to listen in on the electrical activity of their minds, while telepathy is all about transmitting. Both have inherent limitations, which you can relate to the laws of electricity."

"Like, the signal gets weaker with distance," Amelia suggested.

"Exactly," Darren said. "Mind reading is limited to surface thoughts and proximity. I can't probe your subconscious, for instance, unless maybe I'm nearly in physical contact and concentrating really hard, in which case it would be rather obvious. But if you're within range of a few yards or so, then I can pick up what you're thinking."

"The trick there," Feng picked up, "is to find a way to get them to think about what you want. In this regard, well-disciplined minds and crazy people are nearly impossible to read."

"Also it gets difficult if there's a dense or nonconductive barrier in the way," Darren added. "Remember, it's all electromagnetic when you come down to it."

"Now in the case of the Zelos," Feng put in, "from what Observer tells us, collective efforts may be quite possible. Individually the Zelos are very weak and their telepathy very short range, but the more of them there are cooperating together, the longer range and more powerful their telepathic abilities become."

"If that's true of us Humans or not, we don't really know," Darren admitted, "simply because there haven't been enough of us telepaths to find out."

"Well, now you got me to help experiment with," Agent Franklin stated.

"You also have to learn how to filter," Feng added. "For instance, with a crowd of people you could be hearing all their thoughts at once; very confusing at first until you learn how to tune out all but the one you want. Even then, a person might be having a dozen things running through his mind at once, and you have to learn how to tune out all the garbage that you don't want. Takes a bit of practice."

"But, all that said," Darren continued, "if I lock onto your brain's frequency then I can follow your thoughts for a much longer distance, but it requires quite a lot of focus on my part. Usually we have to lie down and go into a sort of meditative state to do it, but it's useful for spying in on someone; like looking through their own eyes, hearing with their own ears."

"How do you lock on," Amelia asked, "what exactly does that entail?"

"Call it frequency locking," Feng told her. "If you want a more thorough explanation then you have to go into quantum mechanics and entanglement, but that's not either of Darren or mine's specialty. We need total concentration to do it and it does take some practice."

"Got it. Now, how's all that differ from telepathy?"

"With telepathy we're transmitting our signal," Darren explained. "Already psychically-aware minds are the easiest to get a clear message through to, or failing that, then someone who is at least open to the possibility of such things. A non-psychic person who's close-minded on the subject will subconsciously block us out. At best he might simply get a feeling about something."

"Like me when I had that urge to go looking for you," Amelia realized, looking at Feng.

"Exactly," Feng grinned. "Now, if you had already known about my abilities, like say Chief Pinyin, and been open to the possibility of telepathy, then I could have gotten through with a lot more detail."

"And what's the range on that?"

"Best we can make out," Darren shrugged, "several miles, though if both people involved are psychics that know each other really well like me and Feng then nearly anywhere in the world."

"Observer tells us the theoretical range limit would be about a light-second," Feng put in, "but we've never really had a chance to test that out."

"That explains why you can only send to me and Feng and not read anyone's mind. You have telepathy, but apparently not the mind reading. In time and with practice, you should be able to send messages to others that you either know really well or are open-minded about telepathy. But you still might develop the mind reading later on."

"We can teach you some tricks to help you focus."

"You mean like the stuff the monks do with the finger, or tapping the sides of their heads or something?" she asked.

"As it turns out," Feng shrugged, "a surprising amount of that sort of thing really works. It's all about getting your brain to complete the correct electrical circuit."

"And how does any of this explain how a person can influence another's mind like the way we saw?"

"Basically more telepathy," Darren told her, "though with images. For instance, I could transmit the image or feeling of a spider into someone's mind and they'll think they see a spider. But to the degree that we have seen so far to so influence or control someone's mind... We're still working on that."

"It would either have to involve some sort of very strong psychic lock," Feng pondered, "or being physically right next to the guy when you telepathically bore into his brain."

"Either way," Amelia agreed, "we're talking one very dangerous person."

A thought to give pause to the discussion, Darren reaching for his drink for a sip, then after a moment Agent Franklin remembered she had a duty to attend to.

"I think we need to talk about the mission now," she broke in. "We're due to land within twenty minutes and I'd like to be sure of the details."

"Twenty minutes," Darren sighed. "When I was a kid it used to take a whole two hours to cross the Atlantic, now under half that."

"Director Forester has arranged for Darren to work as an attaché in the United Nations building in New York where Sir Roberts works," Feng explained. "He'll be just another face in the crowd."

"But if Sir Roberts does have any illicit activities going then he's certainly not going to trust having a new face around his meetings no matter how well he blends into the crowds," Amelia pointed out.

"I don't actually have to be in the same room to spy," Darren reminded her. "Once I get a fix on Sir Roberts' mind then I can psychically eavesdrop on him and everything he sees and hears. As long as he stays within the building then I just need a small office or dark corner to put myself while I'm focusing. Officially I will be the attaché to the office of the British Minister of Finance, inter-nation relations and international economic analysis specialist, undersecretary thereof, local branch office for North America."

"Sounds rather boring. What's it all mean?"

"It is, and it means absolutely nothing," Darren replied. "Just a glorified pencil pusher whose office passersby will leave well enough alone. I'll be free to psychically listen in on whatever Sir Roberts may have going on. And in case I see any faces worth taking pictures of, I have a miniature camera in my tie clip."

"Then while he's doing that," Feng picked up, "you and I will go pay a visit to James Yeung in Cambridge, the young son of my soon to be father-in-law. I'll be judging him for his worth to our little Mars program."

"And me?" she asked.

"You will be looking him over to see if he could be with this little conspiracy we've stumbled into."

"But you can read minds. It should be real easy for you to tell."

"And we recently found out there's somebody that can apparently psychically influence another without us noticing," Darren reminded her. "We need someone that can read intent through body language, we need someone skilled in spy-craft such as yourself. If Feng thinks that James is a good candidate for our project, and if you agree that he's free from certain other influences, then after he graduates he'll be going to a lot more than just my friend's wedding."

"Got it," she said. "Then I'm wondering if maybe I should change into a different set of clothes before we land. My outfit doesn't exactly avoid screaming 'Fed'."

"Then we'll just use that," Feng shrugged. "You're the government agent assigned to escort this foreign person who doesn't speak much English around the city. Just avoid showing off how much more of an agent you are than the normal."

"I'll just act like a few jerk agents I know of," she decided. "Anyone got a pair of dark glasses I can use to complete the picture?"

Feng grinned at the thought and leaned back in his seat for a last sip of his tea before landing.

Once their flight had landed, Darren disembarked and made his way over to an airport limo waiting to take him to his supposed job at the U.N., leaving Feng and Agent Franklin back on the plane while it refueled. A short time after that, the small jet would take off once again, this time for a short hop over to Boston.

The driver punched the destination into the dash-comp then sat back and let the auto-drive system take over. Darren said nothing during his ride, trying to keep focused on his new persona as an attaché from England. He kept an eye on the passing landscape as he imagined someone fresh in from another country would, though after seeing what was on Mars it was perhaps just a little hard trying to look impressed by the century-old buildings towering around him.

The basic skyline of New York had not changed much in recent decades. Some tall buildings had been replaced by more modern gleaming spires of glass and ceramic, the domination of electric vehicles had cleared up a good portion of the smog and haze, but sewer rats and prostitutes were still a part of the New York life. The Empire State Building still stood as a beacon to commercial enterprise, with the Statue of Liberty remaining steadfast in its position as guardian to the gates of the Land of the Free -- despite the great lady being battered and repaired throughout the years.

Darren's ride took him through streets crowded with all walks of life. He rode beneath the artificial cliffs of man that towered high above, past banks and block-long commercial buildings, big theaters and humble ethnic eateries, down streets with more yellow taxis than private cars, and through the veins of a city with seemingly at least as many styles of architecture as ethnic districts. A continuous flow of people seen in very few other parts of the world.

He arrived first at the Roosevelt Hotel on Madison towards early evening; the better to establish his persona at. The hotel's entry much resembled that of a classic theater marquee, the first floor above it a block-long row of ancient windowed archways, the interior a spacious lounge that mixed chandeliers, curtained windows, marble floors, and the elegant décor of a century back, with sleeker lines, modern electric lighting, and information kiosks.

His information had Sir Roberts as staying at the Waldorf Astoria, just a block down; too expensive for a presumed attaché, so Darren had to satisfy himself with remaining within distant sight of his target. Morning would find Darren sipping tea and munching on a muffin at a nearby café while reading an electronic copy of the local paper from a flat-screen built into his table, one eye and his thoughts carefully on the lookout for Sir Roberts. When he finally saw him leave his hotel, Darren finished his tea in a swig and got up, making sure to keep some distance between himself and the man as he carefully studied his thought patterns.

Sir Roberts was a man nearing sixty, fit enough for his age, his white-blond hair precisely coiffed, his goatee and mustache neatly trimmed, and everything about him very well groomed. From the whiteness of his complexion to the expensive tailoring of his suit, it all spoke of British aristocracy, while a plaid sash slung from hip to opposite shoulder suggested a proud Scottish ancestry as well. He even walked with a distinguished looking cane, one which Darren strongly suspected was more for the visual effect than any real need of help in moving around.

While Sir Roberts was getting into a waiting limo, Darren hailed a cab, and quite soon followed in his wake. Flash of his debit card through the taxi's reader, muttering out his destination which the driver punched into his dash-comp then leaned back and let the car drive itself; nowadays, taxi-drivers mostly just took the fare and did little in the way of actual driving– at least in the big cities. It was another drive through the busy streets of New York, Darren more intent on keeping his mind focused on Sir Robert's thought patterns to make it easier on picking him up from a distance. When he was certain that Sir Roberts was heading to the U.N. building, then Darren got out just before it while the limo continued on into the parking structure.

Amidst the near-endless variety of structures about the city, the United Nations building is one of those that stands alone. A singular structure by the waterside, with the row of flags along the wall leading up to the high rising monolith that is both the focus of Man's hopes and the pit of many of his fears. As busy as nearly anywhere in the big city in the mid-morning, Darren was but one of many crowding through the doors. A flash of the ID given him by Director Forester and he was in.

The main lobby looked like a four-level interior mall of white walls, paneled wood, and marbled floors; a city within itself, populated by the denizens of hundreds of nationalities with an accompanying array of styles of dress, mannerisms, and accents. So far Darren had managed to get by without having to resort to his fake English accent, and using a computerized information kiosk definitely helped him avoid the limelight. His was a face amongst the many, his thoughts lightly reaching out in search of those of another as he went over to one of the kiosks and passed his ID beneath it. He was immediately rewarded with a blinking light appearing on the electronic map corresponding to his assigned office space.

"So far so good," he said to himself. "No sign of Roberts yet, though."

He waited around the cafeteria for a short while, picking up another muffin as an excuse for loitering until he could spy Sir Roberts from amongst the many. His patience was quickly rewarded, his mind first to catch a glimpse of the mental pattern he'd studied walking out of the Astoria, and soon he was able to see the white-haired man with the distinguished walk strutting through the crowds with an occasional nod for the few of higher privilege while managing to completely ignore nearly anyone else. The underclasses were furniture to him, which in Darren's mind made things easier for him; easier to remain ignored.

Darren adjusted his tie, snapping a couple of discreet pictures by way of its miniaturized camera within the clasp, then followed several yards behind the man, as with a light brush of fingers to his left temple, he reached out his thoughts to touch lightly upon the back of his mind.

"As soon as he enters the office wing of this place then I can just use the room that Forester– Wait, where's he heading?"

Sir Roberts turned down a corridor, away from the conference rooms and towards a downward sloping hallway, the end of which was marked by a security partition and pair of waiting guards. The sign above read, "Dag Hammarskjöld Library".

"The Library," Darren mused to himself. "So many others around here to get in the way, that might be a bit too far away from my office to sort his mind out from all the others; especially if I want any sort of a good image of what he's seeing. I wonder if my ID is going to get me in *there?* Well, only one way to find out."

Picking himself up into a more self-confident stride, he walked down the hallway, picking up his pace a little to keep Sir Roberts within sight though not enough to actually catch up with him. Sir Roberts passed through the guard station with a flash of his ID, so when Darren got there he did likewise and pulled out his ID.

"I'm sorry, sir," the guard stated with a hard glare, "but the library is not open to the general public.

"My good sir," Darren began, trying out his fake English accent, "I am with the Ministry of Finance, office of inter-nation relations and international economic analysis specialist, undersecretary–"

"I don't care if you're with the Ministry of Funny Walks, that ID of yours is not good enough for entry into the library. You'll just have to get your boss to come back here with you."

"I say, old' chap, I have an appointment and am already rather' late."

"Sorry, still no entry."

Darren could see in the man's mind that he was ready to call in security and the last thing Darren wanted was any sort of public display. So, he gave his best annoyed look, quick nod of his head, then turned away, though not before stealing a glance down the hall from the security point.

At the very end of that hall, before it turned into the library itself, he spied a single door before which hung a sign that had a stick-figure drawing of a man.

"Okay then," he said to himself as he walked away, "Men's Room it is."

The guard may have seen him turn away into the first adjoining corridor, but no one in that hallway actually saw the young man coming out at them. In that very brief space of time, Darren had teleported, as if walking through an unseen door.

He appeared in the bathroom, just outside one of the stalls and in time for the stall door to smack him in the face just as someone was coming out.

"Ow!"

"Oh, sorry ol' chap. Didn't see you there. Apologies."

The map spoke in an actual English accent, then on seeing Darren's picture ID hanging from his lapel, brightened.

"You're from England too? Which part? I thought I knew everyone from our delegation."

"Um, a small town outside of– Listen, this is rather urgent, if you don't mind."

The stranger looked a little sour as Darren pressed past him into the stall, but soon his jovial voice was heard calling through the stall door.

"Maybe later then, what?"

"Yeah… err, what. See you later."

Darren waited until he heard the man walk away and the bathroom door close, then sat down on top of the toilet seat and closed his eyes in concentration, his fingers massaging his temples a bit more deeply now than otherwise.

"Sir Roberts must focus on Sir Roberts. He is in the library…"

By degrees the thoughts of the white-haired man came into some focus. He could see what he saw as he walked to the far end of the library, then from there into a small conference room with a table and eight chairs, each of which was occupied save the one that Sir Roberts himself would take. The door closed behind the English nobleman as the secretive meeting began...

"His name is James Chu Yeung, Dao-ming's younger brother. From what I found out about him, he's just finished his PhD in aerodynamics."

"And he wants to attend your wedding," Agent Franklin shrugged. "What's the problem?"

"Chinese law," Feng related. "At eighteen he was supposed to enroll in the military for a year but he left to pursue his studies in the States a decade ago. Unless he accepts the deal proposed by Chief Pinyin, he will be arrested the minute he returns to China. Let's see... his address was twenty-eight Essex– Here it is."

The neighborhood was like something out of an old movie. Rows of four-story brownstone apartments like aisles of waiting soldiers lining ancient cobblestone streets. A set of stone steps led up to the single-door entry, wrought iron railing to either side. One apartment building just like the many, lost in the ancient byways of the city of Cambridge near Boston.

The interior lobby looked a bit nicer than the outside, still clean, its mahogany wood paneling kept polished. Feng started for the elevator but Agent Franklin immediately steered him for the stairs.

"The elevators in these old buildings rarely work," she explained. "They're also about the size of a small closet. We're better off with the stairs."

The elevator in question was a far older kind than Feng had seen before, looking much like a stylish phone booth enclosed within a gilded cage that ran up the central foyer of the building. The stairs they now stepped up wrapped up and around this same open space, to the very top floor from which he could spy some of the elevator's mechanism poking out from the roof above. The sight of those elderly gears did not give him confidence in its operation.

"I think you're right. Besides, it's only three floors."

Three flights up then down a hall until they came to a door whose room number matched the one on a small card in Feng's hand. With a brief look to Agent Franklin, he pressed the doorbell while she stepped a little off to one side so as not to intimidate with too many unfamiliar faces.

By the second ring the door opened, a young woman on the other side. She looked Chinese, mid to late twenties, long black hair down to her lower back, wearing jeans and a blue blouse, her feet bare. She greeted them with a wary smile.

"Can I help you?"

"Hello. My name is Feng Yusheng. I'm here to see James about a personal matter."

"How personal? I'm his fiancé."

Then from somewhere in the apartment beyond came a male voice calling out, "Jan, who is it?"

"Someone named Feng Yusheng. Says it's personal."

"Feng? *General* Feng?!"

This was followed immediately by the sound of hurrying feet, what sounded like a shin colliding with a misplaced piece of furniture followed immediately by a stifled cry and one foot hopping for a few steps, then the door opening up wide to reveal a grinning young man behind the young woman. He too looked Chinese, at five-eight, he was a little taller than the woman before him, with blue eyes and medium-length black hair. He was dressed in jeans and a well-worn tee-shirt with the MIT logo across it, his feet also bare, and an eager smile splashed across his face that flickered uncertainly.

"General Feng? My sister's told me all about you in her messages. Are you here about the wedding or to arrest me? You're not going to arrest me, are you? Because I'd really like to attend that wedding, but not if– Why are you here now?"

"Easy there, son," Feng said with a soft smile. "Can we come in? I'm here with Agent Franklin of the Federal government."

Here Agent Franklin took her cue and stepped into view, trying not to look overly intimidating for the already nervous young man before her. It was strange for her to see; Feng and James looked the same age, but she knew that Feng was a full ten years older. Just something she was going to have to get used to.

"Oh, yes of course," James offered, stepping to one side with his girlfriend. "Oh, this is my fiancé, Jennifer Tsai Chin."

"Just call me Jan," she said as the other two entered the apartment. "James, are you sure it's okay? If he's from your government–"

"He's also about to be my brother-in-law, Jan. Don't worry, they can't do a thing until I step onto Chinese soil."

The front room of the small apartment was furnished in what might best be described as "starving student" motif. An old grey sofa that had once been white and with more stuffing, a short coffee table that might have been snatched from someone's dumpster then polished up, a handmade bookshelf along one wall filled with a mix of science and comic books, an old flat screen television perched atop what looked to be an even older dinner tray, and finally a scattering of chairs, each of an entirely different style and make. The wall opposite the bookshelf sported a fireplace, its mantle decorated with a smattering of academic awards, then the wall between them both opening up into a small kitchen and a hall into the interior of the apartment. Finally, the remaining wall was a set of tall double-windows looking out over the street outside, a couple of chairs separated by an errant end-table before them. As a whole the place was clean enough, just no two items seemed to match.

"As you know," Feng began as Jan closed the door behind them, "I am to be married to your sister. I know you would like to attend, but there is the matter of your lack of military service before you left China."

"James told me about that," Jan cut in, "and he doesn't deserve to be imprisoned. He's worked very hard to get his doctorate."

"I quite agree," Feng stated. "Which is why I'm here."

While they talked, Agent Franklin had been keeping an eye on both James and his fiancé. Any nuance of body language that might reveal something more sinister, be it a stray flinch at the wrong remark or a nervous stutter. So far both seemed sincere, the girl's concern obviously being for the one beside her.

"If I may," Agent Franklin cut in, "Miss Chin, your English is flawless. Like a native."

"That's because I was born and raised here in the States," she replied. "I'm American."

"Though her Chinese is excellent," James said, nearly boasting.

"But being American," she then continued, "you can understand my concern that James could be ripped away from me by your government while I could be separated from him because of my nationality."

"Exactly the reason for my visit," Feng assured her. "May we have a seat to discuss this?"

Jan looked hesitantly to the two strangers before her then to James; she seemed caught between the need to play the role of hostess versus being protective of her love.

"It's okay, Jan," James assured her. "This is General Feng the astronaut. He's the most famous person in all China. He would never break his word."

"Well then… Yes, of course," she then smiled. "But forgive the furnishings."

"I had my starving student days myself," Feng grinned, "it is quite alright."

They stepped over to the couch where Feng sat down with James, Jan seated to her fiancé's other side. Agent Franklin elected to remain standing, her gaze flicking between the young couple and the apartment in general.

"I would never wish to bring grief to my Dao-ming or her family," Feng began, "so I have arranged a deal with my superior Chief Pinyin back in China. You have just finished your PhD, I understand?"

"We both have," James said, hugging an arm around Jan with a look of affection flickering briefly across his face. "We studied aerodynamics together. It's how we met."

"He and some others were in the school library trying to design the perfect paper airplane," Jan related, her features now softening at the memory. "I flew mine in across the room and watched it land right in his lap."

"Beat everyone else's designs, alright," James finished, "and won my heart."

For a moment their gazes locked, Jan leaning her head into James' shoulder while Feng continued.

"Well, Chief Pinyin spoke with your father and has agreed that you may return to China without threat of arrest, but only if you are willing to work with him as an aerodynamic engineer for a time. Then the Republic of China will forgive your lack of military service."

"Well, that… sounds reasonable," James said with a little hesitation. "How long would it be for and when would it start?"

"The length of service would be for one year, and you would start after the wedding. In fact, there is still some time before the wedding for the two of you to ready yourselves for the move."

"Just so I'm clear," Jan interjected, "after this service he will be free to return to the United States?"

"Anywhere he wishes, Miss Chin," Feng assured them both. "Though I should tell you something that I'm supposed to keep secret for now…"

Feng leaned in closer, his voice lowering a little. Agent Franklin kept an extra careful eye on the pair, ready to note their reactions to what Feng would tell them.

"…It is hoped that you would desire to stay in China longer, because after your one year of service there is a very lucrative and very interesting job that would be awaiting you in Beijing. More than that I cannot say."

"You make it sound so mysterious," James pondered. "It does sound interesting. I would love to return to China, of course, but only if I will later be able to come and go as I please. I would never wish to make Jan a prisoner of my missteps."

"Never when I am with you could I ever feel like a prisoner," Jan assured him, her hand squeezing lightly to his knee. "But what will your father think of me? Isn't it customary in those rural regions for all marriages to be arranged by the parents? I'm not something he'd planned on."

"I'll make him understand," he told her. "Particularly since we may be over there longer than the one year, if that other project is as interesting as it sounds."

"About that mysterious project," she stated, "I've a hunch that it may have more international implications."

"Oh?" Feng said, looking a little surprised. "And why would that be?"

"Because," Jan replied with a nod in Agent Franklin's direction, "*she's* here. You seem to have no problem mentioning such a supposed secret in front of a Fed. That implies something with at least a little international cooperation, as opposed to a purely Chinese secret."

Feng replied with a noncommittal shrug and sideways glance in Agent Franklin's direction.

Bright girl came her thoughts. *I'm thinking a certain project could be getting two engineers for the price of one.*

And I have picked up nothing suspicious in their thoughts, Feng replied. *What about you? What can you see in the way of their body language?*

They're hiding nothing, except perhaps the fact that they were about to have sex when we knocked on their door.

Feng smiled, though for no reason that he would give voice to in front of the couple, then turned that into a remark of reassurance.

"My fine lady, no more can I say but I suspect you will encounter no trouble finding employment as well. Now, do you have up to date passports?"

"Yes," James replied, "but the wedding is under two weeks away. Will we be able to get visas in time?"

"I have connections," Feng assured them, "don't worry about that. Now, I will leave the two of you to discuss things between you, then will return by ten tonight for your final decision. Have your passports ready by then. You will have a day or two after that to pack for the wedding, then after the event, I will arrange for your belongings to be shipped to your new residence in China."

"I'll get to see my family again," James said, perking up.

"And I'll get to see China for the first time," Jan beamed, then suddenly downcast. "I have nothing for the wedding! What would I even *wear* to a Chinese wedding?"

Here Agent Franklin stepped forward, producing a small card in one hand which she then passed to James.

"What's this?" he asked.

"A credit voucher," Agent Franklin replied. "Wedding formalwear appropriate to Chinese custom and the theme of the wedding has been arranged for you both, as well as enough credit for any moving and travel expenses for both the wedding and the arrangement afterward. All courtesy General Feng and his associates."

"Why that's– I don't know what to say," James replied, a bit flustered. "My sister's wedding, a year working in China, and then–"

"And then, it's *our* turn," Jan cut in. "After all, why waste the trip to China? Everyone you care about will already be there."

"Jan," James told her, "in China it is not customary for the woman to ask the man to–"

"So who's asking? I'm just implying. Strongly."

James cast her a grin then wrapped an arm around her for a close hug. Feng took this as his cue and stood up while Agent Franklin headed for the door.

"We will be back later tonight," he told them.

"And we'll have our passports ready and a few things packed," James assured them. "Jan, are you sure you're okay with this?"

The answer she gave came in the form of a kiss, followed by pushing him down onto the couch beneath her. By that time, of course, General Feng and Agent Franklin had left.

The meeting began as soon as the door to the conference room was secured and Sir Roberts had taken his seat. Seven people there besides Sir Roberts, all of which Darren could make out as long as he kept focus on Sir Roberts and what he was seeing and hearing. The sounds of others coming into the bathroom, running water, toilets flushing, all of it Darren ignored as he maintained his focus. Just Sir Roberts and the meeting. What he saw through Sir Roberts' eyes was a little fuzzy, and what he heard through his hears somewhat muffled, but still clear enough to follow…

The first to Sir Robert's right was a white man, his blond hair cut nearly to crew-cut length, his face narrow and clean shaven; a man nearing fifty, his darkly colored business suit accentuating his Germanic features. After him was a slightly younger man, blond hair and looking a little out of shape; just the sort of pudgy pale body one would expect of an Englishman of wealth. The third also looked English, though his body far trimmer, his brown hair partially balding. Opposite from Sir Roberts sat a Frenchman, bald with a mustache drawn to nearly a single fine line, a little portly but with a superior cast about his features. A Chinese man with greying hair came next, a similar air of upper class as the rest. All the men wore business suits of a very expensive cut, all varying from blue to grey. The last figure there, though, was a woman; Japanese, her appearance that of a lady in her thirties though the severe look suggestive of the experience of many more years. Her black hair was tied back into a bun, her red dress in a style suggestive of a kimono but more westernized in its cut and tailoring.

"Gentlemen," Sir Roberts began as he took his seat, "and Lady Kaku, I have some good news and some bad news."

"We know the bad news, Wang got himself killed," the elderly Chinese man spat out. "We'll have no further chance at getting to Feng now. What could be the good news?"

"Easy there, Lee," the lady in the room calmly told him, her voice a cultured pearl. "We will have another chance to stop the Unification talks, or why else would Sir Roberts be here with his good news today?" The Chinese gentleman quieted, though no less pleased, she then turned a seemingly pleasant face towards Sir Roberts, greeting him with the sort of slight smile that could mean either a friendly mood or the promise of much pain if the news is not to her liking. "Sir Roberts, what is this good news of yours?"

"You anticipate me, Chika," Sir Roberts replied with a cordial nod. "Yes, Feng is beyond our reach for now, though rather puzzling is the way that Wang Huang described to me how he apparently rose out of his grave after being knocked on the head, poisoned, tied down in his coffin, then buried. Feng and Dao-ming will be married and under heavy guard even during their honeymoon. By the way, how is our Dao-ming lookalike? She was quite useful in luring Feng."

"No one will find her," the Chinese gentleman assured him with a grim smile.

"Good."

"That covers up our tracks," the balding Englishman there stated, "but that does not help us make *new* ones."

"Agreed," the Frenchman put in. "We need to stop this Unification process *now,* before it goes public. Our profits will be devastated if it goes through."

"Not to mention the general distaste I have for the whole matter," the blond Englishman broke in. "We must stop it before–"

"Yes, before," Lady Kaku said, far more calmly than the rest. "We all know the importance of stopping it, the problem remains in how. Sir Roberts?"

All faces now looked upon the one at their lead for the answer, while back in a certain men's bathroom, Darren had been using their arguing as an opportunity to quickly probe the other minds there.

"Odd," he whispered to himself. "They all feel very strongly about stopping the world unification, but I can't find a single one of them thinking of a reason as to why. Just this very strong emotional fixation that I would think goes well beyond any mere concern for profits..."

Back in the meeting room, Sir Roberts had been calmly awaiting his chance to speak, and now with everyone's attention he began.

"The goal is to break the unification movement, so with our first target of opportunity now unavailable we still have another. Colonel Darren Hildure is Feng's very good friend and he will be at that wedding as well. He will be our new target."

"We can make it look like a group in China resistant to the unification talks is responsible," the Chinese man pondered. "That will drive a wedge between China and the rest. Since the talks are not yet public, all the general populace will know is that their hero from the Mars expedition was slain by a malignant foreign power. There will then be a movement to break off talks with my homeland. A movement which will destroy the talks as well as present an economic opportunity."

"It sounds like it might work," the Frenchman admitted. "But how will we do it?"

"I have obtained a complete itinerary of the events," Sir Roberts explained. "Darren Hildure will be arriving with his parents a short time before the wedding. The wedding would be far too obvious a choice as they will expect another attempt there for Feng, but after the wedding they may be somewhat more relaxed. Colonel Hildure will want to use the opportunity to show his parents around to a couple of favored tourist's sites. I know where they will be going because since Colonel Hildure is considered a visiting dignitary, the Chinese government has already been informed of where they will be visiting so that proper security may be arranged."

"Security arrangements which I will have a hand in," the Chinese gentleman said with a sly smile. "Where would you like him to die?"

"The Great Wall is first on their list of places to go after the wedding, specifically the Badaling Gate," Sir Roberts decided. "The entire wedding party is scheduled to go, so I think that will make for a public enough display. Do you think that can be arranged, Lee?"

"I can arrange for a bomb to be secreted within Badaling's Gate itself," the Chinese gentleman stated. "When he passes through the Gate, it will go off, killing him and those with him but not enough to really damage the Gate."

"Then see that it is activated by a phone call. I will be there myself watching to see when the Colonel enters the Gate. In fact, as a visiting dignitary myself and a member of the English parliament, I will be appropriately horrified and recommend immediate sanctions against the nation of China. No offense, Lee."

"None taken," the Chinese gentleman amiably replied. "If that is what it takes to stop the world unification from happening, then that is what we must do."

"Then we have an understanding." Sir Roberts then picked up his cane and rose to his feet, an emotionless smile out for the ones before him. "In a very short time the attempt at unifying our world will disintegrate and we will have what we desire."

To the nodding heads and voices of agreement, Darren carefully pressed his psychic awareness further in, but try as he might he could find no sign of what that desire could be. Just a pure emotion within each that the unification of the world must not be allowed to happen. Finally he gave up and broke contact, easing his thoughts back into himself alone.

"So they want me dead, and even they don't really know why," he pondered to himself. "Hmm… Still nothing really solid to report to Forester, so I guess I'll just have to present myself as bait for Sir Roberts and play it from there."

He thought for another minute more, then looked up to see a pair of legs showing beneath the other side of the stall door. Standing up, he straightened out his suit, gave the toilet a flush just to make it look good, then left the stall with a brief smile to the man that had been waiting.

"Sorry I took so long, old' chap."

The other frowned in reply then hurried into the stall, while Darren stepped out of the bathroom and walked calmly for the guard station where he had no problem passing through. After all, they were guarding against people with the wrong ID from getting *in*, not leaving.

He would have to tell Director Forester what he had discovered, as well as Agent Franklin, but leave filling in his friend Feng for later. The man had his wedding to concern himself with, let him enjoy it and worry about conspiracies and bombs later.

CHAPTER
SIX

THE WEDDING

September 6, 2050.

"Your wedding is in three days, Feng; you just leave the problems of the world to me and enjoy being the nervous groom. I'll update you on things *after* your honeymoon. The most important thing right now is to answer my dad's question… What about the bachelor party?"

They were driving down the wide Beijing streets in the back seats of a stretch limo, behind them one of Chief Pinyin's security sedans while a pair of men on motorcycles escort from the front. They were fresh from the airport, Darren with his wedding guests, and Agent Franklin there keeping a careful watch on them all. James Yeung sat with his girlfriend Jan while she cast eager wide eyes out at the bright and colorful streets of Beijing, James looking a bit nervous at his return home. For this occasion Jan was dressed up a little, even to bearing through the pain of high-heels, while James was perhaps more formally attired than he needed to be at the current moment. The remainder of the group involved Darren's parents.

Robert Hildure looked like a once-vigorous man recently regaining his youthful vitality, the extra fat around his middle slowly working its way back into muscle, the grey wisps of hair lost amongst his fresh regrowth of dark strands, though the colorful Hawaiian shirt might peg him as someone who until recently had been very much retired. Beside him sat Michelle Hildure, shorter than her husband by a few inches, her shoulder-length hair sporting just as many grey hairs as red, and beginning to look like she could be her husband's senior by a number of years. She wore a full-length red and blue patterned dress, with a green scarf tossed about her neck. Both seemed as preoccupied with their passing environs as James' girlfriend, but at the mention of a bachelor party, Robert's attention shifted… followed immediately by a glare from his wife to which he simply shrugged.

"I am afraid to tell you," Feng now addressed Darren's father, "that traditionally we do not go in for bachelor parties here in China, Mister Hildure. Some say it is because Chinese men end up enjoying so much of a partying life after their marriage that it is not necessary."

"That better not be true of you," Jan said with a light elbowing to James.

"I promise to keep it very much in with the American tradition," the young man promised. "One night of complete debauchery followed by a lifetime of indentured servitude."

This time she gave him a slightly harder thrust of her elbow into his ribs, to which James grinned in amusement.

"It's a pity about the party," Robert Hildure replied, "but I'm just worried about how much I'll stand out at this wedding. I brought my best grey suit with me, but I'm afraid I haven't dusted it off for a while. Michelle here, though, insists on keeping with her usual bright dresses."

"I wear what I want," his wife firmly pouted. "Nothing's going to change me now."

"Chinese weddings are very different from anything back in the States," Feng related. "They are a lot more colorful. Your grey suit would be fine for a funeral, but for a wedding, your wife's dresses would be more the norm. Understated, actually."

"See?" she chided her husband.

"Then, what should I wear?"

"I'll buy you something, Dad," Darren grinned. "You can keep it as a souvenir to show your friends back home."

The view through the darkened windows was starting to speed on by somewhat faster as they took to the broad highway cutting its swath through the midst of Beijing's tallest gleaming towers; the Macau Expressway, that fifty-lane beast that connects all the way down to Hong Kong. Night was approaching and with it, the city took on the look of colorful beacons stabbing against the night while liquid light ran high-speed circles about its feet.

"The drive to the village will take seven hours," Feng then said, "so Chief Pinyin has invited us all to stay at his house. We can leave in the morning."

"That's a pretty long drive," Darren's father remarked. "Whereabouts is this place?"

"A small village in Heilongjiang Province a little northeast of Harbin," Feng supplied, then to the puzzled looks of both of Darren's parents, offered a simplified set of directions, "The far northeast corner of China."

"Ah," Robert Hildure nodded. "That sounds like it could be pretty cold up there, then."

"It can be, but fortunately this is not winter," Feng replied.

"Will we be able to see the Great Wall afterward?" Michelle asked. "I promised some friends pictures of the Great Wall."

"Actually that is on the itinerary for after the wedding," Feng told them. "The first place that Dao-ming and I will visit when we start our honeymoon. We will pass through the Badaling Gate as a symbol of the two of us passing through into a new life together. The entire wedding party is invited, and since it is on the way back to Beijing, no one will have any problems catching their flights home."

"Then we can even visit a couple other places," Darren added, "like the Forbidden City."

"Good," Michelle said with a decisive nod. "I'm not coming all the way to China without seeing the Great Wall and some other Oriental stuff. Now, when do we get to meet the bride? I want to give her a little something to put with her wedding dress. Just a little trinket from my mother."

"We will be arriving at the village by tomorrow," Feng told her, "you will meet her then, though I myself will have to stay away from her until the day of the wedding."

"They got that whole not seeing the bride before the wedding here too?" Robert asked.

"It's a bit stricter than that here in China, Dad," Darren explained. "In the days before the wedding, Dao-ming must live in seclusion with only a few of her closest friends to tend her. She's only going to bend that tradition a little to see her brother James here when we arrive."

"Which gives me another reason to be nervous," James finally spoke up. "I haven't seen my sister or family in years and now it's her wedding, and I have to hope that this Chief Pinyin keeps his word."

"Don't worry," Jan said with a soft stroke of her hand across his shoulder, "I'll tear him a new if he doesn't."

"I should mention that my father is very traditional," James told her. "He will be calling me by my given name of Chu, and will expect my girlfriend to be more demure in public. Not to mention that he will be a bit angry that he had no hand in the choosing of my future bride."

"Well," Jan shrugged, "life has its disappointments, now doesn't it?"

It was with that thought that James cast a worried look out to the highway passing by beyond.

Time soon saw the group at Chief Pinyin's house and a lovely repast prepared by the Chief's wife. Even Agent Franklin sat down to eat, though always with a discreet eye on any window within line of sight of her charges. Mrs. Pinyin took to chatting with James and Jan in Chinese, while Feng acted as translator any time Darren's parents looked a bit confused. They ate in the dining room with the mobile of hanging lanterns, and when it finally came time for dessert, it would be a very nervous James who would leave with the Chief into his study for a private talk.

"A lovely meal," Mrs. Hildure was saying as she dug into a small slice of almond cake. "Though I must say it is different from anything I've had in the Chinese restaurants back home."

"We have fifty-seven regional dialects here in China," Feng explained, "and at least as many local cuisines. You would have sampled two of them back in America."

"And now she's going to be asking for recipes," Robert predicted with a chuckle.

"Well, why shouldn't I?"

While Darren's parents spoke with Feng, across the table Mrs. Pinyin was speaking to Jan in Chinese.

"Jennifer, your Chinese is very good, and yet your parents were both born in the United States?"

"My grandmother took my mom to Hong Kong a lot when she was growing up, then later with me tagging along. Even after she was too old to travel, my grandmother made my mother promise that I would be raised with the language and knowledge of the country where my roots are. I can read and write in Chinese as well."

"One should remain connected with one's origins no matter where you are in life," Mrs. Pinyin nodded sagely. "Is your grandmother still alive?"

"Yes, but not getting around as fast as she used to, I'm afraid."

"Both her and your mother must be very worried about your trip here to China."

"And having to stay for a full year, yes. The only thing that makes my mother feel better about it is that we are here with Feng and Darren. Both are good men that keep their word."

"They are very good men, as is my husband," the older lady said, reaching out a hand to lightly grip Jan's own. "You have nothing to worry about."

Just as Jan was wondering if that was true, James came walking back in the room with Chief Pinyin. She immediately looked up, catching James' gaze, to which he replied with a smile and nod. Jan let out a quiet sigh of relief, then stood up to wrap her arms around her love.

"We have worked out a plan to our mutual liking," Chief Pinyin announced. "Now I suggest we all adjourn to our bedrooms as we must get up early for the trip tomorrow. Housing has been arranged for all wedding guests in the village."

"In that case," Darren said, standing up, "I would like to extend my thanks to Mrs. Pinyin for the good meal and to Chief Pinyin for the hospitality of his home."

As the rest were getting up from their seats to leave for a good night's rest, Agent Franklin caught Darren's eye, as well as his thoughts for a quick exchange overheard by no one, save perhaps Feng if he cared to eavesdrop.

I'm going outside to make a last perimeter check.

I've been scanning around for any other minds other than our own, he replied. *I don't sense anyone, but you never know. Go ahead.*

While Agent Franklin was about her perimeter check, the Pinyin's were showing where each guest was to sleep, though it was with a shared frown that James and Jan found out that Mrs. Pinyin had arranged for separate sleeping accommodations for the unwed couple.

September 7, 2050.

When the black sedan finally pulled up before the two-story Yeung house with the blue ceramic roof, James was clutching tightly onto Jan's hand looking at least three kinds of nervous, while Darren's parents were too caught up in the new sights around them to notice. Agent Franklin was first to get out, along with members of her security team from the two escort cars, giving the area a quick glance around before motioning the others out.

Feng remained by the vehicle, looking longingly at the house, but would not approach. The others, meanwhile, were led up to the front door by Agent Franklin, though Darren paused just a moment or two for a word with his friend.

"Must be hard, not being able to see her for a couple more days."

"It is," he agreed, "but when I do, it will be like the first light of day to a man who has been blind his entire life. She will be glorious."

"Boy, you're in love alright," Darren grinned. "Never heard you get poetic before."

"Have you ever *seen* a girl in a Chinese wedding dress before? We don't just go for the white-on-white look here. You will see, she will be glorious."

"Well, you just keep your mind on your bride and the wedding. After we're certain everything's okay here, Agent Franklin's going to leave a couple of your men with you from now through the ceremony, while she herself remains here to be certain that no one tries anything on Dao-ming."

"For which I am most grateful, my friend. Now it is time for me to wait back in the car lest I catch an accidental glimpse of Dao-ming before the wedding."

As Feng was climbing back into the sedan, a very nervous James was just knocking on the door of his childhood home, Jan tight by his side, while Darren's parents waited behind them with Agent Franklin. Darren was just walking over to join them when the door was answered by Dao-ming's father. For an extended moment Chang looked sternly out at his son, James unsure if to offer a hesitant smile or drop to his knees begging forgiveness. The glare then shifted to Jan by his side, who for a moment let her arm drop slowly from James' side and lower her gaze respectfully, but then stopped, deciding apparently that was not the first impression she wanted to make. Her arm resumed its tight wrap around James' waist and her eyes came up to meet Chang's with a determined ferocity to counter his own. Only a moment would last this contest of wills.

It ended with a smile breaking out across Chang's face, then reaching arms around his son and pulling him close, a hug too for Jan, while muttering heartfelt wishes in Chinese that went completely past the Hildure's understanding.

"I don't need to understand the language to know what just happened," Mr. Hildure said to Mrs. Hildure with a smile.

Father was just guiding his son into his home when another came running in to join them. From the interior of the house, and in complete disregard for her father's sense of propriety, Dao-ming came lunging up to James with a joyous cry upon her lips, flinging her arms around her long lost brother. Tears flowed even from Mrs. Hildure's eyes to watch, and it was Mr. Hildure who held her and Darren back to let the family have their moment.

Even from inside the car by the curb, Feng could sense the joy his bride felt at seeing her brother after so long, and kept his thoughts to himself. He would have plenty of time to know Dao-ming's joy in a few days.

September 9, 2050.

The wedding itself was an event enjoyed by the entire village.

While final preparations were being made, decorations hung out and guests getting ready, Dao-ming spent the early morning first bathing in fruit-infused water. This was followed by a moment of meditation before a pair of red candles; one inscribed with a design of a sinewy dragon and the other of the Phoenix bird in a bath of its own flames. Jane was there in Dao-ming's bedroom to watch as her hair was dressed up in the style of a married woman, which is to say wrapped up into a wide bun about her head, save now with the addition of jewelry dangling from the pinnacles of her hairdo like glittering icicles and a line of sparkly ornamentation draping gracefully between one bun and the next across the forehead of a perfect porcelain face.

"You should take notes," Dao-ming said to Jan while her other friends helped adorn her. "My father has accepted you but will insist that James have a traditional wedding like this one."

"If it means I get to wear all that glittering stuff instead of just the old white dress," she replied, "I'm all for it. But, your hairdresser certainly likes wishing you good luck."

Dao-ming's hair was being dressed by an older lady who was constantly muttering supportive phrases into her ear in Chinese while adorning her hair.

"That is the Good Luck Woman," Dao-ming explained. "When I emerge from my retreat here in my room, she will carry me on her back into the main hall where I will don my wedding apparel, including the bridal Phoenix crown. From there I will be carried in the bridal sedan chair to the site of the wedding."

"I hope that same good luck lady's not going to carry the chair as well, because that sounds a bit much."

"No," Dao-ming replied with a sweet smile, "that will be the job of some very strong men. Escorts. Now, you will be among my lady friends marching alongside the bridal chair with the parasols. It is considered an honor which I talked my father into. He likes you, you know, but will not admit it for some time."

"I got that impression," Jan smiled. "Now let's get you to a wedding..."

As Dao-ming was putting on her finishing touches, Feng was already waiting at the village temple in the older section of town, which in this case was little more than a simple pair of pillars topped by a curved roof and an altar between the pillars; no walls. Surrounded by a carefully manicured garden and ancient stone steps, for this occasion it was decorated with red hanging lanterns, gold and red emblems of family ancestors, and designs of good luck written in older Chinese script. The personal friends and family of both the groom and bride stood circled around the temple amidst a flutter of long gold and red banners, while the rest of the village populace lined either side of the road leading up to the temple.

Feng was dressed in a long red gown, red shoes, red silk sash, and a crown of cypress leaves. Before leaving his home in the village, he had been wearing a silken ball on his shoulder, which his father had ceremoniously removed and replaced with the crowd of leaves, then accompanied Feng on the march to the temple amidst a clatter of firecrackers, loud gongs, and drums announcing his passage, while he was preceded by a young child dressed in red and gold.

Darren was already with the others by the temple and whispering explanations to his parents beside him. Darren's mother was still in her own colorful dress that she had arrived in, though with the addition of a colorful red and blue scarf, while his father looked more than a little uncomfortable in a robe and jacket with as much red and black as the one provided him.

"The child is meant as an omen of Feng's future sons."

"They certainly are a colorful bunch," Robert remarked.

"Wait until you see the bride, Dad."

"In any culture," Michelle Hildure remarked, "the bride is always the star of the show. Though as much like a peacock as the groom looks, I'm curious to see the bride now."

After Feng arrived, bowing to the priest in gold and red robes who would officiate, then kneeling once before the altar, he turned around to face the people-lined road and await the arrival of his bride.

If Daren's parents thought the arrival of the groom had been showy, they would truly be impressed by that of the bride. First came a procession of crimson-robed attendants bearing red hanging lanterns on tall sticks, each lantern inscribed by some ancient symbol, others with banners written with traditional wishes for a long and happy marriage. Then came the musicians; men with a sort of squat wooden kettle drum carried by straps about their shoulders, others with cymbals, flutes, or the rare four-stringed instrument. They played a bright fast-paced tune to which danced a pair of men each wearing an enlarged stylized lion's head that covered most of their bodies, one lion of red and the other of white. They danced and ran about, playing up their roles as if of dragon-lions in flight, heralding the main attraction of the procession.

Behind a cluster of red parasols decorated by golden lettering came the bridal chair. Enclosed in a red and gold box draped with a roof trim of golden tassels, it was supported on twin rows of sturdy bamboo poles to either side of the enclosed chair, carried front and back from the shoulders of strong young men dressed in red coats and pants with black trim. The lanterns parted to surround the temple in a ring as they approached, the banner-bearers stepping away to the sides where the crowds stood to let the rest of the procession pass them by, then the lions giving one last dance about the small temple before finally coming to rest on either side of it. The musicians remained playing but also fell to either side of the assembly near the temple, not stopping their music until the bridal chair would make its final approach.

The chair stopped before the steps of the temple, the ones with the parasols then clustering around one side of it as the bride stepped out onto a red mat but still hidden from view. Before the bride would step any further, however, Chang Yeung came over to talk with another older man.

"What's going on now?" Robert asked.

"Well," Darren replied, "I believe this is where they do some haggling over the bride. That's Feng's father talking to Dao-ming's. When it's done then Feng's father will hand over a red envelope of money to Dao-ming's father. Sort of like a dowry."

"Sounds barbaric, paying someone for the bride like that," Darren's mother remarked.

"It's all in good nature," Darren assured her. "Look, they're already done."

A small red envelope was indeed passed from one father to the next, at which point both men walked back to the altar and at last the parasols would be moved aside to reveal the bride. This was accompanied by another round of firecrackers, a couple of which were gleefully set off by Jan with the other women around the chair.

Her hair looked like someone had captured the tossing of the ocean and frozen it in place then decorated it with fairy dust and glittering stars, golden tassels hanging from her earlobes, atop her head a golden headdress shaped like a bird with flames coming off its spread wings. Her red dress swept down to the similarly-colored shoes about her ankles, overtop a wide-sleeved decorative coat in rose and white flowery patterns that came to her waist. But as beautiful as the adornment looked, it was the one adorned that caught more than the eyes of the groom. For she looked like a perfect china doll, her smile the source of the morning's radiance, covered over lightly by a thin red veil.

For a moment Feng could not say a word, while Dao-ming looked on at her handsomely trimmed man in red, a moment shared as the music came to a final end. Into that sudden quiet, a few nearest to Feng– including Darren– heard his awe-struck remark

"I am marrying a… goddess."

The Good Luck Woman and a few of the bride's friends escorted her to the altar before parting away, leaving Dao-ming alone with Feng before the priest. The priest was a Taoist monk, dressed in colorful gold and red robes with sleeves that draped past his elbows and a long scarf hung around his neck embroidered with dragons and ancient symbols, atop his head a squat conical black hat. The priest began with an invocation that none of the English speakers could follow, though Darren did his best to translate the gist of it for his parents.

"He's bestowing the blessings of Heaven and Earth upon them… and now the bride and groom are giving their thanks to such, as well as paying homage to their ancestors with promises of the success of their union… And now they're bowing and the priest–"

"Darren," his mother gently cut him off, "I think we can follow the rest. The priest gives his blessing and then Feng pulls back the veil and they kiss. Always some variation of that around the world."

"This one might involve a shared cup of tea, I think," Darren replied, "but basically that's it. The ceremony's a lot simpler than the stuff before it."

As the Taoist priest was giving his final blessing upon the couple, Agent Franklin was in the crowds with her security people. One roof within sight had a sniper, another roof a man with binoculars searching the crowds, while Agent Franklin herself had an earpiece with continual updates from her various agents scattered about the crowds.

"Lots of dignitaries here, that's for sure," she said to herself and those hooked up to hear her. "I'm not assuming any of them are safe, so keep eyes peeled, people."

The final blessing was being given to the kneeling bride and groom when she heard Darren's mental voice in her head.

Keep an eye out for Sir Roberts.

He's here with the other ambassadors and dignitaries, she thought back to him, a finger massaging lightly to her forehead as Darren had shown her. *Did you find out what he has planned?*

If I heard right back at the U.N., it won't be during the ceremony but after when the entire wedding party goes to the Badaling Gate at the Great Wall. A bomb will be in the Gate, but Sir Roberts will be there to set it off himself by phone right when he sees me enter.

He's after you, now? Okay, I'll stick to him like glue, but until then I'm making sure that none of his friends have any other back-up plans.

She revealed no sign of the psychic conversation as she patrolled through the crowds, save her steps now taking her closer to the clustering of important dignitaries. This was an important wedding, so naturally there were representatives not just from Beijing but half of Europe. She spied Sir Roberts out of a corner of her eye but made a point of not looking directly at him any more than for anyone else.

The sudden rise of music signaled the end of the ceremony and got Agent Franklin to looking back at the altar and anyone near to it. Darren was busy with his parents, though no doubt with one eye scanning the crowds while a beaming groom and shining bride marched hand-in-hand back to the bridal sedan chair which would then take the new couple away to their wedding chamber at Feng's house across the village.

Agent Franklin used this as an excuse to let her footsteps carry her in the direction of the cluster of dignitaries under the guise of her role as security, but more specifically for Sir Roberts than any of the others. She stayed a respectable distance away, one surely out of most people's earshot but not for those that had been given the physical enhancements over on Mars. If he so much as thumbed a dial button on his cell phone in his pocket, she would hear it.

"Okay everyone," she said with a finger to her earpiece, "I want their entire procession back to their house covered then patrols outside while they do their thing in the wedding chamber. From what I understand there's going to be a lot of partying while those two are busy and Colonel Hildure is going to be too occupied with the celebrations, so it's up to us. I want to be alerted if anyone so much as *looks* in the direction of the bridal chamber, be it local or ambassador. No one is above suspicion save Colonel Hildure himself."

Responses came back into her ear while she smiled just like anyone else watching Feng and Dao-ming being carried away from the temple to their first night together as a wedded couple.

September 11, 2050.

The partying continued for two days, during which time Feng and his bride never left their chambers, nor Agent Franklin her vigil of their environs. Stories were told of the couple by their friends, Darren opting for some more humorous stories, which apparently was not usual for traditional weddings, but being a foreigner it was excused. Various dignitaries mingled amongst the locals, many politely assaulting Darren with questions about his equally famous friend, perhaps with some obscure motive for their own political agendas. Agent Franklin did keep an eye on Sir Roberts, but tried not to be in his direct line of sight; she just happened to always be nearby as a part of her duties. And if she wasn't, then she had other eyes on him all the time; if he checked back into his hotel room for a nap, she knew.

When finally a report came into her ear, she approached Darren where he was staying with his parents at the Yeung house, meeting with him in the backyard garden while everyone else slept off the previous night's celebrations. Some pink flowering bushes, a stand of bamboo, and a few small trees surrounding a little pond were their only observers as they stood there atop the middle of the short brick bridge crossing over one end of the pond, the entire area walled off from public view. Behind them the swept-up curve of the roof of the Yeung house glistened with the early morning light dancing lightly off its edges.

"As much as I saw you drinking, why don't you have a hangover?" she asked at his bright-eyed appearance.

"Same reason you won't anymore," he replied, "Mars. So what's the report?"

"Sir Roberts is on his way to Badaling Gate. On the sly, of course, and way ahead of anyone else associated with the wedding except Chief Pinyin."

"We need to catch him in the act before he can be arrested or he'll turn it into a diplomatic nightmare. Who do you have with you in the way of bomb experts?"

"I got one man that can pick up any sort of radio controlled bomb within a hundred yards of his equipment and have it disarmed inside of five minutes."

"Good. We should all be at the gate by this afternoon. The bomb is supposed to be inside the Gate itself, so before the place opens for the day, here's what I want you to do…"

They arrived later that afternoon, many of the wedding party having driven on ahead while the main contingents traveled by helicopter, the central one of which held Feng and Dao-ming, along with one of Agent Franklin's security men. A vast panorama spread out below, changing from glittering city lights to countryside that seemed to roll on forever. Grassy lowlands with the occasional bamboo forest and sprinkling of small villages like quaint miniatures beneath their feet. Sharp-edged ridges spilling over into another valley and then another, until finally as the team of helicopters brought them into evermore rugged and uncivilized countryside they saw it.

The Great Wall.

A stone snake stretching from one horizon to the next, wide enough for the space atop its length to qualify as a road, punctuated at regular intervals by forty-foot wide watchtowers. A wall several stories high, sheer and unclimbable. A wonder of ancient engineering and determination, a sight like few others. Feng and Dao-ming both gasped at the sight, the new bride pulling in closer to her mate as the first of the contingent of helicopters begins its approach to their final destination.

They were coming to what looked like a fortress in itself; a block of stone at least six stories high and wide enough to qualify as its own castle, topped by a long stone lodge with the usual upward curved lip at the edges of its roofing. On its own, this structure would have been impressive, and yet it is but one part of the Great Wall, a gate through its heart. Badaling Gate.

Darren was out of his helicopter first, there to greet the bride and groom as they step out from their own ride, Darren's parents standing with everyone else around the Gate. Families and friends from both sides of the joining were present, along with the expected dignitaries, all to see this final symbolic step as Feng and Dao-ming pass through the Gate and into a new life.

"I hope you two had plenty of fun," Darren grinned as he led the way from the helicopter. "Everyone's been waiting for you."

"Can't understand why," Feng shrugged good-naturedly. "This is more important to me and my new wife than anyone else."

"Wife," Dao-ming said sweetly, nuzzling Feng, "I like the sound of that word. Wife."

"Not as much as I like having one," Feng grinned, then suddenly dropped his smile and looked up at Darren. "There's something going on, isn't there? What have you found?"

"Nothing that isn't being handled," Darren assured him. "You just go back to being a freshly married groom and leave the dirtier details of things to me and my people."

"Speaking of which," Feng said, looking around, "I don't see Agent Franklin anywhere about."

"Just one of those details that *I* get to worry about. Dao-ming, tell your husband to just enjoy himself for a bit. I've got this handled."

"Feng," she said lightly into his ear, "you have the rest of your life to play hero and savior, but only a very short time to be a caring man deeply in love with his new young wife."

"You're right," Feng sighed. "Okay, let's get through the gate then disappear from public eyes for about two weeks."

"I'm not sure how successful that disappearing part is going to be," Dao-ming noted with a look at the gathered crowds, that now included some photographers and news correspondents, "not with half the world watching."

"Consider me your lift out of here," Darren told them. "After you're finished here I will teleport the both of you anywhere you wish to go to. I dare even the most determined paparazzi to follow *that* trail."

The crowds watched and pictures were taken as Colonel Hildure led his long-time friend and the bride across to join the rest gathered before the Gate, behind them the last of the helicopters leaving the open stone plaza for somewhere less public to land and refuel. The Gate towered before them all, Darren's parents making quiet remarks of shock to one another, several of the dignitaries trying to look impassive and act like they had seen it all before… and mostly failing. The couple posed for several pictures before their friend Colonel Hildure managed to shoo enough of the press of people away to escort them across the open stone paving to the edge of the Great Wall itself.

One of the dignitaries that had been with the wedding party, though, was watching from a bit farther distance. Sir Roberts stood across at the other side of the plaza with eyes on one Darren Hildure and a small phone in one hand.

"Just a little bit more," he said to himself. "That tunnel will focus the blast back on the Colonel and anyone with him. Might even get his friend the General while we're at it; that would really stir things up. Pity about the bride, though, she's such a lovely thing."

He continued to watch, Feng and Dao-ming leading the way with Darren some steps behind. The couple paused just before the gates, some words of significance from husband to wife which Sir Roberts cared nothing about, then hand-in-hand walking into the wide tunnel that cuts through the Great Gate.

A cheer went up once they entered, their passage to a new life begun, whereupon Darren cried out with a smile and motioned the rest to follow as he himself was first to enter in after Feng and Dao-ming.

"Any second now. Come on Colonel, walk faster. Right about…"

Sir Roberts waited while Darren passed into the Gate and a few seconds longer just to be sure he was in the middle of the passage, then with a discreet grin, pressed a button on his phone.

Immediately an explosion of smoke erupted out from the entry through the Gate, people crying out, screams filling the air. The entire plaza was in an uproar, armed men running across from their surrounding posts, others atop the Wall itself looking down to see what the commotion was all about. All the while Sir Roberts calmly watched as a grin curved up from his lips.

"Just perfect."

He brought his hand down to drop it into his pocket, when suddenly something grabbed onto his wrist from behind, squeezing his fist closed around the phone.

"My people have just radioed me confirmation that the detonation signal originated from a phone within a yard of where you're standing, Sir Roberts. If you would kindly hand it over before I twist your wrist off, then I can get on with arresting you."

"What manner of–"

He spun around to discover his wrist being held by a young woman with an amazingly strong grip, running over from some distance behind her two men in suits and dark glasses with guns drawn.

"Young lady, do you have any idea who I am? Let me go this instant!"

"You are Sir Roberts, leader of a conspiracy to break apart the secret talks for a one-world government and guilty of the attempted murder of Colonel Darren Hildure, Feng Yusheng and his bride, and innumerable possible bystanders."

"And where's your evidence," Sir Roberts asked with a sly grin. "That explosion destroyed it all and gave the world the excuse it needs to keep on fighting with itself."

"Oh, you mean the smoke bomb and flares?" she said, nodding once in the direction of the Gate. "Have a look."

Sir Roberts' victorious grin immediately fell as he saw someone walking out from the Gate with hands raised to calm everyone down. That someone was Colonel Hildure, followed soon by Feng and Dao-ming. From grin, to frown, to angry growl, Sir Roberts struck out with his cane at Agent Franklin to wrench his wrist out of her grip, then started running, though not before she was able to snatch the phone from his hand.

Sir Roberts was fit enough for a man of his age, but age and aristocratic dignity do not equate to the physical aptitude of trained agents or soldiers. He ran straight across the courtyard for the nearest vehicle, looking over his shoulder to see Agent Franklin not even bothering to give chase. She just stood there, his phone in her hands, leaning her weight against one leg and shaking her head.

"I'll kill the Colonel with my own hands if I have to," he vowed as he ran. "The world must not unite."

"Well, here's your chance."

He had just seen the Colonel clear across the courtyard a moment ago, but now impossibly there he was before him, the English nobleman running straight into his fist. He dropped, his back hitting the ground hard, cane tumbling out of his grip, nose bleeding as he gasped for air.

"I have diplomatic immunity!"

"Not when you're caught red-handed trying to set off a bomb you don't," Darren stated. "You'll probably get the death penalty, but not before we trace down all your co-conspirators. Agent Franklin?"

Her voice came up from behind him as her slow steps brought her closer to the fallen nobleman struggling to get up to his knees.

"Authorization just confirmed, Colonel," she said with a finger to the comm-link in her ear. "I have some men raiding his hotel room now. I imagine his laptop should be most informative as to the identities of the other conspirators, not to mention this phone of his."

"No!" Sir Roberts finally blurted out. "You can't. The world must not– Cannot– I… Master!"

He'd struggled partway up then fell to his knees as if in prayer, supplicating the heavens with a look of fearful rapture. Agent Franklin stepped back, giving Darren a quizzical look, while from across the courtyard her men circled around them, with Chief Pinyin and his own people closing in as well as keeping the curious back and assuring the crowd of visitors that everything was alright.

Plenty of witnesses for what next came out of Sir Roberts lips.

"Master! I tried and failed. Please hear me."

His face twitched, his eyes widening, then Sir Roberts seemed to notice the people around him as if for the first time. From one to another he looked, wild fanaticism in his every tone and movement.

"The Master will still bring you down. Earth must not unite. It *will* not. He... I will see you all as dust before them. You have stopped one vessel but never them all. Never *me!*"

With that, his body shook as his eyes rolled up in the back of his head. Blood began to drip out of his ears and down from his nose before he finally dropped to the ground.

"Just like the other," Agent Franklin half-whispered.

"And just as dead," Darren followed up. "Which still doesn't answer the question as to who more is behind this all."

"And who this master is," Agent Franklin stated. "At the end there I had the feeling that... it was like another was speaking through his voice."

"Which leaves for some very big questions," Darren sighed. "But that for later."

With a tired sigh, he motioned to one of the attending men in dark glasses.

"Clean this up and get him on ice. I'm curious to see how many of the other conspirators we'll find like this, but for now let's not ruin the day for any of the tourists around here, least of all Feng and Dao-ming."

With a quick nod the man got to work, an emergency vehicle already driving across the plaza, leaving Darren and Agent Franklin to step away and wonder. Who– or what– exactly was behind this? And why?

In the end the news would report of what amounted to a smoke bomb set off in Badaling Gate, the arrest of several others associated with Sir Roberts, a number of which were dead by the time authorities caught up with them, and the successful departure of General Feng and his bride to parts unknown for their honeymoon.

Michelle Hildure thought the wedding was quite pretty but that the failed firecrackers inside of Badaling Gate were a bit much.

CHAPTER SEVEN

REVELATION

February 1, 2051

"Doug Bookman, KLAM Channel Eight News here at Hotel de la Paix in Geneva Switzerland along with about a hundred other reporters to bring you the historic World Weather Conference. According to sources, these talks have apparently been going on for quite some time in secret, which has everyone even more curious. If it's just about some new emission standards, then why keep it so hush-hush?

We're here in the main assembly hall waiting for things to get underway. Whatever the reason for all the secrecy we will be finding out shortly. Before things start maybe I can find someone to get a few words about– Wait, it looks like the chairman of the conference is about to take the podium. Yes, that's French Meteorologist Professor Pierre Simon. With him on the left is First Consular Doctor Yao Ming, China's famed meteorologist, as well as Second Consular Professor Aaron Lipskie of the United States, and Professor Asenath Al-Azhar of Egypt. Let's listen to what they have to say…"

In design the conference room looked much like an old Swiss castle, with high vaulted ceilings, golden tapestries hung over ancient walls, and lines of baroquely carved pillars as stone sentinels standing along either side. Chandeliers brightly illuminated the hundreds gathered within, both the conference attendees sitting in the rows of chairs laid out in semicircles facing the stage, and the herd of reporters of all types gathered at the back of the chamber by the ornate twin doors. The stage itself was covered with a large projection screen, before which stood the speaking podium and the men now approaching it.

Professor Pierre Simon, a man of average height and build with short brown hair and wearing a dark suit. A well-spoken intellect known throughout the meteorological community but by few others outside of it. Behind him other men in suits; a Chinese gentleman sporting a trim looking haircut and cultured manners, a heavy set blond-haired man, and a darker-skinned gentleman with a trimmed mustache and brooding look. They approached the podium with Professor Simon at their lead, furtive glances briefly cast from one to another before settling down into a collective noncommittal look for the cameras, both handheld and the miniature camera-drones hovering carefully above between the chandeliers.

Agent Amelia Franklin stood to one side of the grand room, close to the front within a quick run of the stage, a finger to her earpiece and eagle eye on everyone in the room. As the professor took the stage the hubbub of wondering voices quieted. He looked first out at the assembly of faces before him, then the cameras that he knew would be broadcasting this event across the world, swallowed once, then began.

"Ladies and gentlemen, as some of you are now finding out, for the last three years we have been meeting in secret to negotiate solutions to all manner of weather-related disasters. I am talking about far more than just global warming or global cooling, or whatever the latest trend is, but what happens when a monsoon hits a highly populated coastal region, or the potential threat of an earthquake along the likes of the San Andreas fault-line, or even when a volcanic eruption might occur too near civilization. A dozen different disciplines were involved in this, but contrary to what you might expect, it was *not* to negotiate some world fund to help alleviate any damage or assist victims, nor was it to set quotas for carbon emissions. Rather, it concerns something far more reaching."

He let the statement linger there for a moment, heads turning and voices talking while newsmen quietly made their comments for their audiences, all of them curious as to what exactly the professor was talking about.

"Over the last two years, we have been launching a series of satellites. Part of the function of these satellites is not simply to monitor the weather, but to… control it. Technology exists that allows us to steer a monsoon away from dense population centers and to where it is needed. We have technology to bleed off crustal stress in small measured doses away from where it would do great harm and to monitor the underground magma activity and predict when a volcano will erupt and how to control its flows. We have the ability now to completely control our weather, but that has not been what has taken up the bulk of our time."

Again he paused, the onlookers who had not previously been a part of the secret talks looking incredulous, stunned reporters commenting on this unfathomable leap forward, while others openly scoffed at what was being said. Then once again the Professor continued.

"Our discussions have centered around where we *should* control the weather and to what degree. Weather systems are a convoluted interconnected web; pulling the wrong strand in one place could have disastrous results in another. Fortunately for that, we have had a rather unique consultant; one with over eight thousand years of detailed records of every weather pattern and system on the entire planet. The same consultant from which we obtained the technology to put into the satellites to control the weather. For that, though, I would like to hand this meeting over to a rather famed set of dignitaries that have been key to this project… as well as many others."

Here the Professor and his group stepped to one side while the screen behind them came to life. The first image it showed was of Colonel Hildure dressed in green and brown military fatigues with shoulder patches displaying his service branch… though if one looked very closely then one might spot that one of these patches displayed a graphic of the Earth as a whole with no further indicator of service or even country. Next to Darren stood General Feng Yusheng in his own blue-green fatigues, then standing behind them and blocking any real view of their whereabouts were others: a mid-sized Russian with an untamed mass of white-blond hair, a shorter Japanese man well known in certain geological circles of his homeland, a German woman with straight blond hair and angular features, and a Frenchman whose mostly grey hairs had gone back to being mostly brown while his paunch had returned to a more muscular and youthful appearance than he had previously been known by. Professor Andrii Alexander, Dr. Akio Tomoko, Professor Glenda Hayden, and Dr. Jeremie Claude.

More curious voices began to mutter at this sight. Each of these faces was well known both in their respective fields and as a part of the first successful Mars crew. But to see them now, there seemed something different about them. Younger perhaps, fitter, maybe more confident.

"Hi, I'm Colonel Darren Hildure, and this is my good friend General Feng Yusheng. You know me as commander of the first successful mission to Mars, and in fact, these people behind me are my original crew. What you don't know… Well, there's quite a lot that you don't know. For one thing, the Mars project was far more successful than anyone could have fathomed. You see, we discovered something up here."

"It is an alien installation," Feng picked up, "complete with a robot placed there to tend it and watch over us for the last eight thousand years. His name is Observer, and it is because of him that we have the weather technology."

The view now expanded, showing them the same room that Darren and Feng had first woken up in, off to the left side a humanoid robot covered in a light blue skin and features sculpted to look more human. It stood taller than Darren's six feet and was standing before one wall with a glittering control panel that looked much like a thick obsidian shelf topped with gleaming crystalline specks. The robot gave a nod then spoke in clear cultured tones; not at all the emotionless bland mechanical tones one might expect.

"Greetings, I am called Observer. I have been watching over your world for over eight thousand five hundred years and have been looking forward to this meeting for quite some time."

"Observer's creators were the ones who built this base," Darren continued, "and left him to watch over us for the time when we would be ready. A time when we would need them, but also a time when we would be ready for their help. You see, they have a few rules and cannot give their full assistance to a world that is not yet united, which brings me to the main point of this conference."

Many voices started to rise in the assembly, more than a few wondering what joke was being perpetrated to watch such an obviously fake film. But to what end? Darren raised up his hands for quiet and it was then that at least one of the commentators noticed one small detail in that action.

"Doug Bookman again. The lag time in communications to Mars should be several minutes, but the way that Colonel Hildure just raised his hands for quiet indicates that he has nearly instant feedback on what is going on in this assembly. More like this broadcast is originating from here on Earth. I don't know what the purpose could be behind such an obvious hoax, but it is my speculation that–"

"If you will permit me," Darren continued, "the more astute amongst you will have observed that I'm able to hear all the arguing going on over there in nearly real time. This is thanks to Observer's advanced equipment. But we are not here to discuss such minor details, nor really to discuss the new weather control system. That is just the tip of the iceberg. Observer, if you will?"

The view showed the robot reaching over to touch one of the gleaming specks on his control board. Immediately Darren, Feng, and his entire crew vanished in a blink, leaving just the empty control room behind them. A moment later they appeared once again… right on the stage just vacated by Professor Simon and his people. As solid as any of the others in the conference room, smiling out at an assembly suddenly gone wild. The ones sitting in the front semicircular rows remained calm, for they had been in on secret events for a while now, but others shot to their feet, a couple of reporters dropped their mics, and some of the camera-drones zoomed in for a closer look, one even flying in to lightly tap one of the crew on the head just to make sure he was real.

Into this near riot, Agent Franklin cued her people. Men in suits and dark glasses came out to lightly restrain some of the more physical people, calmly urging them back to their seats, while others worked to quell a potential stampede from the room before it could begin. Darren grinned to them all, Feng making a quiet aside to his friend along the lines of, "They're taking it better than we'd hoped," then Darren finally raising up his voice.

"Now that I have your complete attention, you might wonder why Observer's creators are here at all. There is a threat out in the galaxy called the Zelos, and unless we unite they will obliterate all life on this planet..."

Back on Mars, Observer was tending to his controls, what he might be seeing or doing not something that the still-open feed of the projection system could pick up. A single indicator on his panel lit up, one that drew a curious look as he lightly pressed the stud. Above the panel, the display now floated in full three-dimensional life. First a view of stars hovered before him, then another control and overlaid by a tactical schematic. While Darren was telling the assembly and the world about the Zelos, Observer was busy tracing something his automated systems had picked up.

Something he was hoping he would not see for a few decades yet to come. Immediately Observer turned around to address the projection system and Darren back on Earth.

"Darren, pardon me for cutting you off, but something very important has come up."

He was in the middle of explaining what was known of the Zelos threat, but on hearing such a calm warning from the robot, he immediately turned to face the screen, as did Feng and the rest of the original crew.

"Observer, what is it?"

"My sensors have just picked up a single small vessel. Scout craft would be my guess. It has just passed Mars orbit and should be at Earth in slightly over a minute. Darren, the configuration is Zelos."

"A Zelos scout ship?" Dr. Tomoko exclaimed.

"They must be scouting for their next target," Professor Hayden dispassionately noted.

"And for that very reason it must never get back to its superiors," Darren picked up. "Observer, is the defense grid operational yet?"

"Defense grid?" someone in the audience cried out. "What defense grid?"

"The weather satellites," Feng quickly explained to all listeners, "their other function is as a weapons array to defend the planet from hostiles like the Zelos."

"No Darren," Observer replied, "I am afraid it is not yet fully configured. Estimating the Zelos trajectory now… it seems to be on a heading straight for your location."

Agent Franklin knew her cue and immediately started snapping out orders through her mic pickup as she hurried through the crowds to join Darren and his crew up front.

"All snipers start aiming for whatever you see dropping out of the sky, *especially* if it doesn't look Human. Internal security, form up around this conference room; we need to keep these people safe; they're some of the biggest brains on the planet and I don't want them caught in the fallout… Get me air-defense, I want planes in the air *now.* What do we have in orbit? …What do you mean one of our satellites just went dark?"

The view on the large screen now changed, courtesy Observer, and now showed an overhead view of Geneva with a single black dot falling down from the sky. The fields of pointed roofs stretching across the distance, quaint avenues weaving between them, while a wide promenade ran around the shores of the lake. An old world pearl now threatened by an ominous black dot hovering high above it. Then from one horizon came a jet flying patrol, aiming now to intercept the alien object. The dot changed course slightly to accommodate the attempt.

The black dot flew straight into the jet, coming out the other side and leaving behind it two halves of a jet trailing smoke and flame. The jet didn't even slow it down. This got more than a few shocked and panicked reactions from those in the room, who watched as the dot now came to a hover right above the city.

In basic appearance the craft looked much like a giant beetle, its four legs being landing struts with clawed grippers, no maneuvering jets that could be spotted but its entire shell aglow as it moved. The front where a beetle's mouth pincers would be instead sported what looked like twin barrels suspiciously shaped like gun turrets. Its passage through the jet gave a visual indication of its size, for it was about the same length though much broader.

It paused for only a moment or two, during which time more jets were frantically screaming across the skies to get there in time, while snipers and security personnel braced themselves for a threat they were not ready for. The small craft then shot down, aiming this time straight for the very hotel in which the conference was being held.

"It's coming right this way," Dr. Claude gasped.

"Something about our gathering seems to have attracted it," Dr. Tomoko noted.

"Then I will show them how Russians fight," Professor Alexander boasted, then a bit more subdued, "Anyone have a gun?"

Shots rang out from the snipers, all of which the craft ignored as it bulleted straight for the grand hotel. Its twin turrets glowed as it bulleted down, and from them a pulse of distortion shot out in a path directly ahead of it. Quick distortion of air passing rapidly by, sonic boom in its wake as it slams into the side of the hotel where it continues to burrow on through. The work of a second but now there is a large hole straight through the side of the building wide enough for the alien craft to fly through.

The other end of the pulse was quite evident to all, for suddenly a large portion of the ceiling above turned to dust, chandeliers crashing to the ground, leaving a thirty-foot hole carved nice and neat. Now the assemblage turned into a terrified stampede for the door, while Agent

Franklin and her agents aimed what guns they had straight up at the new hole.

The craft came down, stopping in a hover just within the boundary of the hole, its bottom facing down and neatly plugging up the new entry. The ends of its four landing struts flexed once as if they might grab onto something then from the belly between them a panel slid open.

"Why come *here,*" Professor Hayden pondered. "This is not a military target."

From the open belly they jumped out and the world got its first view of the Zelos from two brave cameramen and the ever-obedient camera-drones. They stood about five feet tall, their tough chitinous body reminiscent of a giant locust, complete with wings and six legs. Equipment was strapped about their bodies, including a clear plastic mask around their faces. There were two, both hovering in the air while bullets mostly bounced off their hides. They spoke to one another in a high-pitched chitter, then one reached a delicately clawed appendage to snap off a small palm-sized black box with one yellow facing and aimed it to the panicked crowds below. From that side a light flashed out, and with it people suddenly spasmed as if from an electrical jolt. Scientists, dignitaries, reporters, and even security personnel all dropped to the ground convulsing.

All except for Darren, Feng, Agent Franklin, and the original Mars crew. They remained standing, shaking a bit but still able to move as they tried to fight off the effects, able to only communicate mind-to-mind as the two aliens flew down, one to Professor Simon's group and the other to the midst of those seated in the first rows.

Feng came Darren's voice into the other's mind, *I can't move. Maybe a finger, but…*

Same here, Feng thought back. *Give me a few moments and I think I can fight it off.*

Feels like a cross between having my entire body dipped in Novocain and putting my fingers in a light socket, Agent Franklin reported. *I'm guessing Mars is the reason we're still standing.*

And the reason why we're going to break out of this and stop those creatures. Feng, where's some of that Asian mental discipline you guys are supposed to have?

I'm a doctor, not a monk.

Only a second or two needed for the rapid psychic exchange, but enough for the first Zelos to land beside Professor Simon's group on its two hind feet and pick up the spasming Professor. It held him as if to study for a bit, then brought him closer until the creature was staring at the professor face to face. All Professor Simon could do was stammer, then from the creature's mouth beneath the facemask something shot out.

A long slimy tendril hit firmly into the man's forehead. The moment it did a scream ripped out from the Professor, but not merely from his throat. Darren, Feng, and even Agent Franklin heard it as a psychic shriek, the terror of a mind being ripped apart, every neuron drained of energy. A moment later the Professor was completely limp, no more convulsing, at which point the proboscis then thrust in deeper, straight through the bone where it began slurping up the soft interior.

The other Zelos had come down to the first row of other scientists and made its own choice from amongst their number, picking up a balding man and meeting him face to face in the same manner. Soon there was a second psychic shriek and another limp corpse.

My God, Feng psychically exclaimed, *did you feel that? I think that thing just ate the Professor's mind.*

It was like his soul was shrieking, a stunned Darren returned. *We've got to stop them before they kill everyone in this room. I can move my hand, what about anybody else?*

I got an arm to work, Agent Franklin reported. *Went for the more physical upgrades than you two did.*

That's it. Thanks for reminding me, Feng replied.

The first Zelos dropped the Professor's body, then reached down for another one– Professor Ming– but instead of feeding on him, tossed up towards the hovering craft above where an invisible force seemed to grab hold of him and gently pull him into the belly of the craft. It then began reaching for the next one in the heap when a voice with a Japanese accent spoke up.

"You will leave them alone."

The Zelos looked over to view the speaker; it was Dr. Tomoko. Apparently his Mars-refitted body had been able to shake off enough of the effects of the weapon to at least speak. This drew the curiosity of the Zelos as it stepped over to the man. Meanwhile, the second Zelos was picking through its own samples from amongst the crowd, rejecting one of the security guards in favor of another doctor and tossing that one up into the air to join with the other.

What both failed to notice, though, was that one of the rods holding up the nearest tapestry was starting to quiver, the tapestry hung from it slowly moving itself to one side.

The first Zelos faced directly to Dr. Tomoko but the man would not flinch. He faced the menace with a proud look and strong chin, to which the creature made a noise that sounded much like a cross between more chittering and... a chuckle. It reached out a claw, thrust its tip into Dr. Tomoko's left shoulder, then very slowly drew a deep bloody line down the entire length of his arm, cutting all the way to the bone.

Now did Dr. Tomoko scream. During this pained cry the alien launched out its proboscis to the man's forehead and once again came the psychic scream, flavored now with physical pain. If to judge from the way the creature's bulbous eyes lit up from behind its facemask, it seemed a lot more pleased with this new meal than the first.

That's when the large curtain rod launched itself. It became a spear trailing a broad colorful trail, piercing into the creature's back, mostly shattering on impact but leaving a small piece jammed into its hard shell. The creature emitted a screaming hiss as it spun around, leaving Dr. Tomoko to collapse to the ground, vacant look on his face. At that moment Darren broke from his stunned state with a loud cry and stumbled towards the alien, while Feng freed first one foot then brought up an arm into which the remains of the curtain rod flew. A makeshift spear into his grip.

Agent Franklin was a couple of seconds later and only managed to free her upper torso for movement. Enough, though, for her to reach for her gun and take aim.

Darren landed on the back of the first Zelos, his strength not yet fully returned, while Feng threw his spear at the other Zelos just as it was reaching for another small yellow-faced box on its belt. The broken curtain rod hit straight into the device, assisted in part by Feng's telekinetic abilities, and drew from it a small explosion of sparks. The creature chittered angrily then dropped to all six legs and charged straight across the room for Feng.

Three shots rang out as Darren struggled with the first creature, from Agent Franklin's gun straight at the Zelos. The first shot missed as it spun around trying to dislodge the man on his back, the second one glanced off its shell, but the third one hit straight into the facemask, cracking it. Immediately the creature went from trying to scrape Darren off its back to quickly covering two of its claws-hands over the mask as it screamed out a sound much like nails running down a chalkboard. Agent Franklin stood fixed with her gun still leveled in both hands, waiting for another clear shot.

At the same time the second creature slammed into Feng, bowling him to the ground and pinning him there with four of its limbs while with one of the other two it reached a claw to the top of Feng's chest.

"Of course," Darren called out. "Their masks!"

Darren immediately changed his tactic from trying to pin the creature down to reaching over with one hand for the straps holding the facemask in place, while Feng was looking up at the thing's ugly face just as the proboscis was starting to reach out.

"Well," Feng actually grinned, "why didn't you say so?"

Suddenly the mask ripped itself off from the second Zelos, just as Darren gave a hard tug on the one worn by the creature he was struggling with. The one over Feng screeched out with lungs afire, forgetting about Feng in favor of running after his facemask as Feng's telekinetic ability had it streaking around the room on a merry chase. The other Zelos began screeching as well as it reached for the mask now in Darren's face, during which time Agent Franklin was able to pull off another shot.

This time the mask shattered, breaking apart into two pieces from the bullet's impact.

By way of the still-hovering camera-drones, the whole world watched as the Zelos chasing his mask started to ooze grey foam from its nose, its eyes beginning to dissolve to the creature's painful cries. Darren finally jumped off his own burden and watched as it frantically flailed around before apparently remembering that it still had its small vessel hovering just above it.

"Oh no you don't," Darren swore.

He made a grab for the creature, while Agent Franklin tried for a leaping kick, but both were still not completely recovered from the effects of the alien weapon, not to mention that the creature could fly. And fly it did as its two attackers met the ground, straight up into the open belly of the craft while its companion finally dropped to the ground screaming as its lungs burned, its eyes dissolved.

"It can't get back to its people," Feng cried out. "They'll know we're here then!"

"I got this!"

That said, just as the belly of the craft was sliding closed, Darren vanished. The world watched from the edge of its collective seat as the alien scout ship darted out through the hole in the building with far less care than when it had entered. Just as it was bulleting out of the hole into the sky, Darren appeared back in the room, this time from a few feet up and tumbling down, his arms wrapped around something. Feng ran over to his friend, Agent Franklin posting herself as the only security currently able to move, gun leveled and ready for anything.

"Safety tip for when teleporting from a moving object," Darren stated as Feng helped him up into a sitting position there on the ground, "momentum is still conserved. Ow."

The first thing Feng noticed, besides his friend's bruises, was the object he held. It looked like a three-foot section of exhaust pipe with a fist-thick mass of glittering wires sticking out of it.

"What's that?" Feng asked.

"Don't know..."

From high above an explosion suddenly thundered across Swiss airspace, the view on the large screen showing a burning cloud where one alien scout ship used to be.

"...but I'm guessing it's important."

The first to recover while Feng helped his friend to his feet, were those of the Mars crew, who in turn rushed about to help others in the room just beginning to stir, except for Dr. Claude who bent down to examine their fallen friend Dr. Tomoko. To the concerned faces of Professors Alexandra and Hayden, he just sadly shook his head.

"Darren, Feng," came the voice of Observer from the screen, now returned to a view of the control room on Mars, "are you both alright? What did you observe about the Zelos? I realize you have some dead to care for but this could be a unique opportunity to learn more about what they want."

"Us," Darren said simply.

"Observer," Feng elaborated, still visibly shaken from what he had experienced, "I felt– we both felt– that thing somehow drain the very thoughts from the Professor's and Doctor Tomoko's minds. It felt like it was sucking out their souls!"

"Followed shortly by literally sucking out their brains," Darren followed up. "Observer, they went straight for the highest concentration of some of the most brilliant minds on the planet and started *eating* them. I think our conference is what attracted them."

"Disgusting to watch," Agent Franklin put in, "and rather terrifying to experience if you're psychically sensitive."

"The Zelos feed on mental energy...," Observer for a moment pondered. "Interesting. I must get this information to my creators; this is the first clue to their motivations that we have ever had. My sensors detect no other craft, hopefully the Zelos will attribute the loss of their scout to an accident or something not worth investigating. You should be fine for now."

With that the image winked out, leaving the three standing amidst the ruins of the room, trembling survivors picking themselves up, and a small flotilla of camera-drones now hovering about Darren, Feng, and Agent Franklin as the center of worldly attention.

"I think," Darren remarked to his friend, "that we have far less time than Observer previously calculated. If they're sending scouts into our region of space–"

"Then we need to get Earth united," Feng agreed, "and that battleship finished, or the Zelos will swarm through us unchecked. One scout ship and two aliens cut straight through everything here. Imagine what their main fleet will do."

Imagining is just what the world would do, as the words echoed through the airwaves, leaving not a person untouched by the images they conjured up, and even the most stubborn critic convinced. The conference would continue, but now with its real purpose as the main topic of discussion: the final logistics of a single unified Earth government and what to do about the Zelos threat.

CHAPTER EIGHT

MIDDLE EASTERN CONNECTION

February 2, 2051

Darren walked into the office of Director Forester, only this time it was not the one located in Washington D.C., but rather her main office right there in Geneva Switzerland, hidden away in a bunker buried beneath one of the stylish old baroque office buildings of the city. More spacious than her CIA office, with a large oak desk a prince might sit behind, two computer flat-screens situated to either side of the plush leather chair in which she sat. Behind her stood a heavy cherry-wood bookcase, its leather-bound volumes an exceptional rarity in an age where books have long since been relegated to electronic media. The red carpeting underfoot was as short as it was said the Director's temper to be, and there were no windows looking out from this room. As far as seating for anyone else, there was none; the Director didn't like anyone sitting at ease before her.

Finally, a small placard atop her desk, bearing not her name but more in the way of a motto. 'You must have a Top Secret security rating just to be in this room.'

She sat behind her desk, her eyes focused on one of her terminal screens as Darren walked in. As usual, she got straight to the point before Darren could even ask.

"Everyone's on board with the unifications but some factions in the Middle East," she said, looking up to him.

"Sounds normal enough," Darren shrugged. "Making trouble is part of their religion."

"These fanatics have stated specific intentions to disrupt the talks with suicide bombers. As close as our other operative could tell, they seem especially fanatical. That wouldn't be anything particularly new except that shortly after his report our operative was found with his brains leaking out from his ears."

"Ah," Darren brightened, "*now* the plot thickens. So we have another lead on our mysterious manipulator of Sir Roberts and the others."

"That's what I want you to find out," she snapped. "General Feng will stay at the conference, with Agent Franklin to assist, while you go to the Middle East and track down the real leader of this bunch. There will be a special ops team available to you under your command should you need it. You'll be making contact with them the minute you board the plane. They've been briefed to follow your orders without questions."

"I suspect after the big public announcement and the appearance of those aliens, they shouldn't have many. At least not as regards my more overt abilities."

"Which reminds me. Has Observer said anything of how that scout ship found us? I find it suspicious that they came upon our world a few decades sooner than his creators anticipated and with such close timing to the conference."

"Apparently they send out scout ships ahead of their intended raiding path," Darren shrugged. "It was just chance they happened to arrive on the day of the conference, then once in the area just headed for the area with the highest concentration of intellect, which would have been the conference."

"Hmm, a possibility," she mused for only a second before snapping back, "which I don't believe for a second. No such thing as coincidence in our business; or much of anything else, for that matter. That's one more thing going on to keep an eye out for. Now get out of here. Your plane's on the tarmac with your travel bag."

"Will do, Erica."

"You're on the clock, so that's *Director* Forester," she immediately snapped. "Now get."

"Pleasant as always," he grinned.

Darren gave a passing resemblance to a salute then turned on heel and left. Soon he would be on a plane with a special ops team headed for the Middle East and the last reported sighting of a very specific terrorist group.

The leader of the special-ops team introduced himself as Major Scott Binder, a strictly military man built like a six-foot-two linebacker, but without the need of the shoulder pads to fill him out. His light brown hair was cut to short military standards, his clothing the expected military fatigues covered by straps of equipment, weaponry, and survival gear. With him were five other highly trained soldiers, each of them checking their weapons and parachutes as the Major filled Darren in on procedures.

"We'll be parachuting into Sanandaj in Iran. That's mountainous terrain over there, but intelligence reports are that's where the group's been hiding out. How are you with a parachute?"

"I won't be needing one. Did you see the opening of the conference? I've got a firm lock on your mind right now, so as soon as your team parachutes down, I can get a picture of your surroundings right from your mind. That's all I need to teleport down."

"I thought that teleporting act was something the robot did."

"For interplanetary distances, yes. But I have my own abilities good for local stuff. The telepathy is also how I'll remain in contact with you in case they take my radio or something, so if you hear a voice in the back of your head, it's me. Any questions?"

"No sir, Colonel."

"Please, the name's Darren."

"Against protocol, sir. We're on a mission. Can't break protocol."

"Then I suppose calling you by your first name is also out?"

"If you wish, Colonel sir, you can call me by Major Scott instead of Major Binder."

"About as close to a first name basis as I guess I'll get, but I'll take it. Okay Major Scott, ready up. We should be arriving shortly."

Twenty minutes later saw the plane high above the drop zone as the side hatch slid open. One by one, soldiers with their parachute rigs and decompression masks jumped out into the clear blue, nothing below but a long drop down to a very rocky end if something went wrong. The Major went last, Darren double checking to be sure his psychic link with the man's mind was holding, then it was just himself alone, waiting until his mind's eye pictured the Major on the ground.

"Okay, this time I've got to remember to compensate for the plane's forward momentum," he said to himself with a nervous intake of breath. "If I don't, I'll appear on the ground going the same speed as this plane is, and that could really hurt."

Another minute more and he saw the Major's parachute hit the ground, then through the Major's own point of view got a good glimpse of what the terrain around him looked like, as well as the other men dropping to the ground nearby.

"Okay, got it. Now just need to get down there."

He shouldered his own backpack, then took in a deep breath, and another, held it for a second, then vanished.

A moment later he appeared on the rocks before the Major, stumbling slightly as if just having come to a stop from a fast run, but catching himself before he could fall.

"A lot better," he remarked mostly to himself. "Still takes the wind out of me a little, but better."

If Major Scott felt any shock from seeing a man suddenly appear in front of him, he showed no sign of it, just finished wrapping up his parachute and tucking it behind a rock before taking out a small palm-sized device with only one button and giving it a press. A light on it started to pulse as the Major came over to report.

"The others will follow my beacon and join up shortly. Terrain as rugged and uncertain as this, it's the only way to keep track."

"Right," Darren realized as he looked at the jagged rocks towering around them, "someone could be just the other side of that cliff and they'd never see us."

"Exactly, sir. You're in charge now, so what's the plan?"

"We need a base of operations to work out of. A good cave will do."

"I've run missions in this region before and know a good cave about two hours from here. It should be within easy range of the reported center of the terrorist activity."

"Perfect. As soon as your group assembles, we head there."

It did not take long for the other five members of the team to find them, after which the Major turned off his beacon, then led the trek through the rugged mountainous terrain.

Jagged stone teeth cutting up to the sky, rocky walls punctuated here and there by ancient footpaths, while overhead the torturous sun beat down mercilessly. It was two hours of climbing through such terrain, in some cases with rope and pitons, all while trying to remain hidden from distant view. When finally they came within view of the intended cave, the Major drew them to a halt and backed away behind a rock while taking out a pair of miniature binoculars.

"Looks like someone else might be using our cave, Colonel," he reported. "We could take them out but it'd be noisy and they might have radios."

"Leave it to me, then," Darren decided. "I'll see what I can do."

A moment later Darren vanished from sight.

"I'm almost getting used to that," Major Scott remarked to himself, then to his men, "Okay weapons ready…"

Darren appeared on a stand of rocks just around a corner from the cave, his feet barely holding onto the edge of his ledge, then carefully sent his thoughts into the cave. There were indeed four minds there to be sensed; men wondering if this cave might make for a good campsite, if Darren read the pictures from their minds correctly.

"Okay," Darren whispered to himself, fingers going to his left temple, "how's about snakes. Snakes… snakes…"

A minute later all four men ran out of the cave screaming and flailing their arms over their heads, running and stumbling as quickly as they could as if the monster of all snakes was right behind them. Darren watched them practically roll down the hill in frantic departure then shrugged.

"I may have laid it on a bit thick. Well, whatever works."

He then winked away, appearing a moment later right beside the Major.

"They should be well away from the cave by the time we get there now, Major Scott."

"I saw through the binoculars," the Major replied with bland regard, "never seen someone run so fast. What'd you do?"

"Classified. But let's just say that they'll be having nightmares for a while."

"Got it. Okay everyone, move out. I want to be in that cave and setting up camp in twenty."

Twenty minutes later the team arrived at the cave, no sign of the recent occupants save some abandoned sleeping rolls and a few guns. Before anyone had moved more than a foot inside, Major Scott called out a command as he blocked Darren's entry with a firm hand.

"Thorough search; mines and booby traps. Go."

As his men went efficiently about their duties, Major Scott gave a quick summary for Darren's benefit.

"This cave is about half a mile long with an underground stream running through the back. If we set up camp in the middle, no one will see us, and as you can see from the mouth we have a view of the entire valley. I'll post a constant watch here as soon as we're established. We'll be able to see any approach long before they get here."

"Excellent. That's when my work starts. I'll be poking around the local villages, trying to pick up anything of our terrorists and their leader. As soon as I find him, I'll just teleport him straight into this cave, where you guys will need to keep him tied down while I interrogate him. In the event that I've run into a lot more trouble extracting him, then that's when you'll be hearing my psychic call. Any questions?"

"Just a suggestion, and that's in the way of a disguise."

"I brought some robes the locals wear with me. They should work."

"All well and good," the Major replied, his gaze now dropping towards Daren's feet, "but what about shoes? The locals are more into sandals than fine footwear."

"These old things? I got them at a discount store."

"To the locals that is expensive footwear. I got some old sandals packed away that I saved from previous missions just in case; use those."

"Well," Darren shrugged, "it sounds like the Director chose you well."

A short time later the cave was deemed safe, only a few piles of old trash from previous generations of thieves and terrorists hiding out to be found, then the camp set up, which consisted mainly of weapons being pulled out, a gun on a tripod set up out of sight near the mouth of the cave, and radio gear with a small dish antenna beside the tripod gun. After that, Darren stood at the mouth of the cave looking down at the villages in the dry valley beyond and called back over his shoulder.

"I'll try and bring you guys back some falafels or something."

He then vanished in a glimmer of light…

Darren walked the dusty streets in a grey robe, hood pulled over his face and sandals on his feet. Squat stone buildings painted with the wear of centuries, carpets hung as walls around some open stalls selling trinkets or foodstuffs of questionable origins, large white sheets drawn overhead across small streets to provide some shade. People coming and going on their daily chores, either selling or buying, making a trip to the town well for an urn of water, or conversing on their way to the local mosque. At first Darren thought he might stand out by his very act of trying to hide his face, but when you're in a country where the heat is over a hundred and ten degrees and the locals specialize in various acts of violence and deceit, hiding your face beneath a hood does not make you unusual but more common than some might want to admit.

The first day as he walked about scanning random minds he picked up little more than images of violent desires against the Christian world in general, here and there thoughts of a recent terror attack but more in the way of local gossip. The second day was much the same, only now fleeting images of some of those involved with the attacks accompanied by feelings of pride. It wasn't until his fifth day out when Darren happened by a man buying a meat roll from a street vendor and caught some telltale images from his mind.

Helicopter. Piloting. Someone of importance. And a name; Abdul Basit. Also, a place in Sanandaj. Darren stayed around just long enough to get some more details from the man's mind before ducking away into a convenient dark alley. A moment later he was walking up to the camp in the cave and Major Scott. By now they had gotten used to his appearing out of nowhere so the man posted as guard by the cave mouth had leveled his gun just long enough to be sure who it was that had suddenly materialized, then resumed his watch.

"Major Scott, I think I have a line on our man," Darren announced as he approached. "There's a helicopter pilot right now that's going to be picking someone up at Sanandaj to drop him off for a meeting in Tehran. From the feelings I got off him it's a man of some importance. Someone named Abdul Basit. Heard of him?"

"Local terrorist figure, as I recall. Very big into blowing people up. Do you think he might be our guy?"

"A lead at the least. Listen, I'm going to see if I can crash that little meeting. I've got a mental lock on the pilot now, all I have to do is wait for him to land with his cargo then use him to home in on his location and teleport over the way I did with the parachute jump. I'll still be able to get back here in an instant if I need to."

"Yes, but we'll be too far out of range to be of any assistance if you need it. It's too dangerous, Colonel."

"But worth the risk. Get on the radio and contact the Director's people. See what they have on old Abdul and anyone else I may be getting the name of. I'll be seeing how rusty by Arabic is."

"Yes sir, Colonel."

"I'll be in the far back of the cave focusing on that helicopter pilot. See that no one disturbs me, I need complete concentration for this."

While the Major got someone on the radio, Darren found a place at the far end of the cave where there was nothing but the sound of dripping water to disturb him, then settled down and closed his eyes, fingers to both his temples. He sent his mind's eye roaming until he came once again to the mind of the helicopter pilot, then from there just took in a deep breath and relaxed, letting his mind cling loosely to the back of the pilot's like a fly on a wall…

Hours later Darren's mind was still with the pilot as he picked up a man wrapped up in flowing desert robes. Shorter than Darren by about a hand-span and a little chubby for his height, with steel grey eyes and an untamed mass of brown hair. He wore a beard, extremely short hugging along the contours of his chin, and from what could be seen of his face his skin was between a light brown and olive coloring. Abdul Basit.

Darren watched from afar as the helicopter lifted off and flew over the mountainous terrain, ducking under radar and weaving its way past known security checkpoints as it came to the Israeli border. Once across the rather porous section of mountain borders, it became just another helicopter on its way to its own destination. The images became slightly fuzzy with distance, or perhaps the emotions of the pilot were interfering, for he seemed to be most enthusiastic about his passenger. When they spoke it was in Arabic and Darren caught enough of it to get the general gist of things. Abdul was to meet with an important financier of some sort.

"A meeting," Darren muttered from his meditative state. "A financier… money for more terrorism. Also… his superior? Yes… Abdul reports to another. Must get closer."

Darren waited until the helicopter had finally landed, getting a good look at the surroundings from what the pilot saw, then opened up his eye, took in a deep breath, and stood up.

"Okay, it's the outskirts of Tehran now."

A moment later Darren was once again gone.

The place was less airstrip and more an empty field of dirt. Structures of a Biblical age stood in the distance beneath far more modern pinnacles of steel and glass. Closer at hand, though, was a single old building with cracking mortar and an old antenna dish fixed to the roof. Nothing else save a single vehicle, and that a white limo with some rather obvious bodyguards standing to either side of the front. Darren appeared around one corner of the old building, ducking back quickly as he saw Abdul Basit walking away from the helicopter towards the white limo.

He called out in Arabic, Darren's very basic knowledge of the language allowing him to follow along, though he did wish that Agent Franklin was around as she seemed to be more the linguist. Still, with his telepathic abilities, he should be able to fill in the blanks.

Abdul called out what either sounded like a greeting or a curse; Darren wasn't quite sure, then one of the bodyguards broke from his immobile stance to open the rear left door. Out walked an Arab, but from his far finer royal blue robes with their golden trim, the checker-patterned head cloth, and the expensive-looking sunglasses, Darren judged him to be one of more princely fashion.

Abdul addressed the man by name; Badi al Zaman. Then their exchange began– something about money– and Darren racked his evolved brain for anything he may have heard of such a man by that name. Midway into the conversation he had it.

Badi al Zaman, he thought to himself, *isn't that a royal of some sort? Yes… Prince. One of the sons of the King of the United Arab Emirates. He's financing this mess? Not good!*

They appeared to be negotiating; the Prince calm and firm, Abdul angrily gesturing. Then finally another name mentioned; two names, in fact. A hotel in the city, and a man. Jad Allah.

Another meeting, Darren mused to himself, *with this Jad Allah character.*

It was then that Abdul was ushered into the limo as the Prince got in with him. With focused glare and two fingers now pressed hard into his left temple, Darren had just a few seconds to get a psychic fix on Abdul before they drove away towards the distant line of buildings.

"Well," Darren quietly whispered to himself, "it looks like I have another trail to follow. Should have just enough time to report back."

A moment's thought and he was gone, just in time for a robed man to come out from the old building and see who he'd heard whispering. Nothing; maybe a phantom in the wind.

Darren was back in the cave, satellite radio in hand as he talked with an annoying but very officious-sounding voice at the other end.

"Colonel Hildure, we have had our eye on Abdul Basit for quite some time now. If you have a chance to grab him then ***do*** *it."*

"It's not looking like Abdul is the head guy," Darren replied. "Some man named Jad Allah. He's going to meet with him shortly."

"And I'm telling you that we've never heard of Jad Allah; the man does not exist. Now, by my authority as chairman of the National Counterterrorism Committee I ***order*** *you to bring back Abdul Basit immediately before you lose him."*

"Sorry, but I'm going to be attending that meeting and see how deep this thing goes. I just called you to see what you guys may have on this Jad character. Besides, my orders come from someone else."

"Impudent! Who else is over there? Go grab Abdul this instant."

"I'm Major Scott Binder," the Major now spoke up, "but my men and I report only to the Colonel. Orders. Besides, we are an impractical distance away from the target and only the Colonel can get to him."

"This is insufferable. We have one of the most infamous terrorists right in our hands and no one will–"

"Listen," Darren cut in, "before you blow a gasket or something, do you know of Director Erica Forester? Because she's where I get my orders from."

Suddenly there was a protracted moment of silence, one that earned a grin across the face of Colonel Hildure.

"I'll take that for a yes. Well, when you talk to her– and before she chews you out for wasting her time– tell her that there's a new face I'm looking into."

A nod then to the radio operator and the transmission was cut, leaving a grin across several faces there.

"I'd love to be around when Forester verbally eviscerates the man," Darren sighed, "but I've got work to do. If I'm successful then I'll be bringing someone back with me on this trip. He is to be assumed as very dangerous, no doubt hiding weapons I'll have missed, and probably extremely pissed."

"We'll have a tranquilizer ready for him, sir," Major Scott tersely replied.

With that task done, Darren got up and once again found himself a corner to concentrate in, this time focusing in on the mind of one Abdul Basit…

The meeting was in a very expensive café with white marble and gold trim all around, high vaulted ceilings and curved archways, tables covered by fine white cloth, and a balcony that overlooked a view out to the rest of the big city. Even more impressive than the high-priced venue of this meeting was that only one table was occupied; Prince Badi al Zaman had bought out the entire place just for this private dinner.

Darren waited until they were all seated– as seen through Abdul's eyes– before teleporting in behind a large planter out on the balcony. He squatted low out of sight, peeking between the large leaves of the potted tree to see what was going on. The prince sat at a table, calmly munching on expensive treats that Darren was afraid to discover the true nature of, opposite him two men. One of them was Abdul, but the other was a stranger. Half a dozen guards with cocked and ready assault rifles stood sentry about the room as extra insurance as to the privacy of this meeting.

The stranger had shaggy dark brown hair to his ears, a slender toned build, and seemed close to thirty. His beard looked like while he didn't usually shave, he never bothered to trim it into a proper beard either. The skin tone of his hands looked to be a light brown, but his face was hidden from Darren's view by a light hood. The rest of his clothing was much like one would see on any be-robed desert wanderer in this region of the world, no doubt the better to blend in with. From what Darren could hear of the conversation and how they addressed one another, this was Jad Allah.

From what Darren could gather, money seemed no object for the Prince, though there were some details that Jad Allah disagreed with. Details, that in the mind of Abdul, could mean that he would not get the credit from his superior for this new arrangement. From Abdul's mind Darren caught concern, fear, and something between reverence and terror about his master, Jad Allah.

That's it, then, Darren thought to himself, *this Jad must be the top terror guy. Now to just get into his mind to double check then maybe I can convince him to just walk out and join me.*

Darren stretched out his mind towards Jad then stopped in sudden shock. He could not penetrate the other's mind! It was like a brick wall. There was just… nothing.

At the same time as Darren was taken aback from this unexpected development, his intended victim snapped his head to one side looking directly at the large potted plant behind which Darren was hiding and pointed an outstretched hand while calling out angrily in Arabic. Immediately several guns spun around in his direction, their owners swiftly taking aim.

"This *can't* be happening," Darren swore.

Quickly he focused, just as the first pair of rifles fired. The planter broke apart, the large plant within it falling down, but there was no longer anyone behind it. Two of the guards immediately ran over to see if he had jumped over the balcony while two more kept their rifles leveled. Just as their attention was on the plant, however, at the opposite end of the room Darren appeared, his right hand grasping onto the

Major's shoulder, his left onto that of one of his other men, both with their own assault rifles in hand and ready.

"Hey boys," Darren called out, "I'm over here!"

The two on the balcony turned just in time to be shot down by the Major's automatic, while the second pair with rifles aimed at the balcony were picked off by the other soldier Darren had brought with him. This left just two guards and the ones at the table.

Abdul shot to his feet, placing himself in front of his superior, while the Prince remained calmly sitting at the table.

"You will not lay hands on the holy prophet," Abdul exclaimed in English.

At the same time, one of the two remaining guards pulled off a shot at the Major's man, the round bouncing harmlessly off his body armor. The man in turn replied by firing his own gun, except he took aim right for the face. The mess that was left fell straight to the ground. Meanwhile, Major Scott had taken aim at the other guard, and very quickly it was over with. All that remained were those seated at the table.

Darren approached the table with a triumphant look, while the Major and his man fell in to either side with guns leveled now at those at the table.

"Jad Allah, our mystery man," Darren grinned. "So you're the one behind all the anti-unification terror attacks."

"He is a holy prophet," Abdul exclaimed, lunging at the Colonel. "He does Allah's work against the unholy infidels!"

"Simmons," Major Scott calmly ordered as the man tried to throttle Daren, "the tranquilizer."

The 'tranquilizer' came as the blunt end of the soldier's rifle slamming up into the Arab's chin. Abdul dropped with an abrupt thud.

"Tranquilizer administered, sir."

Darren spared a brief quizzical look for the Major, who replied with a slight shrug, then turned to the remaining pair still seated.

"Diplomatic immunity," the Prince said in clearly enunciated syllables, a sly cultured smile creasing through his features, "you can't touch me."

"Well, I imagine that might be true," Darren admitted, "if you were a registered diplomat and if we were actually back in my country, which we aren't. I imagine, though, that Israeli intelligence would be very grateful to see you and ask a few questions."

"You cannot do this," the Prince said, indignantly shooting up to his feet, "I am a prince of the royal family of the United Arab Emirates, and I can assure you a diplomatic nightmare if you–"

"Simmons," this time it was Darren giving the command, "tranquilizer."

Slam! Thud!

Now there was only the one left to face, the Prince sliding limply off the table to the ground. Jad Allah had not done much more than calmly watch the events around him, and still radiated an aura of confidence despite now being all alone and at the business end of two assault rifles. Darren made a motion to grab him by the collar but the man put up a hand and calmly stood up.

"No need to grab," he stated. "But what is it you hope to get out of me?"

"An end to your attacks, for one," Darren replied. "I may not be able to get into your mind, but there are other ways of finding things out."

"I imagine there would be," the man replied with an unhealthy grin. He then looked straight into Darren's eyes and for that moment the Colonel could see a fanatical look he was getting to know all too well.

"Please," Jad calmly stated, "say hello to Observer for me."

Before Darren could even bat an eye in surprise, something even more shocking happened. The man vanished, right before everyone's eyes.

"A teleporter?" Darren said with some dismay. "Jad Allah is another teleporter?"

It was a couple of days later that Darren found himself back in Director Forester's Geneva office. The Prince was in the hands of Israeli authorities, Abdul was locked up and undergoing some strenuous questioning, but as to the mystery of one Jad Allah, all Darren had was a drawing of the man's face with some help from a sketch artist; exactly as he had seen it in that one brief exchange. Director Forester was sitting at her desk looking it over as she typed a few keys at her terminal, Darren finishing up his story.

"He had to have been to Mars, Erica. There's no other way he'd have the ability to teleport like that."

"That may be," the Director absently replied, "though I very much doubt that was Jad Allah you saw teleporting; the man does not exist. Here, look at this."

She reached out a hand and turned one of the monitors around in place. Centered on it was the face of the man that Darren had seen, only cleaner shaven and looking less calmly maniacal.

"That's him," Darren nodded. "Jad Allah."

"Wrong," she told him, "that is a man by the name of Alexander Damaris."

"An alias, of course," Darren swore. "That's why no one's heard of him before. It should be easy now. We have the man's real name, we know he had to have been to Mars, we can get everything we need on him, including places where he might head to."

"That's the problem," the Director sighed as she tapped another key, "we know *exactly* where he is."

What came up on the display now was an information bar along the right side of the picture. Complete information on Alexander Damaris, from his date of birth… to his date of death.

"Alexander Damaris was gunned down two years ago by a pair of police officers in Paris, then confirmed dead the next day by an examiner and scheduled for an autopsy."

"I'm guessing the autopsy was never done?"

"Buried at government expense," the Director stated. "So either you were looking at a ghost, or Mister Damaris has some other Mars-given abilities we don't know about and our little mind-raping conspiracy is very good at covering up their tracks. Either way we're at a dead end for now."

Frustration swept through the Colonel, so much so that his fist reached out to slam down onto the Director's desk until a harsh glare from her had Darren stopping abruptly a hands' breath away from the shiny finish. Instead he satisfied himself with a growl not quite under his breath.

"We'll pick up his trail," she then stated. "My agents know what to look for now. Let's just hope that there's not still another layer behind Damaris."

"That does seem to be the pattern," Darren sighed. "One conspirator behind another behind another. When does it end?"

"Worry about that later. Right now I'm told you have a vessel to see to."

"That's right," Darren realized, "it should be nearing completion by now. After ten long years, finally."

"Just some final testing and configuring. Strange to see a ship shaped like a large golf ball, but that's what you, Feng, and the others came up with. They need you on Mars for the final phase. The powers that be have bumped up the schedule and want the first test flight to happen within one year from now, not the three more that was planned for."

"Sounds like we'll have to pull off a couple of miracles to keep to that schedule."

"Miracles are what you get paid for, Colonel," she tersely replied. "Now, I've been informed that the captain will be someone named Eva Gardena, so you'd best get up there to meet her and help out in whatever they need. I'll reassign Agent Franklin to head up the task force looking for Damaris and have Feng on call for when we finally corner the guy, you just make sure we're ready for those Zelos when they arrive in force. If we can get this ship checked out and the planet fully united then Observer's creators just might help us in making a few more."

"Just don't forget to notify me when Damaris is caught; I owe him one."

Director Forester said nothing in reply, just watched as Darren nodded once, turned on heel, and left her office. There was a lot of work she had to see to, and it was looking like there was increasingly less time to do it in.

CHAPTER NINE

FIRST FLIGHT

March 3, 2052
United Earth Ship Odyssey, flight log
Colonel Darren Hildure, reporting.

I guess using the designation "United Earth" is a bit presumptuous, but even as I dictate this, the world's nations are in final negotiations to unite the planet. Logistical details, mostly, and you can well imagine how many of ***those*** *there might be. At any rate, "UES Odyssey" is what we've dubbed this first battleship of space that we've been constructing for the past decade and now it's finally ready for its first test flight.*

I almost can't believe it. So much work in such secrecy and now it's finally here, and the general population is in on everything as well. What a stir that announcement made, backed up by an actual alien attack. The Media's still talking about it; heck, it even booted Hollywood's best-dressed straight off the front page. If this flight goes well, and when the Earth finally unites, then maybe Observer's creators can give us a bit more help before the Zelos show up in force.

The ship is of a rather unusual design, even by the standards of Observer and his people. Picture a giant golf ball, divots and all, and you have the

Odyssey, except that each of those divots is either a weapon emplacement, maneuvering thruster, or engine component. There really is no aft or stern, at least not as far as any outside observers would be able to tell. This means that they can come at us from the front, behind, up or down and it won't matter. That's got to be worth something, right? Of course, one might argue aerodynamics, to which I would calmly point out that in space that sort of thing doesn't really matter. No atmosphere, remember.

The main operative parts of the interior are connected to the rest of the ship through a series of gimbals and inertial dampers. This is so that if the ship needs to turn around in place really fast to present a different array of weapons to the enemy that the bridge crew doesn't get whiplash in the process. When not in battle-mode then the whole thing locks back into place so we can have access to the main superstructure of the ship again, not to mention crew quarters. We don't expect anyone to be sleeping in their quarters during a battle so this part seems workable.

The gimbal system was Feng's idea. The ship does have an antigravity inertial dampening system– again, courtesy Observer– to cancel out the effects of acceleration and motion, but things can get damaged in battle so just in case that fails, we have a more-physical system to rely upon. Also, as it turns out, the gimbal system reduces a lot of the stress the structure of the ship might be feeling from high-speed revolutions.

There are three main types of weapons on the Odyssey. The first is the usual pulse-lasers. Pin-point accuracy, range of three hundred thousand kilometers, high rate of fire, and hooked up to the computer tracking. Next is the Kaon Emitter, which is basically an antimatter particle beam; not as much range but a lot greater punch. In both of these cases the speed of light is the limiting factor, which means they're no good if we ever have to do battle while in warp.

Which brings us to the third weapon, our Photon Pulse Cannon. This beauty borrows a bit of that teleporting technology of Observer's in that it teleports a stream of highly charged particles direct to the target destination. Advantages: range of about ten thousand kilometers with pin-point accuracy and near instantaneous transmission, great for use while in warp, and you can forget about any shields the other guy has in the way. Disadvantage: the rate of fire is a fraction that of the others, which means every shot has to count. Then as I said before, we have several of each of these scattered all over the exterior surface of the ship.

The Odyssey itself is about a hundred meters across, I can't state its maximum speed or cruising range here as that's classified, and all I'm allowed to say about the shields, is that we have some. Electromagnetic deflection field, to be more precise. Oh, and about half of this ship is the power reactor; exact output is also classified but... wow, you should see these numbers!

For this first test flight the mission is simple: go to the asteroid field, shoot up a few rocks, and come back. Just enough to get the kinks out of it and see what else we might need. The crew will be minimal; just Captain Eva Gardena, a navigator, weapons control officer, and an engineer. We've already had a couple of basic systems tests to see if this thing will lift off the ground, but this will be the first one for full flight.

Captain Gardena has proven to be an excellent choice to command the Odyssey. She has a PhD in fusion engineering and mathematics and can think and react ten times better than most people, which makes her a quick decision maker. Not all of that latter, though, is due to her time in Observer's special Chair; she's simply a natural.

For this first flight, General Feng is staying back on Mars as ground control. For the sorts of distance we'll be going, standard radio communications will be impractical, so it is hoped that the telepathic bond between me and Feng well be a more reliable method of communication, though we've never tested it over that long a range before. Observer will still be able to contact the Odyssey no matter where in the solar system it goes, of course, and will coordinate with Mission Command, but apparently installing the same sort of communication system he has into the ship is amongst those little pieces of tech he's not allowed to give us until after the planet's united. I guess his creators have their reasons. Maybe they're afraid we'll overhear their conversations or something?

The large metallic sphere now stood alone in the massive cavern, painted the black of night as it rests atop its twenty telescoping legs awaiting the final countdown. Overhead what had been the ceiling of this supposed mountain cavern now begin to part, the two halves slowly sliding aside as the voice of General Feng is heard echoing down the halls of the alien-human complex.

"Three minutes to launch. All entries to launch bay are now sealed. Communications link to Earth Command is now open through Observer."

While Observer was in his usual small command center, Feng and an assortment of technicians were at their own stations in a long room whose front armor-glass window afforded a direct view of the cavern beyond and the ship all there had been working so long and hard to make possible. Feng himself sat in a command chair, a couple of virtual displays floating to either side of him, while before him the row of techs each ready at their own control station, each busy with confirming last minute statuses of various points of the operation. Voices quietly spoken into their headsets, technical readouts on each of their screens, with the summary of it all appearing before Feng in his own hovering pair of displays.

"Propulsion reads normal, General."

"Weapon's check nominal."

"Satellite tracking is locked on, General."

"All base personnel are clear, sir."

"Darren," Feng finally said through his own headset, "looks good on this end. Any time you're ready."

On the bridge of the Odyssey, Darren had been waiting like an eager child held in restraint while the last launch checks had been made and now finally been set loose to play. The bridge was laid out like a room with a dome, but with the entire domed ceiling and walls above the ring of control stations being one single display system currently showing a view of the cavern around them. Ringed around that were the various bridge stations, only three of which were currently occupied; that of the Navigator, Weapons Control, and Engineering. Each member of this limited crew was dressed in the same blue-green uniform, each with an Earth Services patch stamped onto their shoulders, each a young man that had trained long and hard for this moment.

In the center of it all on a dais raised slightly higher than the main floor is the command chair, set into the floor on a spindle which Darren had been testing out by spinning in place fully around while the base command finishes up their checks. On hearing Feng's voice call out, he immediately got more serious and stopped the chair, looked apologetic at the ship's captain standing nearby, then stood up as he called back.

"About time, buddy. Been like a kid waiting to ride his new bike on Christmas morning."

The Captain who now took the Command Chair was a young woman of medium height, her red hair in an ear-length military haircut, slightly tanned complexion, her good looks kept hidden within her blue-green uniform and frank attitude. Too young to be a captain, some might say, but the times are changing very quickly of late.

A second chair was set up off to one side of the Captain's chair for Darren, but for this first voyage he chose to stand, as if that could get him any closer to pending events. Above and in front of them a portion of the dome's display now changed to a large square with Feng's face grinning down at them.

"Just try not to break that bike, my friend."

"Just a little target practice," then turning briefly to the captain made it official, "Captain Gardena, you may begin the launch sequence."

"Good luck."

The final word said and Feng's image vanished, replaced by the full view of the cavern once again. Captain Gardena, meanwhile, was running her fingers across a couple of controls fixed into the arms of the chair, the result of which was to call up images floating in the air just above the chair's arms. A last bit of fine-tuning to make sure the displays were at her eye level then she called out her first command to Navigation.

"Anti-gravs on, clear all moorings. Navigator, take us up. Slowly."

From the control room, Feng watched with bated breath, as did many there with him, as well as several important figures back on Earth, including Director Forester. She had the views echoed to her own private office monitor and was studying it with as much attention to detail as restrained anticipation. All watched as at first the vessel began to glow; faintly but visible as a subliminal afterglow. This was followed seconds later by the slow retraction of the twenty landing legs telescoping back into the vessel… while the vessel continued to remain where it was. The Odyssey was now floating in place, free of any tethers or means of physical support, and when the legs fully retracted and their hatches sealed over, then the ship emitted a slight pulse of dark light and began to float up. Slowly it rose through the open top of the mountain, ever higher while a world held its breath. High enough until the mountain range below could be seen as a panoramic view spread across the dome-screen of the ship. Another faint pulse of light then one half of the vessel lit up with the fury of a dozen nuclear candles and it shot off into the Martian sky.

In that moment a world cheered and Feng was chief amongst them. Out of his seat he bolted, his feet briefly leaving the ground as the room echoed his sentiments, then quickly remembering himself called out his commands as he went back to his chair.

"Get me full telemetry for as long as we can hold it. How's the interface with Observer's equipment? It won't be long before his is the only equipment able to track the Odyssey…"

Back on the Odyssey, Darren was still standing, grin wide upon his face as the view across the dome-screen showed Mars swiftly distancing behind them with the dark of space growing larger before them. A full view of everything around them.

"Clear of the Martian atmosphere, Captain," Navigation called out.

"Excellent," Captain Gardena snapped, "now let's see what's underneath us as well. Computer, full three-sixty view."

The floor beneath them now shimmered and suddenly it too became a view screen, displaying what lay beneath them. A full spherical view now, save only those parts covered by the ring of control stations around its middle. Darren tapped twice with the heel of his shoe to make sure the view was steady then nodded.

"Nice scratch-proof screen. Wish I had some of this material for my sunglasses. Okay, double-check the uplink to Observer."

"Odyssey to Observer," the Captain called out. "Verify communications and tracking link."

One side of the dome now displayed a large three-foot square showing the face of the robot, behind him the central control room where Darren had first woken up, now what seems an entire lifetime ago. The Captain spun her chair around to face him as he spoke.

"All links secured, Captain Gardena. Is everything operating as expected?"

"Perfectly, Observer," Darren answered.

"Then while we're at it," the Captain decided, "let's test out the full communications capabilities of this thing. Computer, simultaneous links to Mars Command and Earth Command."

Seconds later two more three-foot squares appeared in the dome view; one with Feng's face, the other showing the terse light brown features of Director Forester.

"Looks like the uplink through Observer is working, Darren," Feng stated. *"No comm-lag at all on this end and we should be getting one of a few seconds by now."*

"No lag here either," Director Forester reported. *"Good job, now go to the next part of the test."*

"Will do," Darren replied, then with a glance to the Captain, "At your pleasure, Captain."

Captain Gardena replied with a curt nod, then with a quick swipe of a finger through one line of virtual controls hovering by her right side, dispelled the three images, leaving them now with the full view of space all around them, Mars but a shrinking dot.

"Navigation set a destination into the middle of the asteroid belt. Somewhere nearby one of the larger rocks."

As she was giving her command, Darren finally made his way over to the secondary chair by the Captain and sat down, his mind set now for more serious analysis.

"Coordinates set, Captain," came the reply from the man at Navigation.

"Then let's bring her up to speed. Ten percent light speed… now."

The ship remained steady, but the view before them gave a sudden visual lurch, the stars seen now as if through an atmospheric haze.

"Holding steady, Captain," Navigation reported.

"Engineering, how are things looking from your end?"

"All holding level," came the reply from across the bridge. "Not so much as a twitch."

"Then let's test out the main engines for a short hop," the Captain decided. "On my mark, engage warp engines. Short burst, just enough to get us into the asteroid field."

"Ready, Captain," Navigation reported a second later.

The Captain looked briefly at Darren who just nodded; she gave the command.

"Mark!"

The outside of the ship was a black ball shimmering against the night, shooting like a meteor on fiery tongues, but now something new happened. The unseen force surrounding it brightened to blinding proportions; nothing the naked eye could see and yet still perceived enough to make one turn away. Brighter than like unto a small star… and suddenly gone. On everyone's tracking systems save those of Observer, it simply vanished from view.

The view inside the bridge of the Odyssey was, naturally, a little different. A moment after the command had been given the stars briefly became streaks of light before settling back into a slightly different arrangement.

"First memo," Darren noted, pressing a button on the arm of his own chair to record, "we'll have to come up with a way to adjust the view while in warp. For any extended length of warp travel, seeing everything reduced to vague streaks of light could leave us nearly blind to potential enemies. Maybe some sort of relativistic compensator."

His note made, he released the button, while the Captain went about her own duties.

"Position confirmed, Captain," Navigation reported. "We are within four miles of programmed destination."

"We can do a lot better," the Captain said. "Figure that same percentage error over the distance between stars and we could miss a star entirely. Colonel Hildure, might I recommend another addition to your memos?"

"We are of the same mind, Captain," he replied, once again hitting the button. "Memo; we need a more powerful navigation computer. I would also recommend better integration with sensors to allow the nav-computer to perform automatic course corrections on route... Okay, Captain, let's see about those weapons."

"Weapons control," the Captain next called out. "Let's start with the pulse lasers for some range testing. At your leisure."

"Aye, Captain."

Some miles before them, sensors had picked up a large asteroid, and it was to this the ship now rocketed as one of the many divots across the vessel's surface briefly glowed. A split-second later there was an explosion on the asteroid. This was followed by a turn off to one side and another divot taking aim as the ship spins slightly in place. Another hit scored.

"Good," the Captain nodded. "Kaon Emitters now. See if you can blow a chunk off that thing."

The Weapons Officer nodded then quickly worked the controls hovering before him while the Navigator brought them around for another run. This time the pulse of energy was visible, as was the explosion that ripped off a large corner from the asteroid.

"Direct hit, Captain," Weapons Control reported.

Over at his own chair, Darren was watching some more specific statistics displayed in his virtual interface as he muttered a few notes into his memos.

"Asteroid measures about a mile across, and the Kaon Emitter just tore off about a quarter of it. Targeting display indicates everything within acceptable parameters... Captain, I'd like to see the pulse cannons, then we can try out the roll test."

"As you wish, Colonel. Weapons, crack that rock."

One of the larger divots now glowed; brightly lit tip suddenly fading, followed in that same instant by an explosion of light erupting out from *within* the asteroid itself. In a flash of brilliance the large rock ripped itself apart, scattering chunks far and wide, a few of which came at the Odyssey, only to be deflected harmlessly away by the ship's shields.

Many of the few faces there on the bridge looked caught between stunned and delighted, save the Captain who maintained her trained composure, and Darren who allowed himself only a slight smile at the sight.

"Detonation registered within the asteroid, Captain," Weapons reported. "No trace of anything tracking between it and ourselves."

"I like this weapon," the Captain decided. "Could make it difficult for the enemy to track where it came from."

"That was the idea," Darren replied. "When we saw Observer's teleporter, we asked him if something like that could teleport a beam of energy as well as matter. He couldn't figure out why we would want to."

A short moment to see the fruits of long labors achieved, but shorter lived than expected as Navigation called out.

"Captain, bogey coming in fast."

From one corner of the dome-display, a square drew itself around a small dot of light then expanded into a large window view of the object in question. The object was a ship, shaped roughly like a very large beetle. Daren very quickly called up a small display before himself of the sensor readings.

"Bigger than the one that hit Geneva," he stated, "it could be its companion."

"A sleeper ship waiting to hear back from the scout ship," the Captain realized, "and now it just might know why they haven't responded. Nav, any sign it's seen us?"

"Its course takes it to where the asteroid used to be," came the reply. "I don't think it sees us."

"Investigating an unusual explosion," Darren theorized. "The hull's anti-sensor coating must be working but let's not see for how long. Captain, I know we've just the minimal crew, but that Zelos ship must *not* make it home to report."

"Understood, Colonel. Computer, engage gimbal roll system. Nav, prepare for that roll test and plot an interception course. Weapons, the instant you got a good shot, take it."

"Aye, Captain," came from two different stations, while the one at the engineering station now kept a much closer eye on his systems readings.

As the Zelos ship closed in on the remains of the asteroid, from out of the blackness of space the attack came. At first a barrage of laser fire from such weapons as were within the correct arc, the first of which glanced off the alien hull with minimum damage before it banked quickly to one side to avoid the rest.

"Zelos vessel evading at high speed," Navigation reported. "Altering course to track."

"Can we keep up with it?" the Captain asked.

"Speed-wise, easily, Captain. But that thing's pretty dexterous."

The Zelos ship banked and twisted, coming up from beneath now for the barely-seen spot in space from which the lasers seemed to be erupting and returning with its own weapons fire. Pulses of energy flashed out from the twin barrels of its mouthparts, slamming into the dark hull only to be spread across the whole of the sphere's surface and quickly dissipated. The Odyssey responded with a sudden move sideways from its previous course; no gradual turning arc such as a long arrow-shaped ship might make, but just a different set of thrusters switching on as the previous ones cut off. The move looked to catch the Zelos ship off guard as it abruptly altered its course into a wider swing around to hit the Earth ship at what it might hope to be the rear.

"Shield holding, Captain," Weapons reported.

"That's one good thing," the Captain snorted, "but why aren't we hitting that thing?"

"We have the maneuverability, Captain," Weapons replied, "they're just able to maneuver faster than I can punch the buttons, even with the virtual interface."

"That must be that collective short-range telepathy of theirs that Observer mentioned," Darren quickly put in, "coupled with some sort of direct mind interface, perhaps. They're able to react a lot faster at the controls than we can. Memo: Install that thought-control interface that Professor Hayden's come up with."

"Only one way to it before they escape," the Captain immediately decided, while outside the Zelos vessel continued to attack. "Nav, engage roll maneuver now. Weapons, paint the target and let the computer do all the work."

On the screen ahead of them, they could see the alien ship trying another failed attack run before making a sharp turn away as the glow about it began to brighten a lot more than before. In that same moment, however, something within the Odyssey lurched as the gimbal locks were disengaged, leaving the exterior of the ship free to spin about the interior all it wanted to. The Zelos could see the large black marble picking up speed to catch it, and as it did so, it began to spin in place while all weapons ports started to glow.

"Roll up to speed," Weapons reported. "Firing!"

The first to fire were those weapons faced in the general direction of the Zelos vessel, but rather than wait for them to cycle their energies back up for another firing, it was the spinning of the hull itself that did all the work. One line of weapons fire pulsing out to saturate the region around the dodging Zelos ship, then another row of weapons as the spin of the ship brought them into correct firing arcs, and the next and the next. Spinning black ball sending out a continuous barrage of death, the faster it spins the faster the next set of divots can come into range and fire as it chases after them.

Shower of brilliance saturating everywhere one might dodge to, even for the most maneuverable of vessels the end is inevitable. Several pulses of energy slammed into the hull of the alien intruder, its legs sliced apart, hull scarred, then finally an explosion emanating from within that sends it spiraling. Futilely the front guns start to fire as the ship spins around, only to be hit by several deadly streams of deadly particles from the Kaon Emitters, followed at last by the killing stroke as three different Pulse Cannons center explosions directly within the heart of the vessel itself.

The result to see displayed expanding across the dome-screen as small bits of glowing shrapnel, was rather sobering on several levels.

"Wow, we just… tore that thing apart," Navigation said in an awe-struck voice.

"And it was bigger than the one that hit Geneva," Weapons added, "and *that* one got through every jet they could throw at it."

"Don't get too happy yet," Captain Gardena snapped. "Engineering, report."

"Shielding performed well, despite the ability of the enemy to land a dozen individual shots on us. The portions of their energies that weren't outright deflected were safely absorbed and spread across the entirety of the hull."

"Good. Nav, what is your estimate of their hit-to-miss ratio. How much trouble did the enemy have in detecting and tracking us?"

"Quite a lot at first, Captain," Navigation replied. "They were probably simply aiming for the spot from where our attacks seemed to originate before they got a good look at us. Even then, their hit ratio was only about sixteen percent."

"And Weapons," the Captain finished up, "what was *our* hit ratio?"

"About two percent, Captain," the man replied with a slight sigh. "The ship itself can keep up with them in all respects, but it's just too much power and speed to be handled even with computer aid. At least with the speed and maneuverability of these craft."

His report finished, the Captain then turned to Darren who was ready with a question of his own.

"Captain Gardena, and this is going directly into my memo file as you speak it, what is your personal overall assessment of the Odyssey and how it performed under actual battle conditions?"

"To be blunt, sir, this ship has an incredible amount of firepower, but its weakness is in our ability to control it. The Zelos, as you said, have an ability to coordinate that we cannot hope to match. It took the entire firepower of this ship in a roll maneuver before we could lock onto and destroy that vessel. We need a lot faster interface if we're to have any hope of matching them."

"Agreed," Darren decided. "I'm just glad this came up on such a small scale. Okay then, memo to Feng: tell Glenda we're ready to install a few of those computer interface helmets of hers. Looks like we'll definitely be needing them.

Back on Mars, within the mission control room, Feng stood next to the blond German professor nodding his agreement as the two of them reviewed the recording of the encounter and the Colonel's accompanying memos.

That first test flight was completed after another few days of scouring the asteroid field for any other possible Zelos ships lying in wait, the performance of the Odyssey recorded and transmitted back to Mars Control along with Darren's continuing list of notes for improvements. Most of what he had to say from that point on were in the way of minor technical improvements, nothing more like for their brief experience with the Zelos ship. By the time the Odyssey returned to its hidden berth beneath the Martian mountains, Professor Hayden was already on hand with a crew of technicians to install her computer-interface helmets.

That left Darren and Feng in Observer's control center with an image of Director Forester hovering before the wall with Observer's bank of controls.

"I've looked over all of your recommendations and I agree," the image of the Director was saying. "A two percent hit ratio isn't going to cut it."

"Professor Hayden is already on the ship installing her new interface," Feng explained. "It's basically a helmet that pulls down over the head and allows a direct connection between brain and computer. She's been working with Observer off and on the last few years to perfect it. It will complement the current system by allowing one to instantly communicate commands to the computer via thought. The current virtual controls will still be available, but in times of combat this system will save precious fractions of a second."

"Which as I saw," Darren put in, "can make a world of difference."

"The helmets are being installed at the Navigation and Weapons stations as well as for the Captain's chair," Feng finished up. "Those are the critical stations that will need them in a combat situation."

"Agreed," Director Forester replied. "Observer, what is your own assessment of our design?"

The robot paused for a moment, but when it spoke it was with an edge of what might be termed enthusiasm, if indeed any mechanism can have such.

"I must say that I have never seen this type of ship before, Director. Vessels of Sataran design are far longer but shaped more like a wedge. This new design can make far sharper turns even without the inertial dampers switched on. Additionally, your power to weapons ratio is extraordinary. You could have powered every system on the Odyssey with a power plant less than a quarter the size of the one you built."

"Overkill is our motto," Darren grinned.

"Indeed it would seem," Observer agreed. "Sataran vessels employ weapons of far more sophisticated design but with the available energy density of both your weapons and shielding, coupled with its far greater maneuverability, not to mention the ingenious use you made of the teleporter technology as an offensive weapon, I doubt any of the known races would feel comfortable facing it in combat. I now begin to see why that unknown race that installed the rejuvenation and evolution machine seemed so interested in your people. In the few short years you have had access to what elements of our technology as I am allowed to give you, your people have done impressive things with it. You are a very inventive and creative species."

"Well, thank you for the compliment, Observer," Darren replied with a smile. "We aim to please."

"Observer has consented to allow us to use his hypno-learning device here to more quickly prepare a crew for the Odyssey," Feng explained to the image of Director Forester. "That way we can have a full crew ready in no time."

"Good," the Director replied. "We've seen that these Zelos don't always follow the schedules predicted of them."

"For which I apologize," Observer interjected, "but we simply do not know enough about them. But I have been in contact with my creators and they have a proposal."

Darren and Feng grew curious, but if it was possible for someone to give an icy enough glare of suspicion to make a robot blanch, then Director Forester came very close. It was a very brief, but noticeable, pause before Observer continued.

"I have forwarded the data I gathered from observing the performance of the Odyssey against the Zelos, along with the list of Darren's memos even now being enacted upon, to my creators and they are most impressed. As such they have empowered me to make the following proposal. I will supply a thousand more harvester and construction units to pull in raw materials from the asteroid belt and help you construct two even larger models of this ship, as well as a support fleet. I will further supply the computational assistance required for the design work of such. In exchange, you will supply the design schematics and fabrication details so that my creators may build vessels of this design for their own use on their home planet. They would very much like to start using your designs in combatting the Zelos threat in other places throughout the galaxy."

"We could have an entire fleet of our own in a fraction of the decade it took to make just this one ship," Darren beamed.

"Hold on that, Colonel," the Director snapped. "That's a lot of trust you're asking for, Observer."

"Perhaps," the robot replied, "but I have come to trust you people of Earth."

"I meant us trusting you," she tersely amended, "not to mention Earth's governments as a whole. The possibility remains that you might use our designs against us some day, or even against some other worlds that are not the Zelos."

"I can assure you, Director Forester, that is not the case," Observer replied. "The Satarans view you much as a father would his children."

"Or a puppet master his puppets," she amended. "You have been giving us a lot of things that are just too good to be true, not to mention this mysterious benefactor race of which not even your own people supposedly know the identity or motive of. Are we being helped or manipulated? We don't have the whole picture, and I suspect that neither do you or your masters."

“I begin to see your point, Director,” the robot admitted. “Nevertheless, the offer remains.”

“And I will pass it along to the people that need to hear it,” the Director replied. “In the meantime, while Darren remains on Mars to oversee those adjustments to Odyssey, I have received a message from Agent Franklin that concerns General Feng.”

“Director?” Feng replied.

“It seems as Alexander Damaris has been spotted in China in several different locations of late,” the Director continued. “Agent Franklin needs your help in apprehending the tricky scumbag.”

“Immediately, Director,” Feng immediately replied. “Observer will teleport me straight over.”

“And I’ll get over to help Professor Hayden and the others make those adjustments to Odyssey,” Darren added.

“In that case this conversation is at an end,” the Director replied with a sharp snap to her tone.

She gave Observer a brief glare of suspicion before the image winked out.

CHAPTER
TEN

ALEXANDER DAMARIS

March 18, 2052

The city rose in gleaming towers high above them, the ever-present noise of civilization pressing in from all around. From auto-taxis to rickshaws, if there was a form of transportation it was to be found in the streets of Beijing, all of them contributing their share of the visual and auditory obstacle course behind which nearly anyone could lose themselves in if they had a mind to. Add in the video billboards flashing their ads in Chinese and English, the jungle of neon mixed with projected holographic signage above sidewalks and walkways beckoning passersby into one business establishment or another, and hawkers constantly pitching their wares, and it could be considered nearly impossible to find such a person.

Though if the ones tracking you are General Feng Yusheng and Agent Amelia Franklin, then those odds just might be a tad better.

Agent Franklin's exotic features allowed her to blend in perfectly with the local crowds; a young woman with soft-hued black skin and oriental accents to her eyes and high cheekbones, all she had to do was dress more like the locals to be taken as one of them. This meant a knee-length dark blue patterned dress, wide sun-hat, and dark glasses, though wearing flats on her feet instead of high-heels in case the need for running arose. With her long hair now worn loose instead of tied up as usual when on the job, she could have been anyone except the special agent that she is.

Beside her, Feng had added dark glasses, and a hat with a wide enough brim to pull down over his eyes, to the business suit attire he had adopted, just enough to hopefully hide the face of the most famous astronaut in all of China. The two of them walked together as if a couple, Agent Franklin with a long lock of her hair covering over an earpiece from view, the two of them saying little that most people would catch, though if one could listen to the exchange of their thoughts as well then their conversation would make a whole lot more sense.

"Nearly had him a couple of times," she said verbally, then continued telepathically. *But he kept teleporting away. No way of telling how far away either. What's Darren's range?*

"About anywhere on the planet," Feng replied, then also added a telepathic component. *But they needn't both have the same ranges.*

True… his could be even greater.

"Well, you're just a bundle of optimism today," he faintly grinned. *Though I'll admit that he wouldn't need to go too far to lose himself in these crowds. Have you learned anything more about his abilities?*

They came to a momentary stop at an intersection that had them both for a moment wondering which way to go. Six different streets came together in a sort of English-styled roundabout, with streams of humanity flowing through them like cells in an artery, and a mix of electric and gas-powered cars that hadn't quite gotten the hang of how roundabouts are supposed to work. A mess to navigate, at least until they saw the ramp leading up to the elevated pedestrian bridge that formed a complete ring around the circumference of the roundabout, a full twenty feet above it. They altered course for the press of people heading up the ramp as they continued their conversation.

It's been a little easier ever since you put in the word asking if we could have access to the local face recognition tracking system, she thought to him. *But not by much. We'll catch him on a traffic-cam entering an alley then never coming out the other end. Then two minutes later pick him up again about a block down. He's been popping all over the city that way.*

"Hmm... odd," Feng pondered.

"I just figured that he must be on his way to somewhere and doing it in a roundabout way to lose people like us. Last report had him spotted in this area a short while ago."

The puzzling part, Feng continued telepathically, *is that if, say, Darren wants to go somewhere he'd just teleport directly there and there'd be no way to track him. Our Mister Damaris is doing it in short hops.*

"Range limit?" Agent Franklin suggested.

"Could be. What's the longest distance he's been picked up again after a teleport?"

"Hold on, give me a sec."

As they reached the top of the ramp and the circular walkway, Agent Franklin touched a finger to her earpiece while subvocalizing a request. Feng spent that time leading them over to the inside edge of the bridge for a look around at the crowds below, trying to beat the odds of spotting the one face in their midst, his mind searching out as well for anything unusual. Unfortunately, crowds this thick present much the same problem for a telepath in search of one set of thoughts as they do for a normal person listening for one specific voice from amongst the hundreds.

"Seems to be about a block or two," Agent Franklin finally answered.

"So he has a range limit," Feng replied, his gaze still searching the crowds. "But, he could still just do one teleport right after another to go where he's trying to get to."

"Unless he has to rest between efforts," she suggested. "Let me get some time stamps."

Once again she touched finger to ear and subvocalized her request. Meanwhile Feng led her on a slow walk around the pedestrian bridge, eyes and mind scanning the masses below.

"Even a range limit of a couple hundred meters would explain his success as a terrorist," Feng mused. "That is just enough range to slip right past any sort of security measures. In fact, ... As I recall, the Central Committee is meeting today to go over some finer details of the world unification. Several foreign delegates are going to be present, including the President of your country."

"Got it," Agent Franklin reported, the finger leaving her ear. "It seems as we're able to track him for no more than about fifteen to twenty minutes before he vanishes again. That's just an estimate though, based on the few times we've had more or less continual monitoring of him. There are times when we've lost him for about an hour, which could mean he teleported into a building or something."

"So he has both a range limit and needs to rest up between efforts," Feng stated. "Good. Then if we can spot him and sneak up on him before he vanishes again, we've got him. This means that Darren almost had him back in the Middle East; Damaris probably teleported to just outside the building then ducked into the crowds."

"Well, he's got a lot more crowds to duck into now. His general course seems to be putting him in the direction of your Committee building, maybe we should wait for him there, if that's where he's headed."

"Too many places for him to duck into there. He could teleport into a closet, or the wall directly behind where the President will be sitting, or even into an air duct directly above their heads. At least here we have him out in the open… more or less."

They continued to walk around the circumference of the pedestrian bridge, scanning the crowds below and around for anyone that might look like the terrorist, or at least like someone trying to hide his face from view.

"Wait," Agent Franklin suddenly said, finger to her ear as she paused in her step, "one of my team was just chasing him down one of these streets when he vanished again, but he just reappeared right before a traffic cam that puts him at…"

Her hand drifted away from her ear, reaching out to point at a thick nest of people between one of the streets and the nearest pedestrian ramp up to the bridge, over on nearly the exact opposite side of the roundabout from their current position. But all their elevated angle could show them was the tops of people's heads, though few with hats, so Feng sent out his thoughts to probe.

"Nearly at my range limit, especially with so many people around," he told her, "but there may be something unusual down there. Come on!"

Through the swell of people, they now ran, around the right half of the giant circle, as fast as they could give the circumstances.

Hopefully these crowds will make it as difficult for him to see us coming as we have of seeing him, Feng thought to her as they ran.

I wouldn't bet on it, General. He knows we've been tracking him and will be looking for anyone running in his direction.

Either way, assume we have no more than fifteen minutes to catch him.

They ran dodging and weaving their way through the midday lunch crowd, while below them even more people waited for chance pauses in the flow of traffic or walked from one building to the next. Occasionally an annoyed remark from one person or another they happened to bump, running between conversing couples, around pausing tourists, then getting caught for a precious few seconds by the press of others emerging from one of the access ramps.

I really wish we had Darren with us, Feng remarked into her mind, *make this a lot easier. Unfortunately he's on Mars right now.*

What's the matter, Agent Franklin thought back with a mental grin, *not up for an afternoon jog?*

As they at last came to the ramp nearest the reported location of Alexander Damaris, Feng sent his thoughts out ahead. Mostly he got back an unintelligible mess of thoughts from a score of different people, much akin to the psychic equivalent of white noise, but then as they raced down the ramp he caught something different.

One mind down there is definitely not like the others. Weird pattern that seems to disrupt my efforts at finding him if from too far away. Could be our man.

Can you get a lock on him?

Not a very good one."

Running down the ramp midway to street level, so many people of a similar skin color making it virtually impossible to distinguish one light-brown skinned man from everyone else, the pair paused at the edge of the concrete railing to scan the crowds.

"Too many down there around him," Feng stated. "If what I sensed is him then it's still difficult to pick him out from the midst of everyone else, but I think he's starting to move."

"Then let me try something."

Agent Franklin boosted herself up onto the railing then standing atop the precarious perch, spread her arms wide and called out as loudly as she could.

"Alexander Damaris! We're here to get you."

One face from amongst the many turned sharply, glancing briefly up to see Agent Franklin standing atop the concrete railing looking down in his very general direction. For a moment she saw him, the scraggly beard being just as Darren had described it, then he pushed a passing girl away into the crowds and broke into a run.

"Reflexive action," Agent Franklin grinned, "got to love it."

She jumped down off the railing onto the street ten feet below, landing in a skillful roll up to her feet with no apparent harm save nearly bumping into someone else. Feng was a beat behind her, simply bounding straight up and over the railing and down to the street as had she, the pair now in a race through people and traffic. Voices raised, angry cries, people shoved in their way as obstacles. Then came the blare of a horn as they found themselves in the middle of one of the streets, a driverless auto-bus bearing down upon them. Feng burst into a run, giving himself a telekinetic boost to clear the distance to the other side, while Agent Franklin did a running jump, touching down briefly atop the moving bus only to jump again to the other side. She landed in another tuck and roll, a pace now behind Feng.

Ahead of them, the man with the beard continued to shove his way through the people, who were by now adding their own shocked reactions to the confusion of the chase. Seeing one man make an impossibly long leap across the street while a woman jumps over a moving bus is something guaranteed to have gawkers blocking your way in wonder, some of them quickly taking out their cell phones to snap pictures of the running pair. The chase nearly slowed down to a fast walk as people pressed in for a better look at who could be capable of such physical feats.

With so many people looking in their direction, taking videos of the ruckus, what happened next was inevitable. A voice from out of the crowds, excited exclamation, followed by many others calling out as well.

"He looks like General Feng!"

"That's General Feng."

"It's the astronaut!"

People pressed in close to get a look at their famous hero, to just touch him. Very quickly, Feng found himself nearly at a standstill, while Agent Franklin wasn't doing much better.

"I swear," she said to herself while shoving her way through the crowds, "if I have to punch every person in China to get to this guy, I will."

They could still see Damaris ahead of them, not too far in a straight run, but with so many people packing in around Feng, now to even affect the nearby traffic, a straight *crawl* would even be impossible. A struggle to make their way through when ahead of them they saw Damaris change his course. Suddenly bolting out into traffic, running out between cars and busses, the sound of their honks only adding to what was very quickly threating to evolve into a noisy logjam of vehicles and people, he headed straight for the little park at the center of the roundabout.

"Please," Feng finally called out in Chinese to the people massing around him, "I'm on a very important mission right now."

Agent Franklin was first out into traffic, narrowly missing being hit by one vehicle, dodging around another that paused briefly in its circumnavigation of the roundabout, then leaping over another car on her chase across the street. Behind her Feng finally managed to break away from the crowds to start running across the street as well, his presence finally being the last straw that brought the flow of traffic to a near halt. Honking cars, impatient auto-busses having to resort to manual override to make it through this mess, rickshaws with their tourist passengers in tow now with no way through either people or vehicular traffic. A riot of confusion now spreading wider and wider, and at the center of it all one bearded man in a cloak leaping onto the open grass of the center circle around which it all revolved, running into the middle of it before coming to a halt and turning around to face his pursuers.

Agent Franklin was still working her way around now-stalled vehicles, until she finally decided to make use of the traffic jam by jumping up on the hood of the nearest sedan and leaping from one car hood to another. Feng then took his own route through the traffic jam, preferring to keep to the ground and weaving his way quickly around paused and still-moving cars. The center of the roundabout was in sight for both of them, and so was their quarry. Agent Franklin was close enough to have the best look and what she saw did not make her happy.

The man with the scraggly beard now grew a grin.

"No!" Agent Franklin shouted.

From the last car hood she leaped onto the grass of the central meridian, Feng emerging a pace behind from between two slow-moving cars, then into a dead run she went, leaping the last couple of yards with hands reaching out... The man vanished right before her, and all she caught was grass in her face.

"Almost had him," she swore, as she rolled up to her feet.

"Quickly," Feng said as he ran up next to her, "start looking. He can't be more than about a couple hundred meters or so away. I might still be able to pick up that unusual emanation from his mind."

Eyes quickly searching, one mind reaching out. The noise of a thousand thinking minds, a hundred honking horns, foot traffic atop the pedestrian bridge even coming to a standstill as the curious stop to see the reason for the disruptions below them.

"There," Feng suddenly pointed. "His mind is somewhere up there."

He was pointing to a section of the bridge ringed around the roundabout, one crowded with people looking down at the pair in the very middle of the central meridian. High above them a couple of helicopters had also come in bearing news crews to cover what was quickly becoming one of the biggest traffic jams that Beijing had seen in a very long time. Everyone could now see the one man pointing, while the woman beside him narrowed her gaze in that same direction, searching. Her hat had come off somewhere in the chase, and for the same reason Feng now found himself lost of his own chapeau, but none of that mattered.

"I see him," Agent Franklin said after a moment. "Over there."

Feng shifted his gaze to where she indicated then saw him; Damaris was trying to lose himself amidst the curious crowds, but his identifying beard in a sea of clean-shaven people was as good as a searchlight.

"Feng," Agent Franklin called over a shoulder as she started into a run, "give me a boost."

She started running across the grass in the direction of Alexander Damaris, she on the level of the street and he safely on the bridge a full twenty feet above her head. Sprinting while above her Damaris looked on with a grin, then as she leaped realized only too late the danger. Alone her jump would not make it, but jumping as hard as her Mars-evolved body could manage combined with a strong telekinetic boost from General Feng, had her sailing high into the air in full view of onlookers and news cameras alike, tumbling into a ball, then feet out as she came down feet-first straight for Damaris, where now the crowds he had sought anonymity from had become his trap.

She landed full into his chest, martial cry upon her lips, as he went crashing onto his back with her standing atop him. A stunned crowd suddenly parted from around them, taking videos with their phones, news crews above them getting close-up views of the mysterious woman and the famous astronaut. As soon as Agent Franklin had landed, Feng ran for the nearest ramp. Across the traffic-locked streets, through the watching crowds, then up the ramp and along the bridge.

By the time Feng had caught up with her, Agent Franklin was lifting a semi-conscious Alexander Damaris to his feet.

"I don't think he's going to be blinking away any time soon," she said as he approached.

"Not with the two of us now holding onto him," he said as he grabbed their prisoner by the other shoulder. "If he has limits to both his range and how often he can teleport, then there's probably a limit to how much else he can carry with him as well."

"I'll let Chief Pinyin know we got him."

"I don't think we need to." Feng simply glanced up at the news copters filming it all, to which she shrugged.

"Let's get him out of here," Feng told her. "He's got some questions to answer."

About a thousand people there in person and many more from their television sets across the country watched as General Feng and Agent Amelia Franklin dragged a bearded man down off the pedestrian bridge and far enough away from the roundabout for Chief Pinyin's waiting men to take him into custody.

Alexander Damaris nearly escaped twice from Chief Pinyin's custody.

The first time he had apparently been more awake than his guards had assumed, for when Feng and Agent Franklin were in Chief Pinyin's office finishing up their briefing about the chase, suddenly there was a cry about an escaped prisoner. Fortunately, the range at which Damaris could teleport in a largely unfamiliar place with labyrinthine corridors was about the same range from which Feng could detect the man's unusual mental patterns. Also fortunately, he'd teleported into what turned out to be a closet that opened up into the main squad room.

The second time the man who'd been guarding him just shrugged.

"He said that I should release him and, well, it sounded like a good idea at the time."

"Great," Feng sighed, "he's got some form of telepathic suggestion as well. Amelia, take the front exit, I'll take the back."

"Right."

Feng found him at the back entry into the police station, just about to walk out while a pair of policemen were opening up the door for him with smiles on their faces.

"Stop him!"

The two policemen looked momentarily confused, while Damaris took the moment to make a mad dash for the open and freedom. Once outside, he would have a direct line of sight to any number of places to teleport away to, and Feng wasn't in the mood for another chase. So instead of a flying tackle, Feng simply reached out a hand and gripped it tight as if grabbing onto something, though he was still several feet away. Damaris suddenly froze, unable to move, then as Feng swung his hand back to one side, Damaris went flying back inside in the same direction, slamming against a wall and another bout of unconsciousness.

Next time when he woke up, Alexander Damaris had heavy weights around his feet and hands and was facing Feng and Agent Franklin and no one else in the small room. Nothing but a light and a camera fixed into one corner of the ceiling.

"Now," Feng stated, "there should be enough weights on you to make teleporting very difficult, and no one else in here to influence save myself and Agent Franklin here. So, you're going to tell us everything about yourself."

"Come now," the prisoner replied in a cultured tone, "I'm sure you know that I do not belong here. Agent Franklin, perhaps you would be kind enough to convince the General here to release me?"

For a moment she could feel it; like a tickling at the front of her brain, but a firm effort of will on her part and it was gone, much to the apparent consternation of Alexander Damaris.

"Sorry," she grinned, "but I've been training for people like you. So, how many victims have you been brainwashing like that?"

"It's more like a suggestion," he sighed, "but you're not getting any more out of me."

"We'll just see about that," Feng replied. "Agent Franklin, how's your telepathy coming along?"

"Good enough to link up with you and let you take the lead," she replied with a level expression. "I've never peeled open psychic grapefruit before."

"Me neither," Feng grinned, mostly for Damaris' benefit, "but there's always a first time."

To Chief Pinyin and anyone else watching from the monitor in the next room it looked simply like two people sitting across from the prisoner just staring at him, while Damaris did his best to look stern and unwavering. But from Feng's point of view, he was clawing at a stone wall while Agent Franklin laid hand to his shoulder to lend him what help she could from her own inferior abilities. In their minds Feng was taking a large hammer to the wall around Damaris' mind, leveling one solid blow after another against the unusual psychic patterns of his mind. Feng could feel Damaris trying to reach out and influence his own mind, but the attempt was too weak, Damaris too focused on simply withstanding the assault.

Then the first stone chipped away from the wall, a flinch from Damaris, then another stone and a twitch. By the third slip, words started spilling out from Alexander Damaris' protesting mouth.

"I… I grew up in Greece. Parents… killed in car crash when I was ten. Computer science at Peking University, I…"

"Spill it, Damaris," Agent Franklin scolded while Feng kept his focus. "Who are you *really?* Everything!"

"I… please."

"Talk," Feng levelly commanded.

"I… Engineer, assignments throughout Europe, China, America. Worked… explosives as well. Finally– Ahhh!"

For a moment Damaris' body went rigid, then just as suddenly slumped as Agent Franklin felt the psychic pressure release. Now as the prisoner resumed his confession, it was in a smooth monotone, almost like in a trance. Feng maintained his focused look, leaving Agent Franklin now to walk over behind the prisoner to hold him more erect that the microphones clearly pick up everything he would say.

"Four years ago I was recruited for Mars. I got the full schooling and rejuvenation treatments, then later after I returned, I discovered that I could influence people's minds. More subtly at first, but over time I can gradually alter their loyalties and get them to look up to me as a holy prophet. Only the weak-minded, though."

"Which would be just the mindset of middle-eastern terrorists," Feng put in, his gaze upon the other still not wavering. "What about the teleporting?"

"Discovered accidentally. Forgot my keys in my apartment then next thing I knew was back in there. After some self-training I was able to get up to a range of about a hundred and fifty meters. Still need to recover, though, and can't take much with me."

"Just enough extra weight for a bomb," Agent Franklin pressed.

"Yes… Joined militant group, killed some, influenced others, until I was at the top… Their holy prophet. Easy to get them to believe, all I had to do was teleport in front of their eyes… Made it easier to get into their minds."

"But why did you do it in the first place," Feng asked. "Why become a terrorist at all?"

"I… I… I don't really know. Just decided one day. Not really sure…"

At that point Damaris slumped into unconsciousness and Feng released his concentration. Agent Franklin gently settled his head onto the table as Feng raised his voice for benefit of those watching by remote.

"I'd like to take him to Mars for examination. I get the feeling that there's just something missing in what he's saying. Besides, as soon as he's awake, there's no prison that can hold him down here, and maybe Observer can find a way to limit him."

"Agreed," came the voice of Chief Pinyin from somewhere above. *"Call Observer and have him transported before he wakes up. Agent Franklin, you will need to report to Director Forester to update her on these proceedings, then I suspect she will keep you busy tracking down any other possible conspirators linked to Damaris here."*

"No doubt," Agent Franklin remarked. "General, do you need my help getting him ready for transport to Mars?"

"Don't even need to move him," Feng replied, then called out into the air, "Observer!"

It was not long after that when both Feng and Darren stood before Observer discussing the one asleep in one of the learning chairs across the room, a learning helmet fixed over his head while a med-bot worked on him with mechanical hands bearing scalpels and miniature medical lasers for fingers.

"The Director is eager to see if this rehabilitation process of yours works," Darren was saying. "then Damaris can spend the next ninety years of his current rejuvenation repaying for the damage he's done and the lives he's cost."

"When he awakens," Observer explained, "he will still remember everything he has done but more in the way of a bad dream. With the discrepancies to his personality removed, he should be very repentant. I cannot remove his psychic abilities nor reverse his rejuvenation, though, as that was accomplished by the rejuvenation and evolution machine, which as you know is of alien make. However, I am putting a psychic block on his abilities; he will still be able to access his engineering and computer skills so that he may be useful. Also as you have requested, I have instructed the med-bot to change his facial appearance, cheekbone structure, vocal intonations, and even hair color. He will look and act completely different."

"Good," Darren replied with a nod, "because with all the noise that Feng and Agent Franklin so publically made arresting the guy, his face is pretty much all over the planet right now. He could end up either a martyr or a pariah."

"I will endeavor to arrest the next terrorist far more quietly," Feng promised with more than a trace of sarcasm. "Though it seems a little wrong to completely change a man's personality like this, even for a killer like Damaris."

"I thought I had made myself clear," Observer put in, tilting its head slightly to one side in imitation of a slightly confused Human. "I said I had removed the discrepancies, not changed his personalities."

"Wait, "Darren asked, "what do you mean by 'discrepancies'? And how is that different from changing his personality?"

"I changed nothing," Observer calmly explained. "I removed the changes that I found already performed upon his mind, thus allowing his original personality to resume its normal structure. It was these discrepancies that have been causing Mister Damaris to act in the manner in which he was acting."

"You mean, his mind had been altered? Just like Sir Roberts and the rest," Darren asked in some mild disbelief.

"Yes. If I had to estimate, I would say that a very potent psychic had performed some deep restructuring of his mind. I even found what I would term a psychic kill-switch, where his personality could begin to break down if under certain circumstances, such as being captured. Apparently Feng and Agent Franklin surprised him with the manner of his sudden and dramatic capture so that it was unable to activate. After that, the lock you had on his mind during interrogation likewise prevented it from activating."

"Otherwise he would have ended up just like Sir Roberts and Wang Wei Huang," Darren realized with open-mouthed shock. "Feng, this means that they're all not just involved in the same conspiracy, but have definitely been reprogrammed by a single individual."

"A single very *powerful* individual," Feng reminded him. "Damaris was a very potent psychic able to subtly influence the minds of others, and yet his own mind had been in turn so influenced. There is someone out there pulling all the strings; someone that might even be capable of controlling you and me, Darren."

"I hope not, because that would be bad. Really bad."

"I have data on everyone that has passed through this facility," Observer told them, "and I can assure you that no one developed potent enough abilities to affect the two of you. At least not while they were here."

"And yet, here we are with that very possibility," Darren stated. "Somewhere out there is an anomaly able to control other psychics as well as normal Humans."

"And we have no clue who he is," Feng finished. "That raises some very frightening possibilities. And there was no clue in Damaris' memories as to who that might be? No missing minutes or suspicious people he's met?"

"Not that I can find," Observer replied in his usual calm tones. "Whoever did it was very cautious."

The two men exchanged looks, a shared worry in a single glance, then Darren sighed.

"Forester's not going to like this.

"Since you brought it up then you get to make the report," Feng told his friend with a grin.

"Oh come on, Feng, you were the one who captured him, you could at least go with me."

"Sorry, but I have Chief Pinyin to brief. Besides, one of us has to be around here to give Damaris his new name and cover story when he wakes. Let's see, that was to be a Henry Smith from Houston Texas that's been working as an electrical engineer in California, now transferred back to Texas. Yep, someone's got to get him set up so he can start repaying society, and since I helped capture him that's my responsibility. Sorry, Darren old friend, but I'm afraid the job of trying to look Forester in the eye falls to you."

Darren sighed, grumbled once, then eyed the other with mild malevolence.

"Ya' know, Feng, at times you can be a ripe old bastard of a friend."

"As long as I'm not the one who gets chewed out by the Director," Feng shrugged. "But I will take you out for a drink afterwards."

"Feng, when Forester finishes ironing out my backside, no amount of alcohol will have been worth it."

She did, and it wasn't.

CHAPTER ELEVEN

WARP SHAKEDOWN

December 1, 2052
United Earth Ship Odyssey, flight log
Colonel Darren Hildure, reporting.

This is it, the first real shakedown cruise for Odyssey. I've been overseeing the installation of some minor but significant upgrades these past few months, based on our brief encounter with that lone Zelos ship and the notes I took during that battle. First, our nav-computer is a lot more precise; definitely a necessity for any sort of long-distance voyage. Second, the bridge stations now have the new mind-computer interfaces installed, which in appearance amount to a sort of helmet fixed onto the back of the chair that you bring forward over your head. That should speed up our reaction times significantly, which also is a necessity given the observed reaction times of just that one Zelos vessel.

This time we have a full crew, with Captain Eva Gardena once again in charge. Feng is going to stay on Mars with Observer to coordinate any problem-solving that might arise. Our first test is going to start with a quick jump to Alpha Centauri just to get a good gauge of the speed of our warp engines. After that it will be forty thousand light years in the direction of

Sagittarius, maybe stop by to say hello to our benefactors. I wanted to do a fly-by of the Zelos system, but according to Observer, no one knows the location of their homeworld. Only that when they come and raid your planet, it's always in three ships about one and a half kilometers long each and several thousand fighters. Apparently that's been enough to wipe out entire space-faring civilizations in one of their raids.

Though there is one exception Observer told us about. Apparently there was an alliance of many worlds that came together once with the sole purpose of standing up to the Zelos. They banded against them whenever any of their words were raided and now the Zelos leave their worlds alone. Even then, the most they'd managed to learn was from the capture of one of the smaller Zelos ships, but unfortunately its computer held no information on the location of their homeworld. Or really much of anything about the Zelos themselves, for that matter.

Observer has loaded into the Odyssey's computer as much information as he can provide on what we might find out there, and for emergencies provided a comm-link from him to our vessel. Now, one might wonder how useful a communications link will be given the distances involved but this one operates on a sort of hyper-space principle. In essence, it opens a micro hyperspace portal from our transmitter to a receiver of a specified hyperspatial configuration, which in this case is Observer's. Instant communications in the form of burst transmissions, no chance of anyone overhearing or intercepting it, but also no way of contacting anyone else that might be out there without knowing the configuration of their receiver.

I should interject a short note on the difference between warp and hyperspace at this point. Warp drive encloses the ship in a bubble of space taken from an interdimensional realm where everything can move much faster than the speed of light, allowing us to get to Alpha Centauri in a matter of minutes, but is still impractical for the likes of intergalactic travel. A hyperspace drive, on the other hand, opens up what you might call a portal between one point in space and another, allowing something to pass instantly through to that other place. It's a folding of space, or what some might call a sort of wormhole generator. Advantage: it can carry you over a far greater range of distances in a very short time. Disadvantage: it just does the one transfer; no maneuvering or local moving around of any type. For that, warp or more standard maneuvering thrusters are still the best option. I mention this because a hyperspace engine has been on the drawing board and pending the results of this test flight, will be incorporated into the next vessel that is already being planned. This flight will see how far we can push the warp drive, though, before making that final decision.

The Odyssey was already hanging in space, a black jewel awaiting the final command that would launch her to places no human of Earth had ever been to before. The bridge had a full complement manning all the stations ringed around it, more crew throughout the vessel ready to tend any of its various needs. The launch was being watched by every instrument on Mars and relayed to Earth for all to see. Such an important event in Earth's history, on top of the ominous head of the Zelos recently making itself known, this was something deemed important for more than just Earth central command center to see.

Captain Eva Gardena was at the center of the flurry of status reports and updates coming at her from the various bridge stations, many more flashing across the virtual displays hovering above the arms of her command chair. Darren sat in the second chair, a couple of his own displays echoing a few key systems like engine status, reactor output, and the course already programmed into their navigation. The dome ceiling overhead showed a view of space above, the floor continuing with the view from below, including Mars looking like it was hovering some distance beneath the feet of the Weapons station.

"Gimbals locked in place, Captain," came a report from the engineering station. "We're ready to sail."

"Then we're set. Captain Gardena to Command, we're ready to begin."

The call into the air was answered by three large images appearing strung across one end of the ceiling screen above; the first of Observer, beside him Feng, then the dark-toned severe features of Director Forester.

"In that case, wishing you all good luck," Feng was first to say. "I'll be your liaison for the uniforms back at Command that will be wanting to scream at you for one thing or another."

"Your sacrifice is appreciated, General," the Captain blandly remarked. "I would rather undertake the dangers of space than listen to old soldiers that haven't moved their asses from their desk chairs in a decade."

"I can see why you like her, Darren," Feng grinned. "I'll just tell them the Captain appreciates their interests in this mission."

"Just make sure you don't damage our new ship," now Director Forester said in clipped tones, "or I'll be using someone's hide for reactor shielding in the next model."

"And we love you too, Director," Darren quipped.

"This is a most historic moment for your species, Darren," Observer stated. "I understand it is customary in your history for some words of significance to be spoken that later generations may remember."

"What, me? I'm no speaker. That should be the Captain's job."

To which Captain Gardena swiveled her chair around to Darren's direction and volleyed the honor right back at him.

"You have ranking authority here, Colonel, the honor belongs to you. Not to mention you oversaw this entire project."

"Great," Darren said with a roll of his eyes, "trapped by my own competence."

All eyes on the bridge now looked over in the Colonel's direction as he pursed his lips thinking quickly about what to say.

"Okay then, how's about this. 'Tis a far better thing– No, that one's taken… Okay, one small step for– No, someone used that as well. Praise the Lord and pass the ammunition? Naw, wrong circumstance… I guess all I can say is that this is something that Humanity has always needed to do, been *destined* to do. I would wish that the circumstance that brings us at last to the stars did not involve such fearful tidings, but the stars have always been our destiny. We've lived in space all our lives, when you think about it. Now we're just going to get to know the neighborhood."

He paused for a moment, then shrugged, "That's all I got."

"Okay then," the Captain snapped, turning her chair around to face the Navigation station. "Release all gravity locks and move us away from orbit. Helm, lay in a course and prepare to engage warp drive."

A klaxon sounded off three times, echoing throughout the ship, the three images projected on the screen then replaced once again by a view of the stars as that of Mars began to shrink. When Mars was a large dot in the corner of the bridge, the Helm station called out his report.

"Ready to activate warp, Captain."

"Then engage. Let's take a look at Alpha Centauri."

From all observing from Mars, it looked like the Odyssey started to glow, surrounding itself in a light that started as a dim red, worked quickly up through yellow, green, and blue until finally at violet the brilliant nimbus vanished in an eye-straining flare, and with it the ship. Inside the Odyssey, though, the view was a little different. The stars had stretched out into colored streaks, blurred by the manner of their speed and as visually indecipherable as it had been for their first brief trip out to the asteroid belt. At least until the Captain called out a command.

"Engage our new relativistic compensators. Let's see what it really looks like around here. Wide view."

The dome screen flickered briefly and now the streaks were replaced by a far more distinguishable star-field; colored dots once again instead of the blurred streaks. Nearer stars visibly moved across the field of vision, farther ones more slowly, but they remained seeable as what they are, with one in particular getting closer a lot faster than the rest.

"*Much* better," Darren noted.

"That star up ahead is Alpha Centauri," Helm indicated, himself as awed as the rest, "and the one behind us getting smaller is Sol; the Sun. We… We're really doing it, we're truly out in interstellar space."

"So it would seem," the Captain noted.

To most it looked like the Captain's mood was rock-steady, unimpressed by what they now saw around them, but to Darren's keener observation skills, not to mention his telepathic abilities, he could sense the roiling emotions that she was barely holding in check. They were voyaging between the frickin' stars! She wanted to jump up and cry out, but only her training and discipline held her back.

For himself, Darren was much of the same mind as he watched that star get bigger and bigger, then remembered himself and quickly checked the readings displaying before him.

"Looks like we'll be arriving in a few seconds now," Darren called out.

"Helm," the Captain called out, "confirm."

"Computer is programmed to bring us out of warp as soon as we reach our destination, which should be about the middle of the star system, if calculations are correct. We're going at maximum warp right now, but we can reduce speed to lower warps to maneuver around the system."

"Good," Captain Gardena nodded. "Navigation, I know there's a lot to gawk at but I hope someone's been recording all this navigational data. Things look a little different from this perspective than back in normal space and people will want to see that."

"Yes, Captain, recording since we launched."

"Coming up on destination," Helm now called out. "Emerging in four, three, two, one."

The screen gave a brief flicker then held steady. No more moving star-field, just a steady static view, ahead of them a bright yellow star casting its fiery arms across their field of view. When it was certain their position was steady, Captain Gardena nodded to the young lady at the Science station who began reading off from the display at her station, while the rest of the bridge crew held its collective breath.

"Raw data coming in… The star before us is slightly brighter than Sol, ten percent more massive, and approximately twenty percent larger. Farther constellations remain virtually the same while closer ones have shifted in both location and general appearance. Also recording the presence of two other stars, one of which would be nearly within the solar system if this was back on Earth… Captain, this is Alpha Centauri. We– We did it."

At that point a cheer went up, even the Captain allowing herself a broad smile, while Darren bolted up from his seat to pace across to the star's projected image, as if touching the screen above might be like touching the star itself.

"Attention all crew," the Captain called out after a touch to one of her virtual controls. "You may notice a little change in the view from outside on your monitors. We are no longer in orbit around our sun. That's Alpha Centauri out there, people, and we are the first Humans to see it in person."

Cheers and glad tidings echoed throughout the ship, and for a moment or two the Captain allowed it to be so. She even rose from her chair to join by Darren's side for a quiet exchange.

"Colonel, we did it. We actually did it."

"That we did," Darren replied, as overwhelmed with awe and joy as anyone else. "Though I suppose we should be sharing the joy right about now."

"If we must we must," she sighed. "Comm, get me Observer. Time to spread the news."

A moment later one large rectangle of the dome-screen parted to reveal the steady features of Observer, beside him Feng eagerly grinning.

"You made it?" Feng burst in. "Are you really there?"

"That we are, old friend," Darren replied. "So you can tell the parents that the kiddies have taken their first steps."

Feng let out a whoop of joy, while Observer cocked his head slightly to one side in puzzlement.

"I am somewhat confused by that metaphor, Darren. Are you to mean that my creators are the parents and that Humanity as a whole has taken its first step, or are you speaking this to Earth Command as the parental units and yourselves as their children?"

"And we have another first," Darren chuckled. "A robot who has been observing us Humans for over eight thousand years has just been confused by a multi-level metaphor."

"I am not entirely confused, I just need clarification. Though it is comforting to know that there are still things I can learn of your race."

A last joyous look at the view around them before Captain Gardena resumed her position back in the Captain's chair and had composed herself long enough to once again be a ship's captain.

"Sciences, start recording everything you can. We have an unprecedented opportunity here. We'll stay around here for a bit then move onto Alpha Centauri B for a look around."

"Yes, Captain. We'll certainly have enough to keep the scientists busy for a while."

"That we will," the Captain replied.

"Stream it all through the link to Observer," Darren put in. "We might as well start earning our paycheck right off the bat."

"You heard the Colonel," the Captain ordered. "Let's give them some home movies that *no one* will beat at the next picnic..."

December 5, 2052
United Earth Ship Odyssey, flight log
Colonel Darren Hildure, reporting.

We've spent a few days hopping around our new neighborhood. After Alpha Centauri A, it was on to Alpha Centauri B where we found two more than the single planet suspected of being there. The second planet's about a hundred million kilometers away from the star and the third twice that. The second planet also has a moon that's slightly larger than our own.

I should note how in all of space we managed to detect these worlds. Every gravitational body exerts a pressure upon what Observer calls the 'continuum'. Gravitational continuum, that is, what scientists view as the curvature of space, only it turns out that's slightly inaccurate, but that's another subject. Anyway, the sensors we developed with help from Observer allow us to detect such bumps in the local gravitational fields. When something is moving, like planets orbiting around their star will do, then this creates a ripple, the configuration of which is in direct proportion to the mass of the object and its speed. Thus, planet-sized bodies have their own distinctive signatures, while the continuum ripple from something like a vessel such as ours going at warp speed would be significantly different. Because of this, we were able to detect the presence of worlds that would have taken astronomers decades to find even were they in the same star system.

There are no radio transmissions that we can detect, and nothing in Observer's database says anything about known intelligent life around here, but you never know. We did send in a few probes down to that second world just for a quick look-see and... Well, there's ***life.*** *Nothing intelligent, at least not that we can see at first glimpse, but forests of silvery needle-like trees, lakes of some sort of greenish liquid, and puffy blue clouds across a green-tinted sky. Enough just in those few snapshots to keep the egg-heads back home doing hand-springs for months. I wish we could stay longer, but we've got a mission plan to get back to.*

Still, if this is what there is to be found just circling around this one star system, what else is out there waiting for us? What other marvels are we going to behold? So much to see, not enough time to see it in. Maybe in the future I can make it back here to see more of that strange life down there, or maybe I'll be too busy looking into even more fantastic things yet to come.

Our next leg is to the Sagittarius Arm to say hello to Observer's creators, the Satarans. At forty thousand light-years away, this will take much longer than the couple of minutes it took us to reach Alpha Centauri; about twenty days, based on current calculations. Still, spanning such a distance in under a month's time is an unbelievable achievement. Current estimates have us moving at over five hundred ***thousand*** *times the speed of light!*

Word from Feng is that the entire civilized world is leaping for joy over everything, except for the very few that flat-out don't believe anything they see and think this is all one huge conspiracy to lie to them for some mysterious reason. Oh, and Feng is jumping for joy for more personal reasons: it seems as Dao-ming is pregnant.

"On course to Sagittarius Arm, Captain," Navigation reported. "Computer is automatically compensating for local perturbations along our path."

"Keep on that, Nav," the Captain replied. "The only navigational data we have is based on Earth's own visual observations of an area forty thousand light years away, and Observer's records which may be up to ten thousand years old. Stars can drift quite a bit in that time."

"Aye, Captain," came Nav's reply.

"Cartography," the Captain now spun her chair around to face a different station, "continual mapping of everything we see, fly by, or observe."

"Yes, Captain."

Darren was quite content to let the Captain do her job, besides which he was busy himself taking in all the new data, communicating updates to Feng and Observer, and being generally enthralled by everything. Of course, into any such joyous time, a dark hand must inevitably make itself known.

"Captain," came the report from Science, "sensors are registering a number of continuum ripples from a nearby star system that we are approaching. They don't match up to planets."

"I got it here," Darren spoke up, switching one of his floating virtual screens to the view of the raw data. "He's right. The ripples are too tightly space and coming in too quickly. Something a lot smaller than a planet and moving at… superluminal speeds I would say."

"Our first warp signature," the Captain ventured.

"I would agree," Darren replied. "I would like to investigate this. There's intelligent life behind this, maybe we don't have to go all the way to Sagittarius to meet with Observer's creators."

"Agreed. Helm, alter course for the source of those ripples."

"Aye, Captain. Engaging."

The view of moving stars then shifted, suddenly about twenty degrees to the right as they turned onto a new course. It was not long before another star came into view, larger and larger as they neared. A swipe of a finger across one of her own displays and the Captain had a tactical view of what lay ahead overlaid across the live view of the stars. At first just a simple dot in the star with a line drawn from it to a small square of incoming raw sensor data. As they neared the star, the dot began to move slightly to one side. Closer still and now other dots appeared in the view.

"Detecting three worlds in orbit on this side of the star," Science reported. "The unusual ripples seem to be coming from the second one."

"Adjust course for that world," Captain Gardena commanded. "Weapons: we have force-fields on this thing, bring them up just in case, and be ready with something to fire if worse comes to worst."

"Premonition, Captain?" Darren asked.

"Instinct," she corrected. "Check your sensor data. Do those continuum ripples look like they're leaving the star system or coming into it?"

"Hard to tell with what little we know about how to read these things, but I see your point. The latter could mean invaders."

"Emerging from Warp," Helm announced, "in four, three, two, one."

A world in flames and skies filled with death. Their first view of an inhabited alien world was of a blue-green sphere with great grey clouds welling up from the surface, miles of wreckage hanging in orbit high above, and the remains of a space fleet trying desperately to fend off their attackers. Already ships a thousand feet long were breaking up under the ruthless assault, helpless to stop the great tide heading down to the world below.

The attackers came in swarms, the design of the craft familiar to any who had been in Geneva a year and a half ago. They each looked like giant beetles, the forward guns pulsing out their deadly rhythm. The function of the clawed grippers they had previously seen on the bottom of the landing struts now became apparent as several of them swarmed in around one of the larger of the remaining defending vessels. The claws dug into the hull of the ship, holding it firm no matter how the ship tried to maneuver, then the small craft aimed its forward guns down and began carving into the hull at point-blank range. Some already had their holes craved, into which the five-foot locust-like aliens dove.

While the thousands swarmed around the defending fleet, thence through them and down to the planet below, approaching a closer orbit of the world came the carriers which had launched them. Long slender barges of space, with wings now slowly folding out that gave it the look of a malevolent dragonfly; wings that angled towards the surface far below it. Three such great vessels, majestic bringers of death colored a dark green, now going in for the kill.

Darren said it in a word.

"Zelos."

"Reports all around," Captain Gardena snapped. "Cartography: what do Observer's files say about this system?"

"There's not supposed to be a space-faring culture here," came the reply, "just some pre-industrial age locals, but his archives are admittedly ten millennia out of date."

"Science station."

"Those three long craft are each over a mile long, and from what I can get on those wings they're some sort of weapons arrays. Reading energies of a bioelectrical nature."

"Tactical."

"Judging from the residual ripple signatures and the dispersal pattern of the incoming fleet, this battle can't have been going on for very long, yet in that time what looks to have been a rather sizable fleet and accompanying orbiting defense platform has been brought to its knees. Also registering invader activity on the planetary surface, most of it concentrated around the larger population centers. From the looks of it, I'd say there's between twelve and sixteen thousand Zelos fighter craft."

"Have they seen us yet?"

"Not that it looks like, Captain."

"Weapons. What can we bring to bear?"

"Well, quite a lot, Captain, but I would ask if we should. This is a very good ship but what's out there is overwhelming."

"Which brings us to the moment of decision then," the Captain spun her chair around now to face the one to whom that decision would fall, "Colonel Hildure."

The view was projected all around them, above on the dome and below at their feet. Brightly glowing dust motes in the distance physically carving up the last of the defending vessels, with a clearer view of each of the three main carriers spreading out into position around the planet as their dragonfly wings turn in place. Then the wings started to glow.

"Captain," came the woman at the Science station, "that bioelectric energy is now projecting out from those wings to the planet. I'm reading plenty of life-forms down there but... It looks like whatever they're firing is sweeping across the surface but I'm not reading any signs of destruction. Just... it looks like... I think I can get a visual. Switching to telescopic."

One large square on the dome above shimmered briefly as a view of the world below appeared. A great city of steel and concrete, buildings higher still than the tallest ones on Earth. People in the streets much like Earth Humans, just with a slight orange tint to their colorations. Streets filled with panicked crowds, emergency vehicles speeding about, while overhead the local version of a jet flies by in defense of the citizenry.

Then suddenly all quieted. Thousands dropped to the ground twitching, vehicles crashed as their drivers were struck with paralysis, the jet plummeting uncontrolled into the distance. An entire city helplessly falling to the ground, while from above the first wave of Zelos landing craft descend. The first lands into the street, where a Zelos crawls out and begins grabbing paralyzed bodies to load up, pausing briefly to stick its proboscis into its victim's forehead.

The view then switched to another city, but much the same was happening. Everywhere those wings shone down upon, people stopped moving.

"Just like in Geneva," Darren gasped, "but on a much larger scale."

"I've seen enough," the Captain decided. "Colonel, permission to engage. I can't stand by and just watch as billions of people get slaughtered like this. We're only one ship but at least we can distract them. *Something.*"

"Agreed," Darren said with a slow nod, gaze still fixed on the horrid sight. "Burst transmit all images through to Observer then let's give the Odyssey a *real* field test."

"Aye that," the Captain snapped. "Weapons: engage computer targeting. All bridge personnel switch to helmet interface. Disengage gimbals and ready automatic internal rotation systems. Carve us a path straight to one of those larger vessels, see if we can at least clip its wings. Helm be prepared to make this vessel dance. I think we might have a surprise or two for them they're not expecting."

The new translucent black helmets at the tops of every chair now lowered into place, covering each person's head as their fingers eased back from the bulk of the physical controls, eyes fixed both on the displays hovering before them and that now connecting directly to their minds. No longer were they just operating the ship's systems but now had become a part of them. Man and machine truly as one.

It came from the dark of night, the deep pit of space. A large black orb, soft glitter of force surrounding it, pitted like a golf ball with brightly glowing tips at the base of these manmade craters. Immediately the nearest of the Zelos fighters changed course, flipping over while still in high-speed flight to head in coordinated lines directly for the Odyssey, moving all as if of one body, one mind. Streams of energy were already spitting out, assaulting the strange vessel's force-field as Zelos by the hundreds came in to join the engagement. From the front they came, more swinging around to the rear, above and below. They would soon have the ship surrounded then move in on it just like the others.

"Hold on that a little more," the Captain ordered.

Above their heads, a tactical projection showed the swarms of glowing dots closing in from all around, one after another of them being lit up with a small circle as the weapons computer picked the first of its targets.

"Captain," Tactical called out, "they've nearly surrounded us!"

"Nearly being the operative word," she calmly announced. "Let's wait until they have us *completely* surrounded. Weapons: hold on my mark."

"Captain," Darren said under his breath, "I swear you must have nerves of steel. That, or we're about to get torn to shreds."

"Possibly both Colonel. Now just a bit more and… Fire! All weapons, continuous barrage."

The Zelos had just closed their trap; nowhere for this new vessel to escape to, enough of them to overwhelm its force-fields in time. The only problem they had was in choosing which side of it to designate as the 'front' and a possible location for such critical areas as the bridge or engineering. The answer, however, came from all around it as half of those divots scattered around it fired. Pulse lasers and antimatter particle beams shot out with far greater intensity than one had any right to expect from a vessel of this limited size, cutting through many of the fighters on the first salvo. A fierce defense but nothing the Zelos could not weather.

But then there were the unexpected occurrences. In a few cases it looked like something had fired out from the odd black ship, but nothing was recorded was coming out from it. Then a moment later a discharge would erupt *inside* a Zelos craft, destroying it from the inside out. A hundred Zelos vessels were destroyed in those few precious seconds, and *that* caught the attention of the rest of their fleet.

"Zelos swarming in our direction, Captain," Helm reported. "Looks like about half of them. They're forming up between us and their carriers. Looks like they guessed our intent."

"We can't stand up to all that, but we can at least show them there are some new players in the game," Captain Gardena stated. "New course, engage."

As soon as the course flashed out from her mind to display across the tactical view above, it was initiated. As fast as the weapons of this strange ship had been firing, the Zelos now in their greater numbers could evade; a hive mind coordinating across thousands of vessels that had yet to meet its match. Then it moved, but not in the way of any ship anyone had seen. It did not bank to the left in a gradual sweeping arc the Zelos would have no trouble keeping up with, but suddenly switched from the engines thrusting it forward to an entirely different set of thrusters off to what the Zelos had come to assume to be the side. Forward motion turned into a sharp sideways thrust, the large black ball appearing to spin around in place as it did so, then abruptly stopped and plunged downward into space, the weapons around its upper half firing upwards into the exposed underbelly of the Zelos.

Another shift of thrust and suddenly forward, in apparent defiance of the laws of inertia, and all the time continuing its upward-aimed strafe. The Zelos were quick to react, though, turning end over end to fall into a line of chase, more of their number swinging down from above to join in.

"Helm engage rolling maneuver. Continue forward thrust while firing back at this tail we've picked up."

"Aye Captain."

Orders given just as before, but now with one difference. Nothing had been spoken aloud, but rather transmitted by way of the helmets and the new mind-computer interface. The work of a split second to give and another split second to engage. The Zelos saw the ship's hull now spin up to speed, around and around in place even as it continued to shoot on ahead, and the whole time its weapons firing behind it, timed with a coordinated precision the Zelos had thought only possible of themselves. One row of weapon banks after another as each spun down into range, pulse-lasers like Gatling guns, Kaon emitters cutting down, until the Zelos found themselves flying into a literal wall of focused energy. That did not count, of course, the photon pulse cannons and their ability to teleport their energetic payload directly inside many of the quickly-dodging Zelos vessels. The thrusters too pulsed off in similar coordinated fashion, always the rearward sets firing for only as long as the computer decided they were going to keep the vessel on course before switching to a new set rotating into place.

Then just as quickly, the large black sphere stopped and took on a new course straight up.

"All weapons," the Captain ordered, "new target. Let's clip a couple of wings while we're here."

The rolling of the Odyssey continued, looking like a spherical pinwheel, but now every weapon spinning into position coordinated onto the one target it was coming up underneath of one of the mile-long vessels. Suddenly explosions began registering within the wings it was using to subdue the planetary population with, despite any force-fields and hull shielding to the contrary. More of the swarms that had been meeting against the defending fleet now peeled away, straight on course to come down at the Earth craft from above while the rest chased it from below, but it was too late.

The Odyssey crashed straight through the left-side pair of wings, shattering them into a hundred shards as it continued on its way, firing now at the Zelos attempting to block its way from above.

"Damage report," the Captain called out.

"Shields holding," Engineering reported, "minor structural damage. We've taken out a few of theirs, but projections indicate our ultimate defeat once they all gang up on us at once."

"And we don't even know what other sorts of weapons those big ships may have," Tactical put in. "Or if our force-field is proof against that paralysis ray of theirs."

"Agreed. Colonel Hildure, we've bloodied their nose, recommend we escape to spread the word that these things are *not* unbeatable."

"Confirmed," Darren replied by way of the helmet interface. "We'll need some time to engage the warp engines…." Then Darren got the most delightful grin, nearly evil one would say, as he thought out his command through the interface. "Captain, head us into that star. We're going to ride right through the corona."

"Colonel, with all due respect," Engineering protested, "we'll fry."

"Not as much as anyone following us will when we go into warp while *inside* it," Darren grinned. "Observer warned us that engaging a warp engine while too near a strong gravity well is not safe for the local inhabitants. Captain?"

"I get your meaning," Captain Gardena said with a faint trace of a grin. "Helm engage as ordered. Navigation, plot us a course out of here; something with a lot of random hops to it. Ready on my mark."

That entire exchange took the space of but a fraction of a second; maybe not as quick as the collective hive mind of the Zelos that now surrounded them, but at least enough to challenge it. After the Odyssey came bursting up from beneath the Zelos cruiser, it hovered high above it for only a very brief time before darting straight off towards the sun. Faster and faster it went, still rolling in place but now shooting off its armaments towards the rear. One of the carriers' wing arrays had been damaged past usefulness, but there was enough with the remaining two carriers to consider the subjugation and apparent harvest of this world as a done deal. What concerned the Zelos now, was that there existed a race somewhere that could present such a challenge.

Not to mention one daring enough to fly straight into a star.

The polarizers on the dome screen snapped on, affording them a view without being blinded. Their entire world was now one of fire, their rear view showing the first wave of Zelos to follow them in quickly erupting in brief flares from contact with the corona.

"Captain, force-field stressing to its limits, outer hull heating up," Engineering reported.

"This is your ballgame, Colonel," the Captain told him.

"Right," Darren replied, taking command. "Deactivate all weapons. Once around the sun to gain us some speed, then shoot out at right angles straight at that planet and the mess surrounding it and go to immediate warp. If we do it right, we'll leave them something to remember us with while giving this world a quick burial."

Around the sun the Odyssey flew, picking up speed as it flew. The Zelos saw the vessel vanish into the corona and broke off their chase, favoring the harvest of the world at their feet before anything else might happen. Faster until the view outside was a blur, fire licking out from the ship like a comet, then at one full rotation it shot straight out on a direct line for the second planet. A single mental command from Darren and the Odyssey went into warp immediately.

From the points of view of both the Zelos and the rear view of the Odyssey, as it came erupting out from the star, it drew with it a broad tail of superheated plasma. Barely free of the corona and the ship flashed in colors up through the spectrum, drawing in more of the plasma behind it, until at violet it vanished. The Odyssey popped off like a cork, unleashing a sudden rush of accelerated plasma yanked out by the presence of an itinerant warp field.

In short, a powerful solar flare shot off from the star, drawn on a direct course for the world the Zelos had invaded and the fleet that surrounded it. They would have mere minutes to evacuate, and of their intended prize, that would be forever denied them.

All eyes on the bridge watched the receding view as the Zelos scrambled and a doomed world knew its death; a view quickly cut off by the entry into warp. Helmets lifted off now with the brief battle at an end and it was with somber moods the crew resumed their normal duties.

"Slow down roll and reengage gimbals when able," the Captain commanded. "I've no doubt that little solar flare covered our tracks rather nicely, but let's take the long way home just in case. Colonel."

"Agreed," Darren replied. "And for the record, tell Observer that the world was already doomed, but at least now the inhabitants won't be… Zelos brain food."

"Yes, Colonel," Captain Gardena said with a heavy sigh. "I just wish we could have done more, but there were simply too many of them and we're only one ship."

"Not for long, Captain, but let's save that for later."

December 10, 2052
United Earth Ship Odyssey, flight log
Colonel Darren Hildure, reporting.

The maneuver with the star and the solar flare was very much a Hail Mary play. The Zelos had been whittling away at our shields and would have made it through soon enough, but riding through the solar corona blew them out completely. We also exhausted one of our warp generators, which according to Observer is a normal consequence. Each one has only so many light-years in it after which the engine must be rebuilt or jettisoned before it becomes too radioactive to deal with. Since we're taking the long way home and have no way of immediately repairing it, jettisoning was our only option. We still have enough to get back to Alpha Centauri and from there home to make a full report, but without the shields there's just no way we're ready for another battle. All in all, I would think we didn't do bad for a first outing.

At least until we heard back from Observer in the last burst transmission. We've been taking random hops all over the place to make it as difficult as possible for any Zelos to track us and during rest periods make brief contacts with Observer for any updates. It was during the last such that Observer gave us his own opinion on our performance, and I must say I never expected to see a robot nearly jump for joy before. According to Observer, while there was that one alliance that had beaten back the Zelos, he had never heard of a single vessel doing even close to half as well as we did. He was also impressed with that solar flare maneuver I came up with and agreed that the world was gone anyway.

Anyway, my own assessment is generally positive, though I would definitely recommend that hyperspace engine in the next design, and also recommend some improvements to the warp engine. I don't care what Observer says is normal for warp technology, there just ***has*** *to be a way to design the things to regenerate on their own so we don't have to keep throwing away good warp engines after every long run. Also some tweaks to the power generators would be nice. Right now we're using antimatter reactors, which while powerful enough, run the problem of not finding enough antimatter to power it. I know that Professor Hayden and her staff have been working on a dark energy reactor, which would make our fuel a lot more plentiful, and maybe something we can hook up to the force-fields as well.*

Well, we're coming out of warp now and soon to enter Mars orbit. No doubt there are a few people that will be wanting to hear things from me personally, so I'd best get cleaned up.

The recordings of the Odyssey's encounter with the Zelos fleet were being replayed before the World Assembly, not for the first time being reviewed for every detail that could be gleaned of the Zelos, not the least of which was their easy subjugation of the populace from orbit and subsequent harvesting. Orbiting wreckage that far surpassed anything that Earth currently had and yet it had become as chum to the Zelos.

Director Forester was watching from her office in Geneva, sitting back in her padded leather chair while Darren and Feng stood to either side looking at two screens hanging down from the ceiling; on one the recordings made from the Odyssey, on the other a live view of the Assembly and their reactions as they watched. Director Forester finally clicked both off with a press of a button on her desk and spoke in abrupt tones to the two men that now turned to face her.

"Observer is very impressed with the way that ship handled, but everyone that counts on *our* world is impressed with the Zelos."

"Enough to take Observer up on that offer?" Darren asked.

"Yes," she replied. "We will give Observer the design specs to the Odyssey for him to transmit to his creators, in exchange for which they will provide us with five thousand of their construction bots to do with as we please. They can also build a base in the middle of the ocean if they like, but I understand that doesn't happen until we have finalized our world government."

"The additional construction bots will speed up the building of the next ship," Feng put in. "The designs are based on the Odyssey anyway, just with a few additions like the hyperdrive and also being bigger. It shouldn't take us as long to get it built as for the Odyssey."

"Good then they can also work on adding a support fleet as well," Director Forester snapped. "One vessel, no matter how large, can still not be everywhere at once. We need to stake a defensive perimeter around our entire star system, and certainly our planet. All those fighters the Zelos have are bad enough, no telling any other weapons on board the carriers we hadn't seen them use yet, I'm certainly not going to assume that was the *only* fleet they have."

"Agreed, Director," Darren nodded. "I'll get right on with the new ship. Feng can help me out as before."

"You mean, when he's not looking around for our mysterious brainwashing psychopath out there," she reminded him with a sharp glare. "Agent Franklin is leading the task force for that, but from what I've seen she'll be needing one or both of you to help catch this guy once she finally has him cornered. I don't doubt it will take the three of you just to tie him down without getting your brains dry-cleaned like Sir Roberts and the others. The Zelos are going to be actively hunting for us now, we don't need a second battlefront within our own lines. Now get out of here and get some work done."

A quick nod and both men left, leaving the Director to ponder her own strategies. It was hard to read the Director; they weren't sure if she was pleased at the ship's performance and subsequent addition of all the new construction bots, or displeased that their hand had been tipped in full view of the Zelos fleet. In the end, it was probably both.

Earth had just given the Zelos a bloody nose, but now the Zelos knew for certain of the Human presence.

CHAPTER TWELVE

WORLD UNITY DAY

April 17, 2060

"This is Hal Thurgood reporting live from Geneva Switzerland where preparations are well underway for the celebrations. As you know, World Unity Day is fast approaching and with it, Earth will finally be united. Celebrations are being planned all around the world but the biggest one will be here, the Capitol of Earth's new united government. The final signing of world unity by all the world's governments will be in Sweden and then it will be official: we will, at last, have peace in our time."

"Or at least here on Earth. We have known for a few years, of course, that there are malevolent aliens out there called the Zelos who will one day seek to overrun our world, but plans have long been in the works to prepare for that day. With the help of the small army of construction bots supplied by our Sataran friends somewhere out there, the successor to the Odyssey is ready for launch, with many of its support ships close behind. In fact, the first official test flight of the new ship is scheduled to coincide with World Unity Day. The new vessel is what has been designated as an 'Odyssey-class ship'; based on the general design of the Odyssey– essentially a large sphere– only a lot bigger and with the addition of what they are calling a

hyperdrive system which would make travel to the other side of the galaxy possible. Plenty fast, if you ask me. The new ship will be designated as the 'UES Orion', where the 'UES' stands for United Earth Ship. I think that about says it all: United Earth. This is Hal Thurgood reporting for Channel Six News from Geneva Switzerland."

Darren clicked off the vid news as he came out from his shower towel-drying his hair. Of course he knew more about what they were reporting, and was glad that the part about the Satarans was out in the open– a basic requirement to fulfill Observer's stipulations of unity, when you think about it. But he was equally glad that the full measure of what he and Feng had been involved with the last several years was not yet publically known. They still had a lot to do, including tracking down the mysterious head conspirator apparently able to twist people's minds, and that was best done on the sly.

He walked across his bedroom, tossing the towel onto his bed, when he saw the message light at his nightstand was blinking. Walking over, he pressed a button on his answering machine and watched as a video message appeared on the wall screen opposite his bed. It was his father, looking worried and a bit haggard.

"Son, you have to come over here to the house immediately. It's your mother."

Darren didn't need to hear anymore. In record time he was changed, hair combed, and ready to go. But he wouldn't be using a plane or car to get over to Florida. As urgent as his father looked, there was only one way: he teleported.

He appeared in the living room of his parents' Florida home. The bay-window view of the neighborhood behind him, anteroom through the left-hand side, then the fireplace with the mirror above its mantle, opposite wall with the couch and hallway entry on into the further depths of the house, right-hand side with the sliding glass patio doors. Robert Hildure was pacing before the fireplace when Darren appeared.

"Dad, what's wrong?"

His father gave a start at the sudden appearance then a shake of his head.

"Darren, one of these days you're going to give me a heart attack doing that."

"Sorry, but you made it sound important."

"It is," his father sighed. "Your mother's in the hospital and the doctor said it might be best if we got the entire family together. Darren, she's dying."

For several long moments, Darren could not say a word, could do little more than stand there.

"We knew it would happen some day when she refused the treatment," Robert continued into Darren's silence. "Well, that day has finally come. She's very old now, and unlike myself, is feeling the effects of all those years. Her body is just worn out. She told me that she wants to meet with each of us in private. Your two brothers and their wives are already on their way over there."

"I… I just can't believe it," Darren finally managed. "I just talked to her a couple of weeks ago."

"She's been very good at hiding how much her health has been slipping, son, but I'm afraid the time has come. If you're ready, I can drive the both of us over there right now."

"Of course, of course," Darren absently agreed. "It's still just… I can't believe it."

Darren noticed very little on the ride over, occupied with trying to reconcile the picture he held in his mind of his mother while he was growing up with the old lady she had become. He'd never really looked upon her as being old; in his mind's eye she would always be the young energetic mother he knew when he was six. But now as the car finally drove into the hospital parking lot, he was afraid of what he might see.

Darren was the youngest of three, and so the last to be invited in to see his mother. First there was his father and whatever personal exchange he had with his mother, then each of his brothers. In all, Darren waited for about two hours in the hall outside her hospital room, keeping quiet and trying not to make eye contact with any passing staffers. When the middle brother came out after his own thirty-minute private visit, signaling with just a nod in Darren's direction, then he would have to wait no longer. With an uneasy feeling in the pit of his stomach, he entered the room, letting the door drift closed behind him.

She was lying on the hospital bed hooked up to various machines and monitors, the blinds to the window partially drawn, the television hanging from the ceiling for her viewing switched off. Seeing her so weak and frail, like a withered representation of she who was supposed to be his mother, for a moment it was like looking upon a stranger; just any other old lady of indeterminate age. Then with a sudden resetting of his perceptions he saw true; this very old lady was still somehow his mother. Like any child, somehow throughout the years his mind had refused to see her thusly, always saw the younger woman he'd known, but now he was jolted into the full reality of it.

His mother lay before him, old and dying.

"Darren," she said in a near whisper. "Come, sit down. I have something I want to tell you."

Barely believing any of this was real, or at least afraid to, Darren pulled a chair over to her bedside and sat down, reaching out to hold one frail hand in both of his own.

"Hey Mom," he said, trying to force a smile upon his lips, "I heard you were a little under the weather."

"Nothing a funeral won't fix," she replied with a smile of her own. "I've already told your Dad that it's okay if he remarries should he find the right person. I don't want him to be lonely. It's been bad enough for him having to deal with an old lady like myself while he remains young and vital."

"Mom, don't speak like that. He loves you very much."

"I know, and this is the path that I've chosen, but listen carefully. I had a strange dream last night that you need to hear. I'm not sure if I believe in prophecies or seeing into the future or any of that, but considering all that's been going on the last couple of decades I'm not as willing to dismiss it as I once would have."

"Okay, I'm listening."

She took in a breath, Darren leaning in closer to make sure he heard every word, then began.

"In my dream you were fighting a very dangerous race; like man-sized monstrous bugs. There were a lot of spaceships involved; thousands of them. The Earth was severely damaged and millions of people had died, but so had millions of that strange race. I saw many large round ships, some of them with blue people flying them; or maybe they were robots or something, I'm not sure. Anyway, then I saw you and Feng each flying one of those big spaceships, along with five other ships fighting four vessels that looked kind of like dragonflies a few miles long."

"A light blue woman commanded one of the round spaceships. She was absolutely beautiful; very tall, green eyes, and long white hair. The strange thing was that there was no other living person on that ship, except those blue people-robots. I could see in her face that she was determined to destroy those dragonfly ships. The battle lasted a month before all the ships were gone."

"But I also saw a very small spaceship that looked as bright as a sun. It destroyed one of the large dragonfly ships all by itself. Then later I saw you and Feng in a different universe where apparently those strange creatures are living. After that, I saw you and Feng talking to a blue man who said he was over ten thousand years old. All three of you were talking to a small planet; a *living planet*. After that, I saw you, Feng, and that blue man having a machine inside your body; I don't know what it was doing."

"Finally, I saw you and Feng thousands of years later visiting many galaxies and different universes. Both of you looked the same as now but your bodies looked like they were glowing, as well as your eyes. Darren, I don't understand any of this, in particular the thousands of years and the different universe, but I was strongly compelled to tell you of my dream. I also saw your brothers not listening to you when the war with those strange creatures started and they perished, but their children and children's children were alive because they *were* paying attention to you."

"This vision was a gift, for it assures me that you will turn out fine, and because of that knowledge you should know that I die content. Just remember to take care of yourself, and don't worry about me. I'm fine."

"Mom, I... I don't know what to say. I... I don't suppose you saw anything about me getting married," he said with a slight sniff as a tear leaked from one eye. "Because Feng keeps rubbing it in that he's already on his second child."

"Yes, Darren" she said with a faint chuckle and grin, "but I am not permitted to talk about that. You'll just have to wait for the right time to come. Now what I have told you is for your ears only, and with this I give you a mother's blessing. In the name of Jesus Christ, Amen."

Darren bowed his head for a moment, trying perhaps to hide the sorrow growing upon his face, then felt his mother's hand slip out of his to gently pat him on the head.

"Now go tell your father to come back in. The one benefit of this situation is I get to die seeing the exact same handsome young face that I married."

Darren left with a nod, one last kiss on her forehead before turning away. He left the room with nary a word, just a look and nod in his father's direction. It was three hours later when his father finally came out from that room, and from the dampness on his face and redness of his eyes, all knew that she had passed. A last visit into the room by Darren and his brothers for a last good-bye, the last sight they would ever have of she who had birthed them.

Never had they seen a face more peaceful, and yet strangely alive. Michelle Hildure passed, somehow knowing how it would all come out.

Darren had not finished grieving when he was called to the office of Director Forester. He was met there with Feng, who said not a word about what he immediately sensed of Darren's mood; he just gave his long-time friend the telepathic equivalent of a warm clasp of hands and left it at that as they entered into the Director's Geneva office. The Director was in her usual abrupt mood, her dark red afro curls trimmed even tighter against her head than usual, the slender woman wasting no time and getting straight into it the moment the door was fully closed.

More telling was the fact that Darren and Feng were not the only ones present for this meeting. A tall portly Russian with thick brown hair, wearing a suit with no tie and a heavy jacket and boots. A white man, American, his light brown hair partially balding up front, complexion a little on the pale side, wearing a neatly arrayed business suit. Then finally the elderly Chief Pinyin with his cane topped by the brass dragon's head. All three were already seated, with two waiting empty chairs to complete the semicircle before the Director's desk.

"Darren, Feng; this is Boris Gurov, Russian Intelligence Chief," Forester began, indicating the Russian. "Tim Whittier, Director of the National Counter-Terrorism Center back in the States. And you know Chief Pinyin, the Chinese Intelligence Chief. Have a seat, gentlemen."

"This looks serious," Feng remarked on his way to his seat.

"My friend," Boris said with a slight trace of a chuckle, "you have no idea."

"As you know," the Director began as the pair took their seats, "the final signing is in Sweden, where Agent Franklin is in charge of security."

"A very excellent choice," Darren agreed.

"One of our best," the Director stated. "Every precaution taken, her agents at all key locations, electronic monitoring and sensors, the works."

"I sense an 'and yet' coming up," Darren quipped.

"And yet," the Director continued, "every single one of the foreign ministers present for the signing has vanished. Despite an inhuman level of security, they're all gone."

"The only thing found in each of their rooms was a note," Tim Whittier now spoke up, passing a slip of paper over to Darren. "It states that unless the world government is stopped from forming that they will all be killed, then the Presidents and kings of the world will be next to be kidnapped. My people have been all over this, as have Gurov's and Pinyin's, not to mention Agent Franklin. Not a thing was found, no way anyone could have gotten in or out with those delegates."

"The Director here tells us that the two of you are uniquely qualified to investigate such a matter," Boris Gurov continued. "Is there something about a couple of old astronauts that has been kept out of the popular press that can help us out?"

"There might be," Darren shrugged.

"Besides having led the design and construction teams for our new spaceships," the Director tersely explained, "Darren and Feng are my top two operatives."

"And just how good would that make you?" Tim asked.

"When we came in, Darren and I had already determined that the both of you are not working for certain mysterious forces we have spent many years tracking," Feng replied. "As well as little details like the fact that Boris likes his Vodka… particularly when toasting someone's execution?"

"Partially right," Boris said with a jovial chuckle, "but nice to know your abilities have their limits. If it is someone whose death I did not really want to order, then I give them the toast they deserve. I recently had to do that before this incident arose and was still thinking of it."

"We can only pick up surface thoughts," Darren told him, "but that should be good enough to track down the delegates."

"The two of you have a reservation at the Radisson Blue Royal Viking Hotel in Stockholm," Forester told them. "Your plane is waiting on the tarmac right now."

"Then we'd better get to it," Darren said as he and Feng stood up. "By your leave, Director. Gentlemen."

A collective exchange of nods and Darren and Feng quickly left, off to the plane that would take them to Stockholm Sweden.

Their room at the Radisson had a panoramic view of Stockholm, courtesy of a multi-paneled glass wall; the rows of large square buildings built like a wall nearly right up to the water's edge, peppered through by the occasional steepled tower. It was Summer in the ancient city, the sky clear, the weather crisp and snow-free. Classic old-styled luxury for a two-bedroom suite, accented with such modern amenities as a three-dee television in each bedroom, free Net access, and a plate of complimentary croissants waiting for them on the small table in the common room by the window. The first thing the two men did, of course, was change out of their travel clothes to more casual attire fit for seeming tourists.

"You wouldn't believe this bathroom, Feng," Darren called out as first to enter the facilities. "Free packets of bath salts."

"The croissants aren't bad either," Feng called back as he took a bite out of one of them. "I think we should start our investigation with some basic questioning. Maybe we can prod a few thoughts to the surface that way, catch a conspirator or two."

"You think it's the same one as before?"

"People vanishing in the middle of all the security that Amelia arranged? I'll place money on it."

Darren was just coming out of the bathroom, face washed and wearing a fresh shirt, when they both stopped. The same telepathic voice was calling out to them both.

Darren, Feng; this is Agent Franklin. Don't say another word, just come down to the pool. Your room is bugged.

Not another word did they say, save in the way of misleading ones.

"I could use a bite to eat," Feng stated. "Restaurant first?"

"Fine by me."

Quickly both men changed then headed out to the elevators. It was not long before they found themselves in the hotel pool area.

It was done up to look like a grotto, with walls made to look like old stone well-worn by centuries of dripping water, changing areas entered through other cave doors, towel service from a desk carved out of the stone, and even a steam room accessed through a glass door at the far end of the cave. The room was filled with the noise of a dozen people splashing around in their swimming trunks, which made the presence of a young black-Chinese lady in a dark pantsuit and hair tied up into an efficient bun a bit off-putting and out of place. Nevertheless, no one seemed to pay her any mind, nor the two fully-clothed gentlemen entering to join her where she sat in a small cabana-cave attached to the main pool.

"Okay Amelia," Darren began in a quiet tone as they joined her at the round wooden table, "what's going on? No one even knows we're here, much less where we're staying."

"I know," she replied. "I arranged the rooms personally under presumed names, and yet they're bugged."

"The question is," Feng stated, "do we leave the bugs in or not."

"We could control what they hear if we do," Darren replied.

"Exactly my thoughts," Agent Franklin told them, "that's why I left them in. Just audio bugs, though. No video."

"Of course not," Darren supplied, "the greater bandwidth required would be easier to pick up. Okay then, let's start with the basics."

"I have a list of all security personnel, both local and supplied by each delegation present, all waiters and service personnel even in the vicinity, and anyone else that could have been present or nearby at the time. They've already been interviewed by Swedish police, and myself, but I figured the two of you can dig out a few things none of them would *think* saying."

"What's the matter, Amelia," Feng grinned, "the thought-reading not up to par yet?"

"Getting better," she shrugged. "I can pick up a few surface thoughts if they're focused on just one thing and not actively trying to block anything. You two are the expert mind readers and time is of the essence."

"Shouldn't take us more than a couple hours to go through them all," Darren decided. "Just mention a couple of prompting words like 'delegate' or 'kidnapping' and see what it reflexively brings to mind. What else you got?"

"Security footage. Problem is, each delegate vanished straight from his hotel room and cameras don't cover inside them."

"We'll just have to see what we can find," Darren told her. "Okay, Feng you get with Amelia on the security footage and I'll start with the interviews. First thing unusual you see, send me a direct message and I'll narrow in on any suspects."

"Got it," she replied.

"How come you get to do the interviews and I have to watch all the boring security footage," Feng said as all three stood up.

"Because," Darren shrugged, "I'm more of a people-person."

"Oh come on, if you were a real people-person then you'd have a wife by now and a couple of kids."

"Just *had* to rub it in, didn't you?"

"Any chance I can get," Feng grinned.

The three left the cabana, the two men exchanging good-natured jabs while Agent Franklin kept an eagle eye out on even the most innocent onlooker that might happen to be gazing in their direction.

While Darren walked by one line of people after another, asking them leading questions to get them to think of anything that might incriminate them that he could then telepathically pick up on, Feng was in Hotel Security with Agent Franklin reviewing security footage following every single one of the delegates into and out of their rooms. They sat at one of several three-monitor stations in the busy room, with Agent Franklin at the keyboard as Feng's eyes scoured the passing footage for every shred of detail.

"That's the minister from Brazil going into his room," Agent Franklin explained of the current piece of footage, "and the last time anyone saw him."

"Okay, keep on that but fast forward for a few minutes' worth."

She pressed a key and the video went into fast-forward mode, the counter in the corner of the screen displaying the passage of time. At the two-minute mark another came onto the scene.

"Hold it right there," Feng told her. "Who's the woman?"

"Maid," Agent Franklin said after a moment. "I guess she's entering to clean up."

"While someone is still in the room? And how'd she get past security anyway? Weren't they supposed to have people at the elevators and stairwells?"

"The hotel staff were all cleared through security, as well as searched every time they passed by a checkpoint."

"Hmm... Okay, let's see the next one."

"Delegate from Finland," she said after a moment as a new video replaced the old one. "Into his room and again, never seen again."

"Okay, fast-forward a few minutes."

She did so and once again a maid was seen entering the room about two minutes later.

"Hold there," Feng told her, bending closer to the monitor to study the image. "It looks like the same maid. Well, I suppose they only have just so many people on their staff cleared through security. Let's see some more."

She called up the footage showing the delegate from England entering his room, and once again a maid came two minutes later. France and again a maid. Italy, China, Russia, all the same. Finally, Feng had Agent Franklin display a freeze-frame picture of them all side by side, each picture held at the point of the maid knocking on the door and entering.

"Same maid in every single case," Feng stated. "Who is she?"

Agent Franklin immediately started typing, first having the computer draw a square around her face then flashing by a stream of a hundred other faces in a small window next to it.

"Running facial recognition against the hotel employee database," she said as she worked. "And... Got a hit. Isabella Jacobsen. Age forty-five, employed here for the past year, no prior work history, and also no record of who did her job interview."

"That's unusual," Feng mused. "Okay, get an enlarged picture of her from the video and the employee database. I'm contacting Darren. And see if you can find out where she is now."

Darren, meanwhile, had been spending the morning walking by lines of suspects in the plush hotel lounge area, his mind briefly grazing across the surface of their thoughts then moving on. He was nearly to the end of the last of them when he turned to the hotel manager walking by his side.

"Is this everyone?"

"It should be," the prim-looking hotel manager replied. "Wait, there is one lady not present. I believe the police said she might have been kidnapped."

"Missing? Why didn't you tell me that earlier?"

"I was just informed of it myself a few minutes ago. I assure you, it was not my intention to–"

Before the man was finished explaining, Darren held up a hand for quiet and looked off into the distance. It was Feng's mind-voice he heard now.

Darren, I think we got our lady. Bringing down a picture of her to work from. Her name's Isabella Jacobsen. See if you can detain her.

"This missing lady," Darren then said to the manager, "would her name happen to be Isabella Jacobsen?"

"Jacobsen... Why yes, I believe it is Miss Jacobsen. Reported missing not more than an hour ago. Why?"

Darren met Feng and Agent Franklin at a point midway down a hall leading out of Security, Feng with a couple of printed pictures in one hand, both men in a near run to get to the other. Agent Franklin was already quietly talking into a cell phone as the two men met.

"This is Isabella," Feng said, showing the pictures.

"Reported missing a short time ago. Police think it's a kidnapping, but we don't believe that, do we?"

"She was at the room of every single delegate just before they disappeared," Feng told him. "No sign of what she did to them or how."

"We'll set up a search at the airport and every bus and train station in the city. No, scratch that. In the *country.* Somehow, she managed to spirit away every delegate under everyone's noses, I'm not going to put anything past her. Agent Franklin."

A few last words spoken into her phone then Amelia shoved it back into a pocket and gave her report.

"Her picture is being uploaded into the facial recognition programs for every security camera in Europe as we speak. If you want to cover the rest of the planet that'll take a little longer; about another hour or so. Someone complained about the cost but I just told them to speak to the Director. That shut them up."

"The lady *is* efficient," Feng remarked to Darren of Amelia.

"Better make it worldwide then," Darren decided. "Something tells me this is going to be harder than we think. Oh, and tell them–"

"The facial recognition will be able to see past any makeup or disguises," she replied.

"I'm beginning to think we've all been working together a bit too long," Feng said with a sly grin. "It's almost like we can read one another's minds around here."

Three days went by of tense waiting. When no hits came from anywhere in the Stockholm area that first day, they finished up questioning the hotel about everything they knew of Miss Jacobsen and left to make their command center back in the bowels of Geneva Switzerland, down the hall from the piercing gaze of Director Forester. A room of computer terminals, video monitors, international communications uplinks, and one well-used coffee maker. Agent Franklin's people were monitoring video and security feeds from around the world twenty-four hours a day, while Darren and Feng poured through every computer archive they could think of in an effort to discover more of Miss Jacobsen.

Then on the third day, one of Agent Franklin's security team at the terminals called out a hit.

"Got her at a bus station in Mexico. Local cops saw her but she escaped."

"She seems to have a knack for that," Darren said as he sampled the coffee maker's bitter-tasting product. "Have the locals focus their search on every outgoing bus from that location."

"Yes, Colonel."

It would be another two days before the next sign of her appeared.

"Paris France," another agent called out from his terminal. "Another bus stations"

"Nothing from the airports?"

"No, Colonel."

"Not just Paris, but for *any* airport in France."

"Nothing sir. This is the first hit from anywhere we've had in a couple of days."

"Hmm, odd. Okay, print up the exact location, I'm teleporting over there immediately."

And teleport he did, but as he looked through the Persian airport, quickly scanned about for any traces of her mind, he would find nothing.

The next day it was a warehouse in Madrid Spain. The building was surrounded and sealed off by the local police within fifteen minutes. But even after a full two hours of searching, complete with dogs to sniff out any trace of a scent and Darren appearing there to scan around for any thinking minds unaccounted for, they would still find nothing.

"Feng," Darren said as they later walked back into the command center, "we're missing something. This lady is appearing all over the world but no facial recognition hits at any of the airports, escapes right through any police net we set up… Feng, you know what I think?"

"That she's like you," Feng sighed. "A teleporter, and a very good one."

"Coupled with some skill at makeup and disguise, she's very tricky to catch. Okay, here's the way we need to handle this then. The next time we have a hit, not one local cop is to go anywhere near her. It'll just be the two of us in disguise checking her out first. Maybe we can catch her off guard."

"The only way," Feng agreed.

"Colonel, General," it was Agent Franklin, entering from behind them into the room with an electronic clipboard in one hand, "finally got the scoop on Miss Jacobsen."

"Conference room," Darren ordered. "Now."

Across the command room they quickly moved, past rows of agents staring at screens and speaking into comm-links with other security personnel from around the world, then through a door at the end. Just a small conference room with a single large screen up on the far wall, a long table, and some chairs. Agent Franklin wasted no time with sitting down, just swiped one finger across the screen of her clipboard in the direction of the wall monitor to echo the information she had across the big screen. A picture of Isabella Jacobsen appeared, looking several years younger than her photo from the hotel in Sweden, alongside it a list of pertinent facts which Agent Franklin began to read off.

"Isabella Jacobsen is her real name, but her face was covered in some very good makeup because her age is thirty-three not forty-five. Born in Arizona and has a PhD in engineering from Brigham Young University."

"Definitely a bit more than a maid," Darren stated.

"It gets better," Agent Franklin continued. "Up until a year ago she was working for NASA. Her grandfather's family came over from Ireland and settled in Phoenix Arizona when her father was eight years old. After high school her father went to Arizona University where he majored in criminal law and eastern languages. From there he was hired by a large law firm in Salt Lake City Utah, then three years later was recruited by the CIA. He bought a small one family house in Provo Utah about thirty miles south of Salt Lake City. Two years later he married a girl from Provo and one year after that Isabella Jacobsen was born. Her mother passed away when she was three years old, but four years later her father married the live-in nanny, named Erica, who then took care of Isabella while he was traveling. Isabella loved her stepmother like her real mother. Then three years ago Isabella's father was killed in a car accident. Her stepmother was interviewed and said that she hasn't seen Isabella for the past year, which considering she has a history of checking in on a regular basis to make sure how everything is going, is highly unusual."

"Definitely not terrorist material," Feng stated. "In fact she's about as close to the exact *opposite* of one as you can get. To quit a perfect job like that out of the blue to go become a terrorist?"

"You haven't heard the icing on the cake," Agent Franklin stated. "NASA sent her to Mars for the complete treatment a few years ago."

"And I'm betting she came back with a teleporting gift," Darren said with a look of inspiration. "and from the looks of things as good as mine, which makes her very dangerous indeed."

"It still doesn't make any sense," Feng said with a shake of his head. "To so completely change like that overnight?"

"Not making much sense to me either," Darren admitted, "but we won't know more until we catch her. Amelia, go ask the Director to have some facial recognition cameras installed within good views of every angle of her stepmother's house in case she goes in for a visit. I'll send a message to our friend Observer to be ready with his teleport equipment and a containment facility. The instant I have my hands on her, I want Observer to teleport the both of us straight over to Mars."

"Right," and with a nod Agent Franklin turned and left for the Director's office down the hall.

The next few days Darren spent teleporting from place to place as Isabella was seen. One day she was spotted in Munich Germany and Darren followed only to lose her again. The next day it was Paris, then back to Spain where he was delayed with disarming a bomb she had planted at a train station. Then it was London where he lost her in a shopping center. At last, though, Agent Franklin's people reported a sighting from the facial recognition cameras positioned outside the home of Isabella's stepmother.

When Darren and Fen appeared out of a nearby alley down the street from the small ranch-style house with the covered carport, it was in suits and riding bicycles.

"Just remember, we're Mormon missionaries and this close to BYU no one slams the door in the face of a missionary. I got my PhD there, so I know how things go around here."

"So they answer the door," Feng said, "then the second she shakes your hand–"

"Then we got her."

"And this makeup job your friend did on us? Think they'll really think we're a couple of college kids?"

"At least for as long as it takes to shake hands. Now come on…"

It was around six PM when they rang the doorbell, just in time for dinner in most homes. When the door opened, they could see it was an elderly lady in her sixties who answered it, in the room behind her a partial view of a much younger lady.

"Oh, such fine young men," the older woman beamed. "But can I see our identification, please? We've had a few young men coming through our neighborhood that weren't missionaries."

"Of course," Darren replied, producing a fake ID. A quick glance seemed satisfaction enough.

"Well, you two seem okay. Come on in, you're just in time for dinner."

"Well, thank-you," Darren replied with a warm smile. "We wouldn't want to intrude."

"No intrusion at all," the lady said as she led them into the living room. "Oh, this is my daughter, Isabella."

"A lovely name, Isabella, for a lovely lady."

As Darren reached out a hand, both he and Feng discreetly scanned the surface thoughts of Isabella. Pleasant thoughts, routine; almost too routine. Her face matched up exactly with that of the one they had been chasing, and yet no sign of any of her nefarious activities in her thoughts.

"Have you ever traveled outside of Utah, Isabella," Feng asked. "Say, to Europe?"

"Not at all," she smiled, reaching now for Darren's hand.

Not a single thought to betray her, Darren thought to Feng. *Nothing of the travels we know she's been doing, which means either she has the most disciplined mind around, or–*

Or, it's been altered, Feng finished for him. *You take Isabella, I'll handle her mother.*

Darren grabbed onto the offered hand for a shake and an instant later both were gone. Before the stepmother could do more than gasp, however, Feng quickly placed two fingers to her forehead and froze her in place.

"Isabella had to return to work suddenly, so we left when she did."

Feng left her in a daze, not to snap out of it until he was well gone. A shake of her head, uncertain smile, then she sighed and went about getting dinner for herself.

Isabella found herself locked in a small room with only a monitor to show her a view of the Martian terrain outside. She was confused, angry, and puzzled when there was a knock on the door prior to it sliding open. There stood Darren and Feng, bereft now of their disguises.

"Hello Isabella, my name is Darren Hildure."

"And the other is General Feng," she finished for them. "Yes I know the faces of the two most famous astronauts on Earth, but what I don't know is why I've been brought to Mars so suddenly. You could have just sent me a message or something instead of kidnapping me."

"She really doesn't know," Feng observed. "Isabella, when was the last time you worked for NASA?"

"Silly question coming from the two of you, I still work there. Just been on a vacation the last three weeks."

"And can you tell me today's date?" Darren asked.

"It should be around July twenty-fourth right now."

"And what year?"

"Another stupid question, it's twenty fifty-nine, of course."

"I'm afraid you're off by about a year," Darren told her. "It's twenty-sixty. You can check any calendar or newsfeed."

"What?! But that's impossible. How can I have missed an entire year? I was just at NASA a few weeks ago."

"Actually, you were in Sweden a few weeks ago," Darren supplied, "working as a maid for the past year."

"What?! Why on Earth would I work as a maid? What is going *on* here!"

"Take it easy, Miss Jacobsen," Darren said as he carefully approached. "First know that there is no teleporting out of here, not with what Observer has set up."

"Tele– You *know!*

"Yes. You have the same ability that I have, just as Feng and I can both read minds well enough to know how confused you are. In fact, we can see now that you never told anyone of your ability out of fear of ending up in some government lab."

"Someone has been using you," Feng continued before she could voice any objections. "There is someone out there who is very skilled at placing blocks in people's minds to not just alter their memories but their loyalties as well; make them do whatever he wishes of them."

"You mean like brainwashing?"

"We're not entirely sure how it works," Darren told her. "Only that this person has used you to kidnap all the delegates from the World Unity Conference."

"The Unity Conference," she gasped. "But that's horrible. Are they all okay?"

"We don't really know, which is why we need your help."

"Anything," she replied with honest sincerity written on her face. "But I don't remember any of what you speak of."

"Which is why Observer is going to help us remove that hypnotic block so you can regain your memories and tell us what's going on and where the delegates are being held."

"Of course," she agreed.

"But first," Feng said, producing a small pill as he walked over to the single sink in the room to prepare a glass of water, "we need to give you something to relax. We have no way of knowing what other suggestions might be implanted within you."

"I… understand," she sighed. "Oh this is such a nightmare. I wish I was dreaming."

"For all we know, Miss Jacobsen," Daren told her, "dreaming is exactly what you may have been doing the past full year…"

She lay on one of Observer's learning machine couches in his control room, a metal helmet placed around her head while Observer viewed the alien script that was flashing out across the wall above his obsidian control panel. Darren and Feng stood to either side of the unconscious woman waiting for the diagnosis.

"The person who altered her memories is quite skilled," Observer was saying, "which makes it even more puzzling that such a person exists and yet I have no record of anyone with such abilities coming out from the evolution machine."

"Can you restore her memories?" Darren asked.

"Easily, now that I have her here. She will, of course, remember all that she was made to do, including things she may not want to remember."

"We already talked to her about it," Feng told him, "she wants it all back, no secrets."

"In that case, it will just take a couple of minor adjustments…"

A couple of projected controls carefully turned in place as they hovered above the control board, the flow of colors in the alien graphics altering in small degrees, then as if in a dream, Isabella began to stir. Soft muttered words at first then more audible, the sharp ears of her observers, not to mention some recording devices built into the room, picking up every last syllable.

"Met him at NASA… Said he is my new master. Suddenly wanted to do everything he told me. Phil… Phillipe Moreau."

"At last," Feng said in a harsh whisper, "we have a *name!"*

"Mid-thirties," she continued in her dream-state daze, "short blond hair a little spikey, medium height…"

"If you like," Observer offered, "I can capture a picture of what the man looked like from her memories."

"Do it," Darren snapped. "Isabella, tell us about Phillipe."

"Said he'd been to Mars just like me."

"The delegates," Darren prompted, "where are they?"

"Northern Iran. Mosque in the city of… Gorgan. Catacombs underneath."

Slowly Isabella then began to open her eyes, the look within them filled with the horror of full recollection.

"I remember it all now. I kidnapped all those people, planted bombs for him… It's just *horrible.*"

"Easy there, Isabella," Feng said, laying a hand lightly to her shoulder, "this man has been giving us a lot of trouble over the years, now thanks to you we finally have a name."

"And a picture," Observer said as a letter-sized piece of paper appeared on the panel next to his set of virtual controls. He picked up the picture and handed it off to Darren who took immediate charge.

"Same guy that's affected Sir Roberts and all the rest I bet. Observer get a message off to Director Forester telling her about this development. Tell her that she needs to get a full squad over to Iran to free those delegates. After that I'd like to hide them up here, if that's alright with you, Observer. They need to be protected until we can apprehend this Phillipe Moreau."

"Of course, Colonel Hildure."

"And have your med-bots standing by just in case. Feng, the public doesn't know any of this yet and we still need to keep up with the celebration schedule. My teleporting ability will allow me to track this guy down, but someone needs to command the Orion when it launches."

"I'll be on it," Feng promised.

"I'll help you too," Isabella offered as she carefully sat up. "I need to make amends for what that monster made me do."

"You're a teleporter, not a telepath," Darren reminded her, "I stand a better chance of resisting him."

"I guess you're right," she sighed. "If he controlled me once he could do it again."

"You'll stay up here on Mars for now and tell Observer anything else we might need to know. You're the only one that's been down in those catacombs."

"I'll draw a map."

Immediately she was on her feet, racing over to one of Observer's control panels to draw the map with a few deft passes of her fingers over the panel. While she worked, Darren went over the plans with Feng.

"We have a name and a picture. I'll ask Forester to put both into the facial recognition system. First place his face pops up I'll be there."

"Then meanwhile I'll be on the Orion for a very public event for Phillipe to keep his attention on."

"Just don't forget to test out that hyperdrive. We spent a lot of work on that. Okay Observer get ready to teleport me back to Earth. I'll have this guy tracked down and captured before Feng here gets back from his little joyride."

"Oh, that sounds like a bet," Feng grinned. "Dinner at that snooty place in Paris you're always trying to get me to says the Orion makes a milk-run to the galactic rim and back before you have this guy in custody."

"Done."

They parted on a quick handshake.

By the time Darren was back in Forester's office, the mosque in Iran was being raided by a combination of Iranian troops and Forester's people. Meanwhile the worldwide celebrations had begun, fireworks going off in all major cities, as they awaited the live televised signing that will unite the Earth at last; an event as eagerly awaited as that of the launching of the Orion as it lifts up into Mars orbit with Feng at the helm and Captain Eva Gardena next to him.

Nearly lost in all this glorious celebration was the suicide bomb that went off in Rome, killing the Italian President. The bomber was one of the president's own security guards, but with a strange glazed look in his eyes.

While the world celebrated and Italy mourned, while two caskets for the Italian president and his wife were being interred, a third casket was being shipped off to the States. An American had been killed in that same blast while on vacation in Rome. The casket made it through

Customs in amazing time, arriving in Washington International Airport by fast private suborbital jet two hours later. A driverless hearse drove the casket straight past the turn-off for Arlington National Cemetery and did not stop. Then past a funeral home and two more cemeteries and still did not stop.

It was only once it had arrived in the back of the Veteran's Hospital did it finally stop. Four men with more the look of security personnel than orderlies slid the casket onto a gurney, but it was not the morgue that they would be bearing it to. Into a freight elevator and down into a subbasement clean-room with a full range of medical equipment they went, careful to avoid all contact with any other hospital personnel. There the casket was opened and the body taken out and put onto a medical table. Two doctors in white medical smocks worked on the supposed corpse for twenty minutes before it began to stir, the body's eyes to flicker open.

A man with short spikey blond hair, a strong but nimble looking body, skin a dirty white, and a vicious glint to his sharp blue eyes. He was dressed as a normal American tourist, his clothes casual and nothing of wealth about them, yet as his eyes flickered open and he became aware of his surroundings, the doctors and strong looking guards there all dropped to one knee with heads bowed in respect.

"Master Moreau, we have revived you as planned," one of the doctors stated. "You are in Washington D.C. just as you wanted to be."

Slowly he sat up, looking down at those kneeling around him, his lips hesitantly curling up into a demented grin, his voice sounding like some crazed combination of an orator and a madman.

"Excellent. The time has come to fulfill the wishes of my divine masters. Isabella is lost to us now, but I can still move forward with my plan. Then once the President is dead, their world unity will be worthless. Chaos will reign and the Coming will begin."

As one the kneeling men looked up, the doctor who had spoken leading a chant with raised right fist and a single name called out three times, which the others there repeated in unison.

"Moreau! Moreau! Moreau!"

CHAPTER

THIRTEEN

CHASE

April 24, 2060

Darren was once again standing before Erica Forester, she with her large oak desk, two flat screens, and plush leather chair, the cherry-wood bookcase and its bound contents still behind her. He was dressed in desert fatigues and still looking a little dusty, a fact which earned a sour look from the Director as he made his report.

"We went in with a hundred local soldiers and about twenty of our own people. I was in constant telepathic contact with Isabella Jacobsen the entire time. Her map was very helpful but there are just some things about those catacombs that you need a live person advising you."

"Get to the point," the Director snapped, "did you find the delegates?"

"Yes we did, but I guess Phillipe got wind of our capture of Miss Jacobsen because his people were just starting to move them out. And it looks like his goons were under the same mental programming as the others we've encountered, because one of them driving a van loaded with four delegates, drove himself off a short cliff the minute he saw the troops attacking. Even a few of the delegates tried to take their own lives. Fortunately most of them were drugged up and semi-conscious at best. Still, it was all the men and I could do to hold them down until Observer could arrange transport. A total of eight delegates died from either the actions of their captors or their own hands."

"Yes, this is all becoming tiringly familiar," the Director sighed. "I take it they're on Mars now?"

"With a room that my people have quickly done up to resemble the one in Sweden where the signing is supposed to occur. I asked Observer to have his med-bots treat each of the delegates for any medical problems, as well as helped him examine them for psychic influences, but they're okay now. In fact, they should be starting the signing ceremony right about now. I've arranged a downlink with Observer, so it looks like it's being broadcast straight out of Stockholm."

"Good. And the general public is none the wiser. Excellent except for one small detail… You *could* have cleaned yourself up a bit before coming in to make this report."

"Sorry, Director," he said to her sour glare, "but I wanted to get started immediately on tracing down Phillipe Moreau before he can do any more harm."

"I appreciate the enthusiasm, Colonel, just not the dust on my carpeting."

A last look before tapping a couple of keys in the keyboard on her desk to call up a display on one of her monitors which she then began to read off.

"Phillipe Moreau, born in Paris France but grew up in Egypt. Got a degree at Harvard Law School and is on Observer's list of people that have been to Mars for the full treatment."

"And apparently came out as a strong telepath able to influence people's minds, and from what I witnessed, able to control them from a distance."

"All very unsettling, which is why we need a plan to capture this monster immediately."

She punched another key then turned one of her screens around for Darren to see. It held a split picture taken from a news feed. On the left a man in presidential splendor on the steps of some ancient Roman structure with his retinue, on the right after the bomb blast.

"While the worldwide celebration was just starting to kick up and you were on Mars getting the delegates looked over, a bomb took out the president of Italy."

"I heard."

"Did you hear that the bomb was carried by one of his own guards? A man that has been in his service for about a decade. Loyal to a fault, until the day he decided to strap a bomb around his chest. Now take a close-up look at one of the people in the crowd."

She tapped a finger directly on the screen to one of the faces in the crowd and immediately the picture zoomed in, revealing a man with short spikey blond hair.

"Philippe Moreau," Darren lightly gasped. "I supposed I shouldn't be surprised."

"According to news reports, this was supposed to be a man by an entirely different name on vacation from America. Report is that he was killed in the blast and his body shipped back to the United States."

"Killed by his own bomb? He's not that stupid."

"I had the flight traced," she continued, turning the monitor back around. "It landed in D.C. but after that all sign of the coffin and the body it supposedly carried disappeared. The crew of the plane it was on don't even remember there *being* a coffin on board. Darren, Phillipe smuggled himself into the nation's Capital, and it's not too hard to guess what his next target is."

"He's hoping to derail things by killing the President."

"And with his abilities he could do that just by asking the President to do the job himself, or set up another country by having some foreign minister do the job. Darren, is there any way of protecting against telepathic mind control? Anything that Observer can tell us or anything in your experience?"

"Strong magnetic shielding of the right frequency range. Wang Wei Huang used oscillating magnetic fields to protect himself against my own telepathy."

"Then we'll rig up a magnetic trap of some sort to lure him into. Also, something around the White House. What would you estimate the range of his abilities to be at?"

"Well, I've seen that he can control people from very far away, but using my own abilities as a basis, he would still have to be relatively close to initially set up his control or reprogram someone's thoughts and loyalties. Say, no more than a few feet, maybe even touching, and by its invasive nature it should take a few minutes. Once the link is established, though, the range wouldn't make any difference; he'd be able to send them commands from anyplace on the globe, or just program them ahead of time for what he wants them to do. And he would only be able to focus on one mind at a time."

"So, he needs time, opportunity, and some privacy with his victim. Good; the man has limits. And how would someone like you or Feng fair against him?"

"Against another telepath… Well, it would probably come down to who's stronger willed, but now that I'm aware of him, he would lose all benefit of surprise. Are you suggesting we set up a trap for him?"

"Mister Moreau has already selected the bait himself. He made a play for the delegates, and wants to go after the President, but this time you and a squad of men will be there to catch him in the act. You'll be working with Agent Franklin and her team, since Feng is aboard the Orion."

"Yes, Director, but if you don't mind I have an idea but it's going to require contacting Observer."

"Anything you need to requisition," she replied with a fixed glare, "is cleared, just get moving on this. I want this bastard in a cell on Mars by the weekend."

"Yes, Director."

The look in her eyes, the determined set of her jaw, not to mention her rare use of a cuss word, Darren had no doubt as he gave his nod to leave that the Director was more determined than anyone to get this matter settled.

It's a pity we can't just use Erica as bait, Darren thought to himself. As strong willed as she is, Phillipe would probably bust a blood vessel trying to control her thoughts.

—∞—

The Orion was designed just the same as the Odyssey, but with some significant and rather obvious changes. For one thing, as it hovered in orbit about Mars waiting for the final order to be given, it was five times the diameter of the Odyssey. At five hundred meters across it was a monster large enough for the Odyssey to dock inside of. The layout of the bridge was like that of the Odyssey, populated by a full crew of officers in the same blue-green uniform and Earth Services patch, with Captain Eva Gardena in the Captain's chair, and Feng sitting in the one next to it making his first log entry.

April 24, 2060
Orion Log, First Entry.

The Orion is a very impressive ship, though from what Darren told me of his first encounter with the Zelos we'll be needing a few more of these. Still, it is a very good start. We have a crew of two thousand men and women, one thousand combat-bots that Observer helped us design, and a small army of maintenance bots, and provisions for a full year out in space. There's also a docking port to link up something the size of the Odyssey if the need arises.

Besides the increased size and firepower, there are two major changes from the old ship. First, Professor Hayden and her team, along with Professor McMullen and the boys out of NASA, have discovered a way of regenerating a warp engine while in flight. We won't have to either rebuild or eject an old engine core once it becomes too irradiated but instead now have a way to use the very process of the warp flight itself to keep it recharged. Kind of like how an alternator in a car keeps the battery charged up. We've already forwarded the design changes to Observer for his creators to use. The Odyssey is currently finishing up refits for the new warp engine design.

The other addition is our new hyperdrive. Warp is great for flitting about the neighborhood, as Darren would term it, but still impractical for getting to the other side of the galaxy or beyond, or wherever it is the Zelos may come from. It works by opening up what amounts to a wormhole to the designated coordinates then you're there a few seconds later. The obvious limitations are, of course, that if you don't know anything about where you're going then you run the risk of appearing in the middle of a star or something. That, and it may take some time for the hyperdrive engines to be ready for use again.

We're going to solve that first problem on this trip by using the hyperdrive to transport us to a destination clearly outside of a given star system then use the warp drive for local maneuvering. First, we'll use the warp drive to get to Alpha Centauri as our jumping-off point; if anything goes drastically wrong with the hyperdrive then there's nothing out in that star system to damage. From there we plan a hyper-jump of some seven hundred thousand light years, which should put us out into intergalactic space. Now ***that*** *will be exciting!*

To power both the new engines and the weapons, our power arrangements have changed from the Odyssey. Instead of antimatter, we're using a dark energy scoop to power everything. It's a lot more plentiful than antimatter and has the advantage that we can even scoop the stuff up while in warp. That's part of the reason why we're able to regenerate the warp engines now; it turns out that the Satarans hadn't thought to use dark energy in quite that manner before. Of course that's also part of the reason for the large size of the Orion; between the hyperdrive engines and the dark energy scoop, that's a lot of space taken up. Anyway, we'll see how it goes.

Oh, one last note. On the initial voyage of the Odyssey, Darren came across a planet being raided by the Zelos. Observer has since been in contact with his Sataran creators about the matter and according to him that world was a colony from a race out of the Lesser Magellanic Cloud. It had only been there for about a few centuries at the time, which explains the lack of information in Observer's old records. Nothing else is known about them or the reason for their presence in this galaxy. They appear to be rather secretive and wary of contact, which is unfortunate for them as the Satarans might have been able to at least warn them about the Zelos.

"Are we clear of all moorings and satellites?" Captain Gardena snapped out.

"Yes, Captain," Helm responded. "And course to Alpha Centauri is set."

"Excellent, Mister Thomson. General Feng, we are ready any time you wish to give the order."

Feng looked up from his log entry, pushing the arm of the chair with the screen away for a better look around. The dome and wall screens currently showed the space around them, with Mars behind them and stars all around. His face held the barely-restrained anticipation of a child on holiday, or about to open a Christmas present.

"I know this is old hat to you, Captain, but… that's space out there and we're about to go out in it."

"I don't think it will ever get old hat, General," she replied. "Particularly once we hit the second leg of our journey."

"In that case, you have a remarkable amount of discipline, Captain Gardena."

"So I have been told, General," she replied with the same level features, not cracking so much as a faint grin. "I am actually very excited inside."

He looked over and saw the same even features with not a speck of reaction upon them, and couldn't help but grin.

"Okay, take her out, Captain. And see if we can make it a little showy for the satellite cameras beaming this stuff back to Earth."

"I'll see what I can do, General," she replied, then turned back towards the pair of officers at the forward stations. "Navigator, our course is for Alpha Centauri. Helm, with a bit of flourish if you don't mind."

"Aye, Captain."

And so it would be seen, the Orion surrounded in a glow of its own energy, pulsing in a beat to its own music first red, then yellow, green, and blue. Faster the beat came the brighter it got, until a near constant visual thrum when it hit violet, then a single blinding flash absent of any known color, and it was gone. Nothing but a faint explosion of glitter tossed out by the firing of a couple of its guns for the world to see.

A cheer was heard around the world at this cosmic display of fireworks, as at that same moment the last signature was penned to the Unity papers. But the voyage of the Orion had just begun.

The man with the short blond hair combed into spikes walked down the rain-covered walkway with a large coat drawn about him and a hood over his head, to either side of him a pair of large muscular men, behind him a man in a white coat walking alongside a man with a crew-cut and a military uniform. It was late evening, dark and rainy, ahead of them a wide grassy lawn and beyond that the front facing of perhaps the most distinctive building in Washington D.C., or at least certainly for any military installation.

"My Lord," the big man to the right asked, "if we are here to kill the President, should we not be going to the White House?"

"That was my original plan," Phillipe Moreau replied, "but I have recently learned that he is in the Pentagon tonight. Even better, so are all those delegates. The broadcast from Sweden was faked; they've all been kept here at the Pentagon for safety the entire time. I'll not only get to kill the President but all those delegates as well."

"But how do you know this is true, my Lord?"

Here Phillipe simply pointed a thumb in the direction of the military man walking in step behind him.

"The General here confirmed it not more than an hour ago. He's going to get us in without a problem."

"But once the job is done, how will we get back out again, my Lord? We no longer have Isabella with us."

"While the General here is keeping everyone's attention on his efforts to kill as many people in there as possible, I'll be working my power on a convenient source of escape. General, who would you recommend?"

The General's eyes held the same fanatical look as the others, as Sir Roberts or Wang Wei Huang; a loyalty now alone for the one before him.

"An M.P. should do it, my Lord," he replied. "He'll be able to sneak you out to the motor pool or one of the secret emergency exits."

"See?" Philippe smiled. "Problem solved."

They came to the wide grassy lawn, a sidewalk to either side of it leading up to the front doors to the Pentagon itself. Ahead in the rainy dimness they could see armed soldiers lining the front, a few stationed along the walkways leading up to it, all of them in long black raincoats and wide-brimmed hats drawn over their heads as they stood at attention with rifles ready. Philippe pulled the hood of his own coat more over his head then motioned to the General.

"Please be so kind as to make sure we make it through unmolested. I'm sure there's any number of hidden gun emplacements we can't see as well as these soldiers."

"My credentials will get us through easily enough, my Lord. Then I can locate which room the President and delegates are in so that I may go in there and kill them."

"It would be easier with a bomb, my Lord," the large man to the left stated. "Guaranteed to take them all out."

"Yes, but with all the chemical sniffers that must be at work in that place and no Isabella to get us past them, we wouldn't get three feet before being picked up. We shall simply have to rely on the good General's handgun and anyone else I have time to pick up in there. General, after you."

He stepped aside to permit the General to walk out before him, then followed along with the rest of his people in a bold walk down the left-hand walkway, the General ignoring the first of the guards as he led the others direct to the Pentagon's doors. A long walk down, Phillipe keeping a discreet eye on the guards just in case. He couldn't see much of their faces, but then that meant they could not see much of his as well. All good.

Nearly to the front doors and the line of guards stationed there, when one in the middle of the line stepped forward.

"I.D.," the guard called out in a strong tone.

The General pulled out a plastic ID card hanging at the end of a chain looped around his neck and held it up next to his face as he gave a cold reply.

"General Taylor and party, now move aside, soldier."

At first the soldier did not move as he regarded the ID, then as he took his first step closer, from behind the General, Phillipe narrowed his gaze and raised up a hand in the soldier's direction.

"You are mine," Phillipe quietly intoned to himself. "I am your new Lord…"

"All systems reading normal," Helm called out. "Star mapping systems confirmed; we have arrived at Alpha Centauri."

Feng stood up from his seat, starting into a slow walk around to see the view now projected all around them. One star in full view, two more distant ones, the constellations not quite as he had known them. A grin slipped wide across his face, as indeed across the bulk of the bridge crew who had not been on Darren's first trip in the Odyssey.

"I'm actually here. Alpha Centauri. I can't believe it. Are there any planets around here? Maybe some of them are habitable. Oh the possibilities!"

The Captain let Feng revel in the moment for a bit, actually suppressing a grin of her own when no one was looking, before recalling the duty for which she was here to perform.

"General, I am told that once we have some more ships constructed that we may be sparing one to explore our immediate stellar neighborhood, but the mission currently at hand is to test out the hyperdrive. Or, do you not wish to see what intergalactic space looks like?"

For a moment Feng had lost himself in the glory of discovery until reminded of the reminder of an even greater event forthcoming.

"Yes," he reluctantly sighed, "you are right, of course. Science– uh, Miss Tanaka– what's the reading on any continuum ripples we've left in our wake?"

"Miniscule for the small distance involved," the young Japanese lady at the Science station replied. "The new engine design appears most efficient."

"Now that's funny," Feng grinned. "We're actually considering four light-years as a small distance. Okay, time for the big one. Captain, by your pleasure."

As Feng marched quickly back to his seat, Captain Gardena thumbed a button on the arm of her own chair and called out an announcement now heard throughout the entire ship.

"Attention all crew. We are preparing for hyperdrive jump. This will be the first field-test of the engine and we have no way of telling what manner of effect we'll feel. As such, everyone is to strap in and secure themselves. Engage all automatic emergency systems. Helm, ready the drive and countdown from thirty."

"Aye, Captain."

The Captain released the intercom button then did as Feng and others were already doing and buckled herself into her seat; full seat and shoulder harness just to be sure. A klaxon sounded off once throughout the ship, then the British-accented voice of Mister Thomson at the Helm began counting down.

"Hyperdrive engine warming up; launch in thirty, twenty-nine, twenty-eight..."

Every passing moment was a buildup of excitement for Feng, his every cell eager to fly through the stars, be as the ship itself and feel the hyperspatial winds. At twenty he could feel a static charge in the air, and at fifteen the exterior of the ship began to glow a bright white. By ten the view around them of space was starting to fog over, the stars themselves seeming to begin drawing visibly closer.

"...seven, six, five..."

The stars now started to race faster and faster in towards their common point of the Orion and with them farther stars previously unseen being pulled into view. All of space itself being sucked down into the singularity that the Orion was fast becoming.

"...three, two, one. Engage!"

Racing stars become a panorama of streaks and lines, space itself rushing inward until it all blends down into an explosion of white that encompasses all. For the very briefest of moments nothing but brilliance to challenge even the automatic polarizers, and then…

Existence once again.

For a moment Phillipe held his pose, his eyes narrowing in to hold the gaze of the one soldier, seeing beneath the hood to the eyes glaring impassively back at him. Eyes, as the soldier turned his head to regard the ones before him and seemingly Phillipe behind the General in particular, that looked to be a pupiless yellow.

"What's this," Phillipe puzzled to himself. "I can't sense a mind. Not in that soldier or… any of the others with him."

"Identity confirmed by facial recognition," the one soldier stated in a flat voice.

"Good," General Taylor began, "then you will kindly permit us to–"

The soldier's rifle immediately came up with an inhuman efficiency, aimed directly at the man with the short blond hair.

"Identity has been confirmed. You are Phillipe Moreau. Please surrender immediately."

The voice so flat sounding, and no mind that could be sensed for, then a chance gust of wind blew back the hat away from the face of one of the other soldiers, revealing no face of flesh and bone, but metal and plastic with brightly glowing yellow eyes.

"Shit," Phillipe swore, "some of Observer's robots! Protect your Lord!"

General Taylor immediately brought out his pistol and started firing, as did the two large men and the doctor in the white coat, forming themselves into a wall between their lord and master and the robotic soldiers before them. Coats were shrugged off as rifles brought to bear and now to see, much to Phillipe's horror, not a single living mind there for him to affect. Robots with the basic outlines of humans, with two legs and two arms, but little beyond that in appearance now that their disguises were gone. Bullets fired only to be ignored by the machines. The intruders had brought no heavier weapons than pistols with them, for Phillipe's main weapon was his mind.

But here there was no mind for him to affect.

While his mind-controlled minions fought to protect him, Phillipe started to back away, quickly looking for a way out.

"If Observer programmed you then you may not harm a living creature," he finally realized with a mad grin. "You may detain but not kill."

"No, but *I* sure can."

"Huh?"

"Sa!"

The martial cry came along with a pair of feet flying through the air as one of the soldiers shrugged off its coat to come leaping through the air. A soldier with exotic eyes and facial features a softly-hued black, her long hair tied back into a bun as she came feet-first into Phillipe's chest. He went down with a cry, rolling over with his opponent to finally land on his back with Agent Franklin sitting atop him, knees into his stomach and hands pinning his shoulders down.

"You are hereby arrested under authority of the new world government. Kidnapping, murder, heck we'll even make up a few new laws just to apply to *you.* Any last words before nap time?"

He said nothing, just looked up into her eyes with a malevolent grin.

"Now *you* have a mind, and as they say where there's a will, I get *my* way. I am your new Lord and master."

For a moment she held there, uncertain. Thoughts began to form in her mind, memories not her own that with each passing moment became increasingly harder to tell one from the other. She felt memories forming that she at first knew to be false but then became real. She… had always known him as her Lord and creator. He had… created her and now… came to reclaim her. There is nothing more important than his desires and safety. Those other memories of her life, *those* are the false ones, the lies.

She found herself standing up and backing away enough to allow her prisoner to quickly get back up to his feet. While his other minions were trying unsuccessfully to deal with Observer's robots, Phillipe found himself looking at a new minion, his gaze never leaving her own as now he reached up a hand to touch lightly against her temples.

"Agent Franklin, is it?"

"Yes, m-my... Lord."

"Better. Now to just get this fixed in place and maybe *you* can get me what I need."

"Yes I... No, I am supposed to capture–"

The struggle was written clearly across her face, a war to see which set of thoughts would be her own. A part of her knew that what this man was doing to her was wrong, that he was the most cunning criminal she had ever encountered, but another part was certain that it was Phillipe Moreau who had come to set her free from the tyranny placed into her mind by Observer and the others.

"You're a feisty one," he grinned, "well trained, but in the end it will do no good. They all succumb for I am the master, granted the power by the divine ones."

"Yes, my– N-no, you are Phillipe Moreau, you are..."

"Amelia, no!"

Another came bursting out from the line of soldiers by the front of the Pentagon, though this not robotic but quite human. A man with a strong frame and short dark-brown hair. He was running down the walkway with a pistol in one hand, frantically waving his free hand out for attention.

"Ah, that would be the good Colonel Hildure," Phillipe smiled. "I'd recognize his picture anywhere. Agent Franklin, he will be trying to invade your mind, but you will ignore it and instead *shoot* the Colonel. That's the one thing about getting one of strong enough will finally under my control, is not even the abilities of the Colonel or his friend will be able to get her back so easily."

Darren was twenty feet away and closing when he saw a blank-eyed Amelia Franklin slowly lifting up her arm and aiming it in his direction. He tried thrusting out with his thoughts to snap her out of it, but try as he might, standing so close to Phillipe there was nothing he could do to penetrate the psychic block around him. And to telepathically attack him directly? Maybe if he had Feng with him perhaps, but this one's mind was far stronger than anyone had feared.

"Good-bye, Colonel," Phillipe grinned.

Agent Franklin slowly began to pull back on the trigger.

Nothing around even of stars, at least not as they were used to seeing them. It took a few seconds for a confused crew to put things into perspective as they gazed about in wonder but then they saw it, Feng first to voice it. A single stellar body as large appearing as a full moon, but one like a flattened disc of stars.

"The Milky Way," Feng gasped.

Even Captain Gardena had forgotten her usual composure and slowly got to her feet to gawk along with everyone else. Space blacker than anyone there had seen it, save for that single sight they could perceive, that of their home galaxy. It was nearly a full ten seconds before anyone said a word.

"Someone record the date," Feng stated, "this is historic."

"I'll say," the Captain absently echoed, then remembered herself and sat back down in her command chair to resume the face of discipline. "Nav, sensor readings on anything available. Miss Tanaka, do I even have to ask if you're recording everything you can?"

"Already on it, Captain," she replied, her fingers flying across her controls. "Magnetic readings, stellar cartography, radiation, the works."

"Excellent," the Captain stated, turning to Feng. "General, how long do you want to stay out here before making the jump back?"

"Will forever be long enough?" he grinned. "First let's get some navigation beacons to set our bearings by. I know the Milky Way looks big from here and kind of hard to lose, but we're one hyper-jump away from being completely out of sight of it. One of the parameters of this mission is to help set up a practical coordinate system for future explorations."

"Captain," Miss Tanaka cut in, "significant continuum ripple reading about… twenty thousand light-years from here."

"How significant?" the Captain asked with a measure of suspicion in her tone.

"Well… is there a small galaxy around there we don't know about? Because that's what it looks like."

A swipe of hand across the controls and the sensor view appeared in a squared off section of the dome-screen, with one green dot as the Orion's position and a bright blinking dot for the mysterious object.

"Wrong position to be one of the Magellanic clouds," the Captain mused, "and far too close to be Andromeda. General?"

"Take us to within half a light-year of it, see what we got," he decided. "Maybe we've already discovered some new stellar phenomena."

"Right," she started. "Nav, set course for within half a light-year of that continuum ripple. Helm, engage warp drive when ready. Let's give the hyperdrive a bit more time to rest."

"Aye, Captain."

"Better use the hyperdrive again," Feng suggested. "Warp drive for this distance would take about two weeks and this might be a temporary phenomenon."

"Mister Simonson," the Captain said, turning her chair around in place to face the man with the light brown hair at Engineering station, "can the hyperdrive take it again so soon?"

"All looks fine, Captain. A short hop like this shouldn't tax it any."

The engineer was grinning at the word 'short', and even Feng couldn't help but smirk a little, but the Captain had regained her disciplined features and spun back around towards Helm with a nod. Mister Thomson responded with his fingers working the controls before him.

Once again the exterior began to pulse its way up through the visible spectrum, until with a final flash the stars in their view– or in the current case, galaxies– shrank down into a singularity for a brief moment before snapping back into normal view once again.

They were still outside the Milky Way, but now before them hung what might have been a glittering ornament of space. It might have been a normal star, except for its presence so far away from anything resembling a star system or gas cloud that it might have formed out of, until Miss Tanaka put it into perspective as she read off the data coming in.

"Judging from our estimated distance and our viewing arc, what looks to be a star would fill Jupiter's orbital. That radiance is bright enough for a star, but... Hmm, nearly all of it is concentrated on a relatively narrow band of frequencies. And all of it photon emissions, nothing really in the way of particle emissions."

"That's impossible," the Captain stated. "Stars don't work like that."

"Agreed," Miss Tanaka nodded, her eyes still fixed on the data floating above her station as it scrolled by, "but there's more. Enormous magnetic readings, but... no mass."

"What?!"

Feng was now on his feet, perhaps trying to see if the Science Officer was joking, but Miss Tanaka looked back at the General with as serious and confused an expression as he had seen.

"Confirmed, General. Whatever that is, it has no gravitational field whatsoever. No gravity, no mass."

"Impossible," Feng pondered, slowly sitting back down, "and yet here it is. What manner of object gives out light in so specific a range and no gravity?"

"General," the Captain suggested, "maybe it's not an object at all."

To Feng's wondering look, Captain Gardena called out to the Helm.

"Warp engines; bring us right up next to that thing. Miss Tanaka, see if someone can ready up one of the combat-bots for use as a probe."

"Yes, Captain."

"Course set, Captain."

"Engage."

A moment later the strange object began to grow with swift nearness, until it filled their view entirely before stopping.

"We're parked about a hundred thousand miles away, Captain," Helm reported.

"Launching robotic probe," the Science Officer announced. "Close-up data coming in now..."

All eyes were fixed on the screen as a new square carved itself out of the dome to display the reams of data now streaming in which the Science Officer interpreted for everyone there from her own station.

"...it seems to have a definite boundary; more so than any star should have. Like someone had drawn a line across space with a razor blade. Confirming no gravity, and the light, while bright, carries no heat that would be of harm to any vessel. Also picking up–"

Suddenly the viewing window disappeared, replaced by more of the surrounding view of space. Heads turned just as quickly but the Science Officer was just as puzzled.

"Captain, the probe just vanished."

"As in," the Captain replied, "something not simply flash-frying on the spot from temperatures at the core of a star?"

"Yes, Captain. The instant it passed the boundary of that thing, it was gone. But Captain... Now I'm picking up some telemetry from it. Sensor readings are still absent but we got her ID signal."

As the Captain and others pondered over this mystery, dawn was starting to break across the face of General Feng.

"Captain," he ordered, "set course straight into that thing."

"General?"

The Captain's expression flickered with more than a trace of disbelief.

"Have Helm keep a careful lock on our exact trajectory into that thing, but head right in. I think I know what it is."

"As you say, General," she conceded. "Nav, set a course directly in and keep a watch on our tail. Helm, engage when ready. Slow forward with all shields up."

"Aye, Captain. Slow forward, all shields engaged."

The Orion eased forward. Quite fast by any terrestrial measure of speed, but still far slower than its warp drive could handle. The object grew to fill their entire view, then nothing around them but light and a sensation of falling. Falling down an infinite well, until with a sudden popping they felt more than heard, the light vanished and they were in the darkness of intergalactic space once again.

"Nav," Feng immediately ordered, "confirm our position."

"Checking sir... Sir, there's– I don't understand it."

"Explain, Mister Subramanyam," the Captain ordered.

"Well, Captain... the Milky Way, it's gone. Oh, there's a galaxy out there, but it's not ours."

"Confirming," Miss Tanaka put in. "Long-range cartography recording the presence of distant galaxies, but none of them are placed as the ones we know of should be."

Confusion was settling itself across the bridge crew, save for Feng who was sporting a slowly widening smile.

"That's got to be it."

"General," the Captain began, "if you have something then now would be–"

"We're in a different universe, Captain," Feng began. "Observer once told me and Colonel Hildure stories from other races of instances where two universes can overlap. An inter-universe singularity, you might call it. The stories told of people from other long-ago cultures who would find such portals and go through them to a different universe, then return. We're actually in another universe entirely."

"Another first for Earth-kind," Captain Gardena agreed, "but might I ask if the stories told of how one gets back? You might notice that we seem to be lacking something in the way of an exit on our end."

Sure enough, from the new view now surrounding them on the dome and wall screens, there was a galaxy out there that looked visibly different from the Milky Way, and other far more distant objects placed other than how they had been left in their home universe, but of a bright star-like object with no mass, there was no sign.

"They are said to be of limited duration," Feng stated, "but I don't think we'd be unlucky enough to have gone through just when the thing was closing, we may have simply been flung out of it a bit farther than planned. Miss Tanaka, start scanning for continuum ripples."

"Got one," the officer reported almost immediately. "Twenty light years from here."

"Take us there," the Captain ordered. "As fascinating as being in another universe might be, we can sit around and see how long this doorway remains open from our *own* side just as easily as from here. Engage warp drive."

"Aye, Captain."

With little more than a single galaxy or two to be measured against, the only sign of motion came as a distant pinprick of light began to swell, until just as before it began to fill their view.

"That's it," Miss Tanaka confirmed with a look at the sensor readings scrolling across her station. "But Captain, we have three more continuum ripples. Much smaller but in the same vicinity as the... object."

"Let's just call it a 'Breach'," Feng suggested. "Now get us a view of those– Wait, you said *three?* Would they be about ship-sized?"

"Well, yes sir, but they'd have to be pretty big ships. Wait, view coming up now."

Before it even came into view, Feng had a most unnerving feeling in the pit of his stomach. At first the view showed just three small specks hovering around the edge of the Breach. Then a flicker as the view magnified and they resolved into three very long vessels.

"Readings coming in," the Science officer reported. "Three distinct vessels, about a mile or two long. Difficult to make out from the visible radiation, but from the looks of them–"

"They're Zelos," Feng said in a near-quiet hush, gaze fixed on the one image before them. "It's their entire fleet... Now we know why the Satarans could never find their homeworld."

"General?" the Captain asked.

"They aren't even from our universe," he continued in quiet tones. "They must make use of these Breaches to raid worlds in *our* universe. No way anyone can trace that."

"I would guess that they know how to trace *us,* sir," Helm announced, "because those ships are turning around directly in our direction."

A quarter-turn around the edge of the Breach from their current location, they could see the first of the three immense vessels slowly turning around to face them as a storm of smaller craft launched out from its decks. They had discovered from where the Zelos come, but it would seem the Zelos were determined to keep their secrets.

"Agent Franklin!"

From the struggle flashing across her face, it was clear that she was trying to resist, but Phillipe Moreau's power was undeniable and Amelia Franklin was no longer certain what was real anymore. She seemed to hear Darren's voice distantly, as if calling through a wall of mattresses muffling his voice, but there was a growing disconnect between what she heard and what her mind was telling her she saw.

"Maybe another way," Darren realized.

He stopped in place, lowering his gun, then raised up a hand in her direction and thrust out with the power of his mind like he had never done so before. Phillipe simply grinned as he calmly took out a pistol of his own from his pocket and leveled it in Darren's direction.

"You think to break my power with your own? Mine is granted by the divine ones. My masters who even now speak to me of their glory. We are food and raw materials for their engines of war and when they come they will ravage the Earth. Minds such as yours, Colonel Hildure, will make for a rare tasty treat for them."

"No," Darren realized with sudden shock, "it can't be! The Zelos. You're in contact with the Zelos!"

"Our all-powerful masters," he grinned maliciously. "Now do you see why you can never hope to overcome my influence? It sources from the *gods* themselves. I am but their prophet, their herald, my purpose to ready the Earth for their coming. And it begins with Agent Franklin killing you, Colonel, and there's not a thing you can do to change that."

"Actually I wasn't planning on it," Darren called back, "just using it a little."

Before Phillipe could question by what he meant, Agent Franklin's view of the world suddenly resolved itself. She saw her target standing right next to her; Colonel Hildure raising up a gun and calling, "Shoot me," while nearly twenty feet away Phillipe Moreau gave the same command, to shoot the Colonel.

"Yes, my Lord," she absently replied.

Then she pulled the trigger. The one next to her reeled back as a hole blasted through his face, his hand spasming up with gun in hand to pull off a wild shot at the other before falling to the ground. In that instant the world suddenly spun back around, the influence upon her mind abruptly gone. But as she looked down in brief horror, the one she had thought to be Darren was actually Phillipe, bleeding away the last of his life, while the more distant figure now with a gunshot wound in his chest was in reality Darren Hildure.

No time for shock, though, she dropped her gun and ran over to the Colonel while calling out to one of the robots just finishing up dealing with Phillipe's men.

"Tell Observer three to teleport over to Mars and have a med-bot ready. Hurry! Colonel, I–"

"Knew I couldn't break his control over you," he said, both hands grabbing onto his bleeding wound as he lay there on the ground, "so I bent it a little. Made you think that Phillipe and I had switched places."

"Well, it worked, now hurry up and stop bleeding."

She slammed a palm down onto the wound and closed her eyes in concentration. Within seconds the blood oozing out from between her fingers slowed down to a trickle, then when her hand came away it held the slug that had been in his chest. Daren's eyes widened with surprise.

"I thought you could only *sense* health."

"I've had a few years to practice," she shrugged. "But this is just a quick fix."

Two of the robots came walking over, one to pick up the remains of Phillipe Moreau, the other to help Agent Franklin get Darren to his feet. Moments later, all had vanished.

"Nav," the Captain quickly decided, "set course directly through the middle of that thing. Helm, I want full warp. Engineering, release all gimbals, weapons start setting targets, and everyone with helmets on. We're going through them hot."

Even as everyone on the bridge pivoted the translucent black helmets fixed atop their chairs down into place over their heads to initiate the far faster direct mind-computer interface, the Weapons Office interjected his concerns.

"But Captain, even with the helmet interface, at the speeds we'll be going there's no way the computers can accurately target anything."

"Won't matter, Mister Jones," she said with a dismissive wave, "with as many bogies as there are out there, we'll hit *something.* Ready to engage full rolling maneuver… *Now!"*

It came like a comet, spinning around in place while shooting out a constant barrage at anything that even looked like it was coming in its direction. A comet accelerating up to light-speed trying to make it to the Breach before the deadly weapons of the three large carriers could draw a target. Zelos fighters by the thousands drawing closed their net, skillfully evading the bulk of the oncoming weapons fire yet always more to come. Rolling fire, cosmic energies boiling forth, never stopping to see what had been hit.

The Orion crashed straight through the wall of fighters before it, leaving in its wake a trail of antimatter particles and tumbling craft, behind it the three carriers punching out with their own waves of force to just tickle the rear of the Orion before it plunged once again into the Breach. The universe spun as before, but the light of the Breach had barely faded from sight when Captain Gardena cried out her next command.

"Helm! Hyperdrive *now.* Any point in the galaxy will do, just so they can't follow us home."

The view of the Milky Way before them started to collapse into a singularity, while from behind them they could just begin to see the first of the carriers emerge from the invisible hole in space. Then it all winked away.

When the skies cleared they were once again surrounded by stars, the Helm mopping his brow before calling out his report.

"All clear, Captain."

"Matching up stars to maps supplied by Observer," Nav then announced. "I should have our position in a few moments."

"When you do then take the long way back home," Feng told him. "Ten jumps at the least, using the warp drive if you have to. They mustn't track us back to Earth."

"Yes, General."

That done, Feng then turned to Captain Gardena for some quiet words.

"Captain, that was some very quick thinking you did back there. I'm impressed."

"That's why they gave me the captaincy of the Odyssey," the replied. "My Mars treatment resulted in my synaptic responses being ten times faster than human norms. I can put my mind in a sort of hyper mode, but it requires some nutrition afterwards. For some reason usually ice cream."

"Then allow me to treat you to a cone the first we arrive back at Earth."

"You haven't seen the mess hall on board," she said with a slight grin. "Why do you think I asked for an ice cream machine installed?"

"Then as soon as we know where the heck we are," Feng told her, "and as soon as we get back, we've got something that *everybody* will want to hear. We now know where the Zelos come from... Only problem is, with the way that Breach probably moves around, how will that help us?"

The Orion made the first of several jumps a few minutes later and would be a full two weeks making its roundabout way back to Earth... during which time Feng found out that the Captain's preference in ice cream leaned towards butterscotch.

CHAPTER
FOURTEEN

DEBRIEFING

May 10, 2060
Colonel Darren Hildure, personal log.

Phillipe Moreau was dead on arrival at Mars, but Amelia's miraculous abilities at healing kept me from bleeding out long enough for Observer to fix me up. I've spent the rest of the time telling Director Forester about the outcome, then repeating the same story for nearly every other intelligence Agency chief on the planet. Fortunately after this, now with a single united Earth, there will be only one main intelligence chief I'll have to report to. Unfortunately that person will still be Erica Forester.

Feng took his sweet time getting back. Seems as he had a tailwind he had to out-race... which means he's paying for dinner at that place in Paris. At least we know now why not even the Satarans could find the Zelos homeworld. An entirely different universe, who knew?

Anyway, we're all back on Mars now with an interplanetary conference call set up for a last debriefing on everything. Feng's just finished giving his report so I guess I'd better hang up this psychic dictation machine and start paying attention…

The meeting was taking place in Observer's main control center, his learning machines and the evolution machine in the background, Observer off to one side watching while Agent Franklin, Feng, and Darren faced the projected images of several of Earth's top spy and security directors. Boris Gurov of Russia, Tim Whittier of the United States, Chief Pinyin of China and of course Erica Forester of… well, no one's really sure. Feng had just finished his debriefing and was stepping back in line with his friends as silence briefly settled upon the room.

The image of Director Forester was first to speak.

"If Phillipe Moreau was in contact with the Zelos all this time, then besides being responsible for the likes of Sir Roberts and the others whose minds we found influenced, it would not seem improbable that he is the reason why that Zelos scout ship happened upon our solar system. Observer, how possible is this supposition?"

"I would say that you may be partially correct, Director," the robot replied. "To the best of our knowledge, the Zelos do not operate well in smaller groups and their long-range telepathy certainly has its limits. More likely is that their connection with Phillipe Moreau allowed them an approximate area and they have been in a search pattern trying to discover Earth's exact location. That was no doubt one of several such scouts sent to a range of systems in this sector."

"But how do you explain Moreau himself?" Boris asked. "Such phenomenal psychic powers that the Colonel even had problems with, and all under Observer's nose? I thought everyone going through the process up there undergoes an evaluation."

"They do," Observer replied, "and according to my records Mister Moreau did. It is possible that the evolution machine triggered a slowly evolving latent insanity that was not at first detectable. This growing ability then put him into contact with the Zelos, who perhaps fed him knowledge of how to further his powers and used him to disrupt Earth's plans until they could use him to locate it. They knew then that Earth existed, and posed a very sweet treat for their tastes, but they did not know exactly where it was located."

"They would have been able to learn everything that Phillipe knew," Darren continued, "but he knew nothing of stellar navigation and had no reference point to give them. All they could do was try and triangulate our position using him as a single reference point."

"And if they had yet succeeded in that process then we wouldn't now be sitting here," Director Forester summed up. "Now with Moreau dead, they have no more reference point to go by."

"The man became a tool through no fault of his own," Boris sighed. "For the safety of all Earth he would have had to been executed anyway."

The image of Boris sat back, one hand now coming into view with a single filled glass which he then put to his lips in a silent toast. Observer took this opportunity now to speak up.

"The pattern of the Zelos raids now makes sense, once you take into account the intermittent appearance of that interdimensional breach. It may even be that the breaches follow a regular course such as an orbit around the outside perimeter of the galaxy, and that orbit dictates how soon they will come into range of the worlds they will raid. They have a limited window to make it through a breach, raid a world, then make it back. If we can map out the course and frequency of these breaches then we could someday meet them when one opens."

"The Orion went through that one breach pretty hot," Feng interjected. "We were firing everything we had while we entered it at full warp. Could that have thrown off the pattern of the breaches?"

"Unknown," Observer admitted. "But it does give my creators a starting point for further investigations."

"I'd just like to thank them for patching me up," Darren said with a hand scratching at his chest. "Agent Franklin here did a great job stopping the bleeding but it was your machines here that did the final job."

"Actually it was the rejuvenation machine," Observer replied, "that which you call the evolution machine. Remember it was built by forces unknown for reasons just as mysterious. It had never been tested on missing limbs or organs before, and while as you say Agent Franklin did repair some of the damage, your heart still needed to be rebuilt."

"Rebuilt?" Darren asked. "How?"

"Cloning using existing tissue from your body," Observer told him, "as well as the insertion of a small generator which I believe to be composed of some sort of nanite technology. In fact, it had already prepared itself for the operation by the time I placed you within it."

"So... I have a machine in my heart?"

Being only a machine, though a very sophisticated one, Observer couldn't realize the significance of Darren's pause, slight though it was, though even from an entire planet away through a projected image Director Forester glared suspiciously in his direction.

"Well then," Feng picked up with a friendly slap to his friend's back, "we'd like to thank *them* for saving my friend's life."

"Then I wish you luck in finding them," Observer told them. "Thousands of years crisscrossing the galaxy in search of them has still yielded no sign of their presence."

"With what General Feng discovered," Agent Franklin added, "they could very well be from that other universe."

"That thing knew when I needed an extra regeneration," Darren added with a thoughtful look, "not simply at the same interval as everyone else in my original crew. It was ready for my heart operation... It *knew.*"

"You know what you're implying," Feng realized, "they could be watching us even now."

Before anymore commentary could be given, however, a chuckle sounded out across the room. It came not from any person there, though, nor even any of Observer's robots, but from the very back. All heads turned to see that the laughter originated from the alien rejuvenation machine itself. The laughter then died down and from it a voice spoke, rich and full.

"I like you people. Such a young race, so full of energy and new ideas. Always thinking, unlike so many other races. Someday, Darren and Feng, you will find me, but in the meantime I will have a lot of fun watching you. We will see you in the not too distant future."

Another chuckle then the machine was silent... along with the rest of the room as all eyes drifted in Observer's direction.

"Observer," Darren was first to voice, "forgive the language, but... What the Hell?"

"I assure you, Colonel, that in the entire ten thousand years this machine has existed that it has never before talked nor given sign of having the capability to do so. I will have to report this to my creators immediately."

While Observer hurried over to one of his control stations, Darren turned back to face the images of the security chiefs to see that Director Forester still had her gaze locked directly on him.

"Colonel," she said, "I've a feeling you have something you may need to tell us. You paused when Observer described you as having a machine in your heart. Why?"

Now all eyes shifted to the Colonel. Everyone there knew of the Director's instincts, that even before Mars not a person alive could long keep a secret in her presence. Darren dropped his head with a sigh, then explained that which he had thus far told no one.

"On my mom's death bed she told me of a vision she'd had the night before. A dream with particular significance for me, and I think Feng as well. She saw us battling what sounds like the Zelos, including four dragonfly-shaped spaceships a few miles long."

"Not sure I like where this is going," Feng quietly interjected.

"One of the large ships got destroyed by a small very bright ball, and there were millions dead on both sides. There were also five very large ships with robots in them to fight on our side, one of which was commanded by a woman with some robots with her. In the dream my mom saw that this woman was very determined to destroy as many of the Zelos ships as possible."

"Sounds like a future ally," Feng stated.

"There's more," Darren continued. "She went on to tell me that she saw Feng and myself in a different universe fighting the Zelos race, and... Well, apparently we'd met a blue man over ten thousand years old. Then some stuff about talking to a living planet and having... machines in our bodies. It was thousand as of years from now and Feng and I look just as we do now but with our eyes glowing like fire. Some of it I don't understand, but most of it seems to involve the Zelos. Still, though, the vision had *four* of their ships, but we know they always come in threes."

"Hmm," Director Forester pondered once he had finished, "a blue man in another universe… Colonel, didn't Observer tell of a man that went off to another universe?"

"Why, yes I did, Director," Observer replied as he walked back over to rejoin them. "And it was indeed a blue man. He left ten thousand years ago in search of the makers of the rejuvenation machine and never returned."

"And now he's appearing in my mother's dreams ten millennia later," Darren said thoughtfully. "I'm thinking that he's found them and surviving all this time from their technology."

"Observer," Director Forester snapped, "I think it's about time we know the name of this blue man that seems to like appearing in people's dreams. Is that still in your records?"

"Why, of course, Director," Observer replied. "You just never asked before."

"Then what is it?"

Observer paused for but a moment, everyone physically and virtually present focused on the robot for the answer he would give.

"The man's name was Morpheus."

All remained silent as they contemplated the meaning of such a name, except for Darren who voiced a light chuckle then explained to the inquiring looks.

"Of course… Morpheus is the Greek god of dreams."

EPILOGUE

Out in the depths of space beyond the galactic rim, three very large ships gathered outside a hole in space. In the dark shadows of their bridge their commanders gathered to consult, their collective insectoid minds pondering their position with a combination of telepathic exchanges and the clicking chirps voiced from their mandibles.

We have lost the connection to our tool on the planet they call Earth.

He was discovered and killed then. Were we able to triangulate his psychic signal yet?

The answer came after a pause and consultation with their instrumentation, then one of the mind-voices giving reply.

Not precisely, but we do have it narrowed down to a sector...

ABOUT THE AUTHOR

Uwe Jaeckel, currently technical supervisor, has a bachelor's degree in engineering from the Hochschule in Munich. This is his first publication and more to come. He and his wife, Leona, have three children and live in Nashua, New Hampshire.